HONEY

"Tristan's hustle isn't easy, but her money is"

MEKO

ISBN: 9780692859834
Library of Congress Control Number: 2017903793
Eagle Life Publications, Dallas, Texas

CHAPTER 1

After watching my mom and dad argue and fight almost every day like they hated each other. I knew that things were going to be different when my mom came and told me that she and I were about to move out of town to go and live with her mother.

And although I was only five years old, I knew that I wasn't going to see my dad again, even before my mom told me that I would never see him again. But at that age, I was just happy about the fact that we were about to go and live with grandma, because I barely saw my dad anyway.

Not knowing that my grandmother would pass away only four months after we'd moved in with her and my uncle Snap. – He had moved in with her a few months before me and my mom came, but we all continued to live under my grandmother's roof after she passed away, since we were all family.

And things were going okay, until one day when I was sitting on my uncle's lap and felt something weird. And when I tried to stand up, because I wasn't sure what it was.

He had picked me up and sat me back on his lap. Then told me that everything was okay, and I believed him because he was my uncle. So I knew that I was in no danger from whatever it was, so I just sat back down and didn't think much of it.

Then he asked me a lot of questions like if I knew the difference between right and wrong, and did I know what sex was.

And with my mom being more concerned about my dad than me, although they weren't together anymore, and she had other boyfriends by then. I could honestly say that I didn't know much of anything besides my toys and coloring books.

But my uncle Snap was sure to educate me in his own way when he watched me for my mom one night while she went on a date. He started touching me in private places while explaining to me how much he loved me and needed for me to keep our secret.

He used to say that he was like a dad to me. And I can remember him telling me that I would never see my dad again, and that he would be my uncle and my dad too. He said that I just had to make sure that I kept our secrets and never told anybody because that's how all dads are with their daughters, but it was a secret.

And as bad as it may sound, I was okay with it at first because he really was like a dad to me. And at that age, I just wanted to make him happy. And we were only touching each other with our hands and mouths at that point. It wasn't until one day when I saw him bring out a yellow jar of Vaseline from his bedroom, and that changed everything.

He had opened the jar, then greased me between my legs right before he penetrated me at the age of six years old. And I can remember crying because of how bad it hurt, but he said that it only felt that way because he wasn't my real dad, but I would be okay when he finished.

He kept calling me Honey, and telling me how sweet and thick I was while he talked about how honey lasts forever. – He explained how pure honey is, and how it will never spoil or rot, just as long as you never mix it with anything. It will last forever.

During the entire time as he penetrated me, he compared me to honey and explained how that moment would last forever, just like honey. And from that day forward he gave me the nickname, Honey, and everybody thought that he called me that because I was so sweet.

I was shy and never really said very much, so everyone. Including my mom started calling me Honey instead of Tristan, because they said that I was such a sweet little girl.

And during that time in my life the sweetness slowly began to bitter after my mom had gotten sick the night of my seventh birthday party. I thought that she had just eaten too much cake, but she had been sick for a while and everyone knew how ill she was but me.

But no one ever really explained much of anything to me besides my uncle Snap. He was the only adult who would ever really sit down with me and try to explain anything.

Until we had to go to the hospital, and on that day a lot of people came to me and explained to me that my mom had died of Cancer. – And since nobody could locate my dad, and my uncle Snap didn't have a job. Child welfare services eventually took me away from my uncle and kept me because they couldn't find anyone who could afford to take me in. Until I'd turned eleven years old, and was sent to live with Momma Bass.

Momma Bass was a foster parent who already had other kids living with her who didn't have parents just like I didn't, and that's when I met my two foster brothers and my little foster sister.

And we all got along great, and Momma Bass genuinely did love us, and she had more money than my entire family had all together as a whole. Which means that I was able to live better than I'd ever lived during my entire life. Although she wasn't super rich, she made sure that my siblings and I had everything we needed. And I mean everything we needed and wanted.

So to us, we were super rich and as happy as we could be.

We always played together, and I was honestly able to tell child welfare services that I was happy. And that I would love to be adopted by Momma Bass if it was okay with them, because she had literally stepped up and became a real mom to me.

But there was a meeting held regarding me before I'd even asked to be adopted by Momma Bass, she had already told them that she wanted to adopt me if I would agree to it, so everything ended up working out perfectly.

She already knew that I would agree to being adopted by her because there had been several occasions when she and my siblings would always talk about me permanently staying with them, ever since I spent my very first night at her house.

It was like we were already a strong family from the first day we met, and everybody everywhere, even at church they would tell Momma Bass that she was a strong woman. And that they admired how well she was raising three teenagers and a little girl, because after a while of doing a lot of paperwork and etc., my adoption was final. – My brother Don was sixteen, my brother Deon was seventeen, my sister Sabrina was eight, and I was thirteen by the time my adoption was officially finalized.

We all took the last name Bass, and I was truly able to say that I had a family who loved me and no one was abusing me.

We were all adopted by Momma Bass because we had no parents, and there was no one willing to take us in. But Don and Deon are biological brothers, because they have the same mother, but she died in a car accident.

Momma Bass stepped in and adopted them even though she had just adopted Sabrina after her mom died in a house fire. – But Momma Bass was already some sort of important well known social worker before she decided to stop working and adopt us four and raise us as her own.

Although every now and then she would still have to leave us to go and help child services with a few cases when she was asked to do so. But after a while, her love for children and her good heart was being taken advantage of. And she should've turned down some of those cases because it became easy to get her to do things after you've really gotten to know her.

And due to her past, she had money so she always worked for free when she would leave us to go and try to help other kids. And she knew that she could leave Deon in charge of us because he was the oldest.

And because she would always have family meetings with us due to her experience with working with so many kids, that did play a big role in our lives because she did things like sit us all together as a group, as well as talked to us individually to make sure that we were all on the right path. – We all pretty much knew everything about each other, just like we knew that sometimes she would have to go and help other kids.

But we knew the rules and understood that Deon was in charge when she wasn't around. And one day we saw some kids on the news because their mom and dad were cooking drugs, and running a prostitution ring from out of their home, similar to Don and Deon's case.

And we saw Momma Bass on TV doing an interview about what was going to happen with the kids. So I asked Don and Deon did they ever miss their stepdad after he lost custody of them for having sex with those underage girls in their home.

Because in Don and Deon's case, before Momma Bass adopted them. The police went to their home to tell their stepdad that their mother was just involved in a fatal car accident, and she died. But unfortunately, when the police pulled up to their house, a sixteen-year-old girl was fighting a seventeen-year-old girl over some money that Don and Deon's stepdad had just given them.

While there were also a few more underage girls inside of their home stripping and having sex with adult men, and a few teenage boys for money.

And although Don and Deon was not inside having sex, they were too young to be inside of that house watching everything as it appeared to be something that happened regularly at their home. So they were taken away from their stepdad and put into a foster home since their mom had passed away, and there were no other family members willing to take them in.

But Don told me that he didn't miss their stepdad because he had other things to worry about. He said that he only used and abused their mother anyway, so he really didn't care to think about him at all.

While Deon said that he didn't miss their stepdad either, although he did teach them a lot when it came to women, and how to use them to their advantage.

I then inquired more and more about their past life before Momma Bass, and they began to ask me questions about my past life before my mom died. And although we all somewhat already knew of what our past lives were like, we began to talk about some of the deeper stuff concerning our past that we'd never discussed with Momma Bass.

Don and Deon explained in detail how their stepdad allowed them to get lap dances from the girls, but only if they didn't tell their mom about it. They said that their mom knew about their stepdad having the girls dancing in the house because she was getting money from them also, but she would have been so mad at him if she would've ever found out that he had let them get a few lap dances from time to time.

And for the first time ever, I then brought up me and my uncle Snap. Since he was the only part of my past that I never really talked about, ever. But I told them that I don't miss my uncle Snap, or the way that he used to make me do things to him.

And I gave them just as many details as they'd given me on what they had been exposed to, and as you can imagine. I left my brothers mouths hanging wide open, as well as my eight-year-old sister because they had no idea that my uncle had done any of those things to me. I even remember explaining to Sabrina how she's lucky that she's never had a dad or a stepdad because dads are evil, but it's just a secret.

And by me opening-up so much to them, my brothers decided to follow my lead because after the shock of everything that I'd told them began to settle into their minds.

They also began to share more of their stories, and that left only Sabrina's mouth hanging wide open because she was looking all kinds of confused. But I had already been exposed to just as much as they had been exposed to, just not the recruiting of the girls or the lap dancing parts.

But the porn videos, sex, and the masturbation part of what they were saying was nothing new to me, but it did bring all of us even closer together because we began to share a lot of secrets.

And that brings me back to how easy it was to get over on Momma Bass, no matter how much experience she had because on that same day. Don and Deon took me down to the basement of the house and through some double doors that Momma Bass had blocked off.

And there was a stairway that led to a large storage shed, and at that time I thought that Momma Bass didn't even know about the shed. Because it wasn't until I'd gotten older when I realized that she had to have known about the shed, because it was on her property. But nobody had used it in years judging from how it looked from the entrance through our basement doors.

But Don and Deon had found the shed, and they had fixed it up without any of us knowing anything about it.

And they used it all the time because Deon's girlfriend Autry even knew about it, and they had called her over to the house that same day as well.

But that was after we had made Sabrina go to her room during our conversations, so she really didn't find out about the storage shed or any of the extremely graphic stuff until she'd gotten older. And even then, she still only knew very little concerning anything bad like we'd experienced because we would always send her to her room after that day.

And although Autry was twenty-two years old, Deon was more like her daddy, because she did whatever he told her to do. While Momma Bass, me and everyone else thought that she was nineteen years old. Because Deon was only about to turn eighteen during that time, but that day I found out her real age as they were hiding so many things from us.

And since Momma Bass loved to see her children making money, Don and Deon had us thinking that they made their extra money by doing yard work and washing cars. — While I braided hair, and did art work through my paintings so that Momma Bass could sell them at the local flea markets.

While she had also framed a lot of my freelance paintings throughout our house that looked professionally done hanging on the walls. But little did we know that Don and Deon had started their own miniature strip club right in Momma Bass's storage shed, and they had money that we knew nothing about.

The first day that I walked into the shed, I can recall them telling Autry to turn on the stereo, then Don told me to go back upstairs and into the house to see if I could hear the music. He said that they would leave the volume as it was, but they wanted me to listen hard to see if I could hear anything.

And when I did it, I honestly couldn't hear anything, and the TV wasn't on or nothing.

So when I went back downstairs while following the path back to the shed, I told them that I couldn't hear the music at all. – While they explained the reason that I couldn't hear anything was mainly due to the expensive red and gray soundproofing insulation that covered the walls.

And then they asked me how did I feel about dancing, and I told them that I didn't feel anything about dancing. I told them that I could dance, but I've never danced while taking off my clothes at the same time.

Then Autry asked Deon if it was okay if she showed me a few moves on one of the poles that they had in the middle of the floor, and Deon told her that I already knew more than he knew about getting dirty anyway. So he told her that I can speak for myself on if I wanted to see her dance or not.

And as Autry didn't exactly know what he'd meant by that, because she didn't hear me telling them how uncle Snap would hold me upside down while we orally did things to each other as if I was an adult.

All Autry knew was the hair braiding Honey who loves to paint, although she did eventually ask him what did he mean by that, but he told her that he didn't care what she showed me. Especially if I said that it was okay from my own mouth, so when she asked me if I wanted to see her do some dance moves on the pole without needing my brother's approval.

I paused and still asked Don and Deon what did they think about it, and again, Deon said that I knew more than he did so it was totally up to me.

But then I asked Deon why did he keep saying that I knew more that he knew? And he said that it was because he didn't know that his thirteen-year-old sister had been exposed to so much already. – Don then asked me if I knew the name of the sexual position that my uncle Snap and I were in when I was being held upside down, so that his mouth was on me and mine on him. And I told him no, then he said that as my big brother he just didn't know what to say or do.

He said that I knew so much, but I still knew so little. And that's when I told Autry to show me some of her moves because I wanted to see how she could dance on the pole and take off her clothes at the same time, while staying on beat with the music.

She then looked at Don and Deon and saw that they really didn't seem to have a problem with her showing me her moves. So she then began to move her body to the music while looking at me, and my eyes were immediately glued to her because I saw art.

I saw her moving so smoothly to the beat, then she slowly but surely began to remove her clothing. And it didn't seem hard at all, the art was forming in my head as she continued to perform by climbing up the pole then sliding down while her art was coming alive more and more right before my eyes.

She was awesome, and I wanted to mock her, and they all laughed at me when I told her that what she had just done was a work of art and I liked it.

Don said that not only through my paintings, but absolutely everything that I see or do is a piece of art in my brain.

Then Autry asked me if I wanted to give it a try to see if I would fall off the pole, but I was too nervous to try it.

But then Deon said that it was okay, and that they wouldn't laugh at me if I didn't do it right. So I eventually ended up getting on the pole, but not exactly how they expected me to. — I started out dancing regularly and only took off my jacket while I danced to the beat of the music. And I had grabbed the pole a few times, but not in the same ways as Autry did.

Then suddenly Autry walked over to the stereo and stopped the music, then she told me to act like Don and Deon weren't sitting there, and that I should pretend that they were invisible.

She told me to look at what she had on then take a look at myself and what I had on.

She was almost naked, only wearing a bra and some thin and nearly see through boy shorts. And I was still fully clothed, so I explained to her that what she did was art mixed with sex, but I wasn't sure if I could do that. So I was just dancing and taking off my clothes. They all then laughed and said that I didn't take anything off but my jacket, and that I was still acting scared.

My brothers asked me if I wanted them to leave and go back into the house if I was uncomfortable, but I told them no because I was going to pretend that they were invisible.

Then Autry said that if she showed me sex and art, then that's what she wanted to see me do. Sex and art on the pole while taking off my clothes, just like she did.

She also asked me what song did I want her to play, but I told her that I listened to so much music when I was painting. That it really didn't matter what she played because art is art, and I would just follow the beat of the music.

And when the music came on, my sex mixed with my art came forward on not just the one pole but on both poles that were posted near each other in the middle of the floor. I stood between the two poles and danced to the music while slowly but surely taking off my clothes, and I kept my eyes glued to Autry as if she was my canvas.

They had a total of three poles in the shed, but the other pole was on the other side of the room, so I looked at nothing or no one but Autry and those two poles.

And while Autry stared back at me, she didn't move, she'd sat in a chair and watched me as I stripped all the way down to my bra and panties.

She and my brothers sat through two songs as I swung from pole to pole.

And then I hung upside down at the end of the second song in attempt to mock Autry and what she'd previously done, but just in my own amateur style.

But when I had stopped dancing, neither Autry nor my brothers said anything. The three of them just sat and stared at me, even when I told them that I was getting scared. And had begun to quickly put my clothes back on due to how much the entire mood of the room had changed because of their silence.

Autry eventually said that I had to be lying to them because there was no way that was my first-time dancing in a sexy way, nor was it my first-time dancing on a pole.

She said that there was nothing that I could say to make her believe that was my first time, and my brothers agreed with her. Deon told me to continue to put my clothes back on, and then he told Don that he just couldn't believe what he just saw.

He told Don that he really hoped that he wasn't thinking the same thing that he was thinking, while Autry told them both that she knew exactly what they both were thinking. And that she was thinking the same thing, but they needed to remember that I was their sister, and that I was only thirteen years old.

I stepped in and told her that I would be turning fourteen in a few weeks, and that I really wanted to know what they were all talking about because I really didn't understand anything of what they were saying.

I just knew that I was feeling very uncomfortable, especially after they all started acting like they'd just seen a ghost.

And Deon kept telling me to hurry up and put my clothes back on because I was too young.

Then Autry decided to take it upon herself to tell me how Don and Deon only cut enough grass and washed enough vehicles to make it seem like they really be working hard on lawns and vehicles.

But she said that most of their money comes from her and a few of her friends that comes into the shed to strip for a lot of different guys, and Don nor Deon said anything.

They just let Autry talk, although Deon was still making me feel nervous by how he was acting. But seeing how Autry was the only person talking, I asked her why did they all start acting so weird? Especially after I'd taken off all of my clothes, because I was only doing what they'd asked me to do. And she told me that whether I was telling the truth or not about that being my first time ever dancing like that, she said that they were all thinking about making some serious money with me. But the problem was that I was their sister, and that I was too young, so Don and Deon didn't know what to do or how to act at that moment.

She told me that my body was unbelievable at my age, and that my brothers were just beside themselves because they didn't know that I was so physically developed, and neither did she.

The three of them eventually started talking to me all together, and told me that I was a natural at dancing like that, because I'd just put on a show for them without anyone having to teach me anything. They said that I was too young to be that good on my first try, but I told them that art is just what I am. And just like Autry, I'd mixed my sex with my art while taking off my clothes.

Yet they stood in amazement while Don asked me how I felt about dancing like that again with the room being filled with people. And I told him that I felt scared, and that I would never do that with the room being filled with people.

Then Autry asked me if I would do it for four hundred dollars, and I seemed to have heard her say four million dollars because at that age.

Four hundred dollars was just the same as four million dollars to me, because that truly was a lot of cash for a girl like me. –

Cash that would be placed into my hands and not Momma Bass' hands like the money that I get from braiding hair and painting.

Because I was already making a lot of money, even four hundred in one day. But Momma Bass had separate accounts set up for all of us that we had to put most of our earnings into it.

But I knew that four hundred dollars would be immediately mine to spend however I wanted to, so I told Autry that I would like to have the four hundred dollars, but I was still scared.

Then Deon told me that I didn't have to do it if I was scared, and that he just couldn't believe what I'd just done in front of them because I wasn't shy about it at all. He said that he wished that they would have never brought me into the shed or revealed anything to me. Then Don told him that he felt the exact same way, although there was still no denying what they'd just witnessed.

And thanks to Autry explaining things to me in general, she told me that the point was that I could make myself and them a lot of money by doing what I'd just did for them. But the room would have to be filled with people. – I then asked her if I could come and see her and her friends dance like that with the room filled with people first. Before I decide to do anything else, because I wanted to see what all they did.

And after about two weeks from that exact day, we did just that. We waited until Momma Bass was busy, and we knew that she would be away from the house for a while. – My brothers then had just about everybody who came to the shed to park their cars up the street from Momma Bass' house, mostly in a twenty-four-hour grocery store parking lot that was around the corner from the house. And they didn't mind walking that short distance to get to us, because it wasn't far at all. And I saw them all paying Don and Deon a fee to come inside of the shed.

While Autry and three of her friends eventually came from behind a big fancy curtain and danced.

The guys started taking money from their pockets and throwing it at Autry and her friends because they weren't just secluded to dancing on the poles alone. – They were dancing on the poles, each other, and the guys while I watched them receive a lot of money just for dancing and taking off their clothing.

And when they took a break and let the crowd mingle amongst themselves, Autry came looking for me and asked me what I thought and how did I feel.

I told her that I felt fine, then I asked her was she scared and she said no. She explained to me how Deon wouldn't let anyone come inside if he felt like they didn't have any money, or if he felt like they didn't know how to act in such an environment without causing trouble, so she had nothing to be afraid of.

While she also explained how it was usually the same guys that came on a regular basis, because she would only see new faces every now and then. And those new faces were generally laid back older guys who didn't make much noise, while at the same time she was sure to inform me that she knew that Deon had purchased a gun with a silencer from her brother, and he wasn't afraid to use it. Because one time they had to stop Deon from shooting a guy that had come into the shed and tried to adjust the speaker volume without their permission.

Deon got mad when the guy wouldn't listen to what they had to say about not touching the music, and he was about to get him until Don and some other guys stepped in and set the guy straight before they threw him out.

Then Autry told me that it was a good idea that I'd asked to come and watch what happens first before getting in front of everybody, because the things that I do with my body would surely catch them off guard. And that's why they knew that I would bring them more business.

She then asked me if I could see the difference in how they danced versus how I danced, and I told her yes.

I told her that I tried to be different on purpose, but still sexy and confident like her. While I also explained to her how I'd danced in a sexy way before, but never on a guy's lap like her and her friends were doing.

But she laughed and said that I'd said the exact same things about never been on a pole before, but I was excellent on it, and that she could only image what my first lap dance was going to be like.

Then she told me to still be sure to watch everything that she and her friends were doing, and to not do anything that night even if somebody offered me money to do it. But I told her that she didn't have to worry about me doing nothing because I wasn't about to do anything for anybody anyway. And as the night went on, Autry and Don continued to school me throughout the night on things that I knew nothing about, and I can say that I truly learned how much control a woman's vagina can have over a man.

Along with how much money and power a woman could potentially possess with her body if she really wants it, so needless to say from that day forward. I've viewed money, power, and sex in a whole different way.

Starting with going back into the house and up to my room later that night after everything was over, and I thought about that four hundred dollars that I could get that Momma Bass would know nothing about.

Then I called Autry and told her that I wanted to dance with them, but I would only do it if they gave me five hundred dollars.

And that's when she told me that she and her friends have to give my brother's their first fifty dollars or more sometimes, depending on the size of the crowd. But they must pay my brother's whatever their fee is first, then they get to keep whatever else they make after that for themselves.

She said that I could probably get whatever I wanted from them at that point, and that I was smart to ask for more money, because once I get on board with them.

She told me that I too would also have to pay Don and Deon their fee first, before I would get to keep whatever money that I make for the night.

And I was cool with that because I knew that if I'd shocked them as much as I did while feeling as nervous as I was, then I was confident that I would be able to make a lot of tips once I'd gotten a little more comfortable with everything.

I really didn't care about having to pay my brothers first, especially if it wasn't an extremely large amount. But I was sure to make it known to them that they weren't getting any of my five hundred dollars for accepting their offer to dance.

CHAPTER 2

A few weeks had passed and my courage was up enough to go into the shed without any fear to perform my art in front of everyone that had been coming to see Autry and her friends. And I had studied them all, along with several internet videos long enough to know exactly how and what to do.

So when the time came, I went behind the thick curtains where we changed into our dancing clothes. Then Don came behind the curtains where we were and asked me if I was ready to do it, and I told him yeah because I'd been practicing in my room on some lap dancing moves that I saw on the internet.

And although they asked several times, I wouldn't let him or Autry see anything that I was planning to do, so they just decided to trust me.

Then after double checking on me, Don eventually left from behind the curtains and he didn't come back, and that's when I told the girls that I lied to him because I was very nervous. But I was also still ready and eager to go out there and dance, I just didn't want to tell Don how scared I was because he probably would've made me wait a few more weeks.

And with them all knowing that I was the youngest in the room, or even more so the youngest in the building for that matter.

They all stepped up and helped me out by telling me to relax and just be myself, especially after they saw that I was going to do it with or without being nervous anyway. But they said that they wanted to see what Don and Autry had been telling them about as far as my dancing, so they gave me a lot of advice and encouragement.

No one told me not to do it, or tried to persuade me to do anything different, so I began to accept everything good about what they were saying about my art. And I really wanted to see how much money I could make, because even they were saying that it would be a lot if I stuck to it. But I would have to get comfortable enough with people watching me and sometimes touching on me.

But then Autry told me that I had to pick out three feature songs that I wanted to dance to, but I told her that I felt the same way as I'd felt weeks-ago about me dancing to any songs. It really didn't matter to me what they played, but then she explained how the five of us would individually get on the poles on three different songs of our choice throughout the night. And that it would be better if I picked out some songs that I was familiar with because nothing would be like it was weeks-ago, when the room wasn't filled with people.

But I had already mastered how to twerk and how to move my hips and everything else very well, no matter if the song was fast or slow. Therefore, I told her that the crowd could pick my songs because I still didn't care what they played, then all of the girls tried to warn me and suggested that I pick my own songs out for my solo dances.

But again, I informed Autry that if they wanted me to mix my dancing with my art, then I would just follow the beat with whatever songs they choose. Then while no longer hoping that I would eventually shake off the nervousness, I became relaxed and mainly determined to show them that I could be sexy and dance to any song. – And when we gathered to come from behind those curtains, I really saw just how much my brothers were all about making money.

The music was loud enough for everyone to hear it, and the crowd of people was just so unbelievable to me.

And I was so glad that Momma Bass wasn't at home, although even if she would've been at home, she probably would've ignored it and thought that it was just my brothers and some friends hanging out. But regardless, they always had someone inside and outside watching just in case she ever popped up.

But on this night, they had us to come from behind the curtains by name one by one, and of course I came out last, and with a bit of a special introduction. And the crowd had no idea on whether I could dance or not at that point, although my brothers did tell everyone that they had a bona fide newbie that had joined the crew. But they didn't tell anyone my real age, or that I was their sister.

But when it was my turn to come from behind those curtains, I knew that everyone was expecting me to get the party started immediately, and the girls all stood to the side while asking the crowd what song did they want the newbie to grace their presence with.

And once they chose a song, I began my art and worked my body and those poles to the best of my abilities, before the other girls decided to join in with me.

But when I noticed that this crowd wasn't just throwing out one-dollar bills, I saw some five-dollar bills, and even a few tens in some of their hands. And that made me turn up the volume on my performance. – I started flipping, splitting, and especially twerking along with the beat of the music.

And by the time the second or third song went off, and another song came on that had a different flow.

I had asked Don to come over to me and pick up my money while I go and do my first lap dance. I then went into the crowd and over to the section where I saw the most money coming from, then I'd picked out a guy who looked like he could afford to give me more money, judging from how much he was holding in his hands.

I made him sit in a chair while I seduced him and gave him everything that I could as the crowd became eager and started pushing each other while trying to get a better view of what the newbie was doing to him. And from that night forward my life changed because during the day I was sweet little Honey who loved to paint. Then on certain nights, I became sweet little seductive Honey, who receive my first five hundred dollars from my brothers like they promised. But added to that I made a total of almost two thousand dollars in one night on my first night dancing, at the age of fourteen years old.

So as you can imagine, money was no longer an issue for me from that night forward, and Momma Bass was still giving me a percentage of my money from selling my paintings.

And I was still braiding hair whenever I felt like it, so I was very happy with how my life was. Especially after seeing how the money that I'd made from years of painting and braiding hair was pennies compared to how much I'd made after only a few months of dancing in the shed.

Don and Deon had even put up another thick curtain in the shed that was only used for private lap dances given mainly by me, after they saw exactly just how seductive my dances could get, depending on the tips.

They knew that those guys would pay us to come behind that curtain to watch me get damn near completely naked while dancing on them like they were my boyfriend. Because I did a lot of touching behind the curtain, and I would really get up close and personal with whomever I was dancing on if the money was right, although they were very limited on how much they could touch on me.

Although sometimes I would sneak and let them get away with touching on me a little more than Don and Deon allowed. And I didn't mind telling on any guys or girls who would try and be disrespectful by aggressively touching on me after I'd asked him or her to stop. Because I knew that my brothers didn't play any games when it came to anyone disrespecting me or any of us.

Nonetheless, that didn't really happen to often anyway, because I would usually speak up for myself if I felt uncomfortable. – Don told me a long time ago that I must speak up for myself in that type of business, or people would think that they could come at me any type of way. So I became very stern and very direct when I would speak to anyone that I ever had a problem with.

Although after a while, everyone who came into the shed on a regular basis knew that I wasn't afraid to say anything to anyone. And while behind the curtain, being aggressive was mostly fun anyway so I just let people enjoy themselves while I got paid and let them have their fun.

What they didn't know was that I wasn't old enough to be saying or doing any of the things that I was doing to them. Despite the fact of a rumor that was started about me being under age in the beginning, but nobody cared to see if the rumor was ever true or not because it was never an issue.

Until after I'd turned eighteen years old, and wanted to open a bigger and better building and location for us to dance in. Because even after we had expanded the storage shed, it still didn't help anything because we could no longer turn the music up as loud as we could prior to me coming on board.

And my brothers were cool with my ideas of us moving out of the shed and into a better location, because it would give us all more freedom.

What they weren't cool with was how I'd applied everything that was taught to me by them, on them when it came time for us to make some serious business decisions. Because even though I was only eighteen years old, I felt grown and didn't let them treat me like a teenager.

And after I'd graduated from high school, I demanded a say in when and how we would shut down the storage shed and privately open a bigger place. Because after a few years of watching how much control my brothers had over Autry and her friends. I never gave them total control of my life like that, regardless of if they were my brothers or not. While every now and then I did take advantage of the fact that I was their sister, so I did get away with a lot of things that the other girls couldn't.

But in my opinion, although they were all older than me. Autry and her friends just didn't have a real say in anything, period.

But throughout the years, Don, Deon, or Momma Bass didn't raise a fool. And that's why I stood up for myself anytime any money business came up, just like they taught me to. I just did it in my own way, and I never forgot how my brothers totally believe that women are one of Gods most powerful creatures.

But as Deon told me, we are indeed powerful, but if a woman lets a man get into her head without her standing for something. Then if he knows what he's doing, then he can control everything about her, no matter how much power she has. — He said that she will give him complete control over her life without even realizing what she's doing, if she's not careful.

Whereas I wasn't very easy to control, and my brothers knew that so we sat down and came up with a plan on how to transition out of the shed together. Although during that time of us planning to open a real strip joint, Momma Bass wanted me to go to a Performing Arts college after I'd told her that I didn't want to go to a regular college.

But eventually I lied and told her that I'd gotten a job working about an hour away from the house at a lawyer's office, making almost twenty-three dollars an hour as my starting salary.

And she and everyone else was happy for me, and they were cool with me being a lawyer's assistant. Instead of going to college because I kept selling my paintings at the flea markets, and at a few other places that Momma Bass had set up for me by then.

They just didn't know that the lawyer that I was working for was a regular customer of mine who had been coming to see me for a long time to get a few private dances, every time he and his wife would fight.

But one night during a serious conversation with the lawyer, I told him my real age, and he'd promised me that I could work for him after I graduated high school. And could type at least sixty words per minute with little to no mistakes.

So a little while after I graduated, I went to work for him, but I was only getting paid eighteen dollars an hour starting out. Not twenty-three dollars. And the job wasn't an hour away from the house, I only told Momma Bass that so that I could go and live with Deon during the weekdays. Because by then, Deon had his own apartment that was located not too far from home. But it was still almost on the other side of town, much closer to my job, or at least that's what Momma Bass thought.

Although the truth was that it took me just about the same amount of time to get to work from home as it did from Deon's apartment. I mostly just wanted to be out of the house and living on my own after I graduated high school, I just wasn't ready to live completely alone, whether I could afford it or not.

And Don had re-did the storage shed and revealed it to Momma Bass after he'd set it up to look like his own little studio apartment. And it later became Sabrina's apartment, because she'd moved all of her stuff into the shed as soon as Don moved out, and he'd done such a good job that it had no signs of it ever being a strip joint at all.

And Momma Bass was just happy with how well he'd cleaned it up, not knowing that we all had done some pretty wild things in there for years. – But overall, Momma Bass never found out how badly we'd behaved back then, as everything was going so well in our lives at that point.

Even at my day job things were good because none of my coworkers knew that our boss was a strip joint lover, and that I was his calm me down girl. Because at that time cash ruled everything around me, so he didn't have to ever worry about me saying anything to them about any of it, period.

Because even if they would have found out and brought it to our attention at work, or even if his wife would've come to me personally and asked me anything about him, or what he does outside of work. I would have said nothing and acted like I honestly didn't know anything about what she was talking about until the death of me.

There was no way that I would've let her mess up my cash cow by divorcing him, because it would've eventually messed up my daytime pay and my deep cash flow at night after they fought. My mouth and everything else that he needed to be locked and sealed was, and he knew it. With the weird thing about our friendship being that he never actually tried to have sex with me for real. No matter how much I touched on his penis when I danced on him, I can honestly say that he's just about the only man that I've danced on, and have literally felt and saw his penis hard several times. He's even pulled it out for me to see it, but he's never asked me to have sex with him.

While my brothers were over protective and wouldn't have allowed us to have sex even if we would've tried to. We still could have found a way if we really wanted to, but my seductive dancing. Mixed with a few naughty grips of his penis every now and then satisfied the both of us, and he would immediately leave me to go home and have sex with his wife.

And as there were several other hard-working businessmen just like my boss that would come into our club for a private dance when they were having life problems, I always gave them every bit of what they wanted as I whispered into their ears and tried to take their minds off of their issues.

Unequivocally by the time I'd turned twenty-four years old. I had gained so many male and female customers that trusted me with so much of their personal information that I didn't need to visit any websites, or get onto any social media networks to find out anything.

They all brought their joys and their sorrows to me whenever we were in private, especially after I'd customized a few things to fit mine and their needs in our new location. I was then able to do a lot more than I could do when we were in the shed as my clientele continued to grow.

And after some time passed, I'd asked Autry and her best friend Mia to see if they could find Storm and Booby. — And try to get them to come home to visit our new location since they'd stopped working with us and moved away after they had a huge argument with Mia over some money. Because when Storm and Booby got physical with Mia, Autry jumped in it and that made them both quit and they never came back.

But Deon and I had been discussing how we wanted to celebrate how well the business was doing, and I thought that bringing Storm and Booby back would be a great idea since they were the two sisters that used to dance with Autry and Mia before I joined them.

And although by that time we had already added a few more dancers to our crew after Storm and Booby left. But I knew that me, Autry, Mia, Storm and Booby were the original dancers from the shed who had given Don and Deon such a great name in the streets for having the best girls in our area to do what we did.

Therefore, I really wanted the original five of us to come out and do a big show like we used to do in the shed when we were working for a big amount of cash to split as a group. On top of that, Don's twenty-seventh birthday was coming up, so that made me really want to turn everything up a notch.

Especially knowing how the five of us would always put on such a grand show for our audience every time we would link up together like that as a group. – Not to exclude our other dancers, but I had an exclusive plan in mind for Don's birthday bash.

And with the greatness of social media, Autry found Storm and her sister Booby within two days of me asking them to help me find them. They ended up calling me and we all eventually linked up because they'd put aside all of the foolishness that had taken place the last time they saw each other, and we were-able to come together as a group just like we used to. But then a week before Don's birthday party, he came and told me and Autry how big of an impression that he wanted to make on some rich guys that he'd invited to the club for his birthday.

Not knowing that we were already planning to put on a big show that would bring him more money anyway, although in our minds the show was intended for him and the success of the club, not some rich guys that we didn't know.

But I knew that it would all work out perfectly because we were all ready for whatever, and with his invites added to the others whom we knew were coming, that would really give our other dancers a chance to do their thing that night as well.

While Don told me and Autry that he was specifically depending on me and her to put on an impressionable show for the guys as a birthday gift from us to him, so of course we told him that we would impress his guests to the best of our abilities as his gift. Then after practicing and preparing all week leading up to his birthday party, and the success of the club.

We not only showed up and showed out, but we all received an extra one hundred dollars from Don personally, on top of the money that we'd already made by the end of the night.

Because although it was his birthday, Don had given us money because he said that we had just put more money into his pockets than we knew about, after leaving the bachelor's dad so happy.

He told us that he had invited the guys to come out and party with him because of some business opportunities with the dad, but also because one of them was about to get married and was looking for some entertainment. But then I told him that I had gotten with all of the girls and with Deon to help me put together a night that he or the rich bachelor would never forget.

While I also let him know that he didn't have to pay us anything extra because all of the girls agreed that our extra efforts were our gifts to him, but he gave us the money anyway.

But what really made his night a great night was how he didn't know that I had also secretly taken Storm and Booby out to dinner their first night back home, so that I could get some extra help with my gift to him other than the big club birthday party. Because I remembered him talking to me one night about how he wished that he would have had sex with either Storm or Booby.

He told me that they both were some bad chicks and that he wished that he would've gotten some sex from them both, but he didn't want to come between sisters. He said that he couldn't choose which one he wanted the most, so he just didn't touch neither one of them. So as his little sister, being the freak that I am, I could hear it in his voice how much he really wanted them. But he knew that he couldn't touch them without a lot of drama being attached.

So I asked both Storm and Booby if they would surprise him with a threesome, because I knew for a fact that he really wouldn't be expecting anything like that to happen no matter what's going on. And I knew that Storm and Booby would do damn near anything that I asked them to do, especially if I'd promised them that it would be kept strictly between the four of us forever. Unless they opened their mouths to tell anybody about it, and before our dinner was over they not only agreed to the threesome. But they both had guaranteed me that they both would suck him and ride him until he wanted them no more.

While unbeknownst to my surprise, while successfully granting one of Don's wishes. — My life received a big surprise that night also that forced me to make a few permanent changes in my life that I never saw coming.

While usually I place myself in a mental zone that puts a smart and strict wall between me and my audience, although I still allow myself to seductively connect with whomever I want to connect with while I performed. And I didn't care who the males or females were, or how much money they had. I always set limits on intimate feelings when I'm working, and that's why I was so shocked and nervous when my heart sped up and my mind went blank when I first laid eyes on Rico at Don's party.

I immediately felt something strange, and the walls that were built to block everyone out came crashing down because none of that applied to him. I instantly felt like he was my real boyfriend, or my husband, or somebody like that as soon as I saw him. – It seemed liked everyone disappeared for a moment, and we were the only two in the building.

When in reality, I actually did see him standing still in the middle of the big crowd as every person in the building was feeding off of me and Autry's stunt show. And I couldn't do anything but stop and stand still when he had approached me and said that it was nice to finally meet me.

Right then being unaware of what he meant by that, since I'd never met him before in my life, so I didn't know who he was or what to say. I just knew that I wasn't about to block him out like I would normally do to anyone else, even Autry looked at me and asked me was I okay, and why did I stop dancing.

But since I knew that we were right at the end of our sexy stunt show, I told her that I needed a break. And that we should stop and do our own thing, or she should just go ahead and bring out the other girls.

She then signaled for the other girls to join us while I stopped and talked to Rico, as he stood right in front of me. I then asked him why did he say that it was finally nice to meet me, and how did he know me.

He told me that he didn't know me, but he knew that he had just found his wife. He said that his uncle, as well as his best friend, who have both been married to their spouses for several years. They told him that whenever he met the right one, then he would know it.

And at that moment he was convinced that there was no way that he would be leaving that club without getting my number, he said that he just knew that I was the one that he was going to marry one day. And then after talking to him for a little while, and seeing how our feelings were very mutual, although we've never met or even heard of each other at all before that night.

We became completely attached to one another within only a few minutes of us meeting.

Then Don came over to us and asked if he could speak with his little sister privately for a minute, but then Rico jokingly said. "Hell no, she belongs to me!"

We all laughed, and continued to laugh when Rico looked at Don and told him that if I was his real sister, then he was so happy that he was going to be welcomed into our family.

I then told him that Don was my real big brother, while I walked away from him as we all continued to laugh at the look on his face after finding out that Don is my brother for real.

And while Rico firmly stood exactly where he was and waited for me and Don to finish our conversation.

Don and I had to walk a little further away from him since he was still close to us and could've heard Don when he came close to me and said. "Honey, please tell me that you are feeling Rico like he's feeling you?"

We walked a few more feet away from Rico, then I told him that I was feeling like it was love at first site with me and Rico, and that it felt kind of weird because I've never felt like that before about anybody.

But I liked it, so I told him that I wanted to see what was up with him, and to my surprise. Don really liked the idea of us together, because his purpose for pulling me to the side was because he wanted to tell me who Rico was, and why I needed to make him a frequent visitor of the club.

But then he said that there was no need for him to target Rico anymore, since I seemed to have already pulled him in, just in a different way. And with me seeing how happy Don was for my newly found friendship with Rico, I wanted to know more about who he was, and how did Don know him.

And I was getting excited about the fact that he and I connected so quickly, as well as the fact that Rico is a guy that Don and Deon may actually approve of.

Therefore, I was really intrigued. And I wanted to know more about him so Don then told me that his name was Rico Stevens, and that he was there with the bachelor party.

He said that Rico's family owns a chain of hotels in several different states, and that he was one of the groom's best friends.

And usually if Don gets excited, or shows interest in any males. The guy is usually some sort of pimp, rich, or just a plain ole powerful human being period. So I knew that things were about to change in my life, and with Don liking him so much. I was just happy about the fact that Rico may be my first potential 'real' boyfriend.

While Don on the other hand turned out to be just as happy as I was that night, because I later found out that Storm and Booby had given him one of the best gifts that he's ever received in his life. – While in my opinion, I think the three of them have had several threesomes together even after his birthday was over.

But I can't prove it, so I just don't speak on it too much, no matter how weird it was that Storm and Booby had both moved back home immediately after his party. – And they began to hang out with Don more than they hung out with me, Autry, or even Mia since they'd made up and has been friends longer than any of us even before their dancing began.

I told Don that it was strictly his business when it came to having threesomes, but I warned him to be careful and practice what he preached and not get his feelings too caught up into something that he should clearly see that wasn't meant to be long term. – Although ultimately, I stayed out of it and just enjoyed the fact that I seemed to have gained a friend for life on Don's twenty seventh birthday, because Rico and I had become inseparable ever since that night.

He was genuinely content with me dancing, because he never tried to interfere with anything once we really started seriously dating. And his family even purchased a lot of my paintings to put on the walls of their hotels.

So I can honestly say that my life was great, and it seemed that nothing could bring me down or make me unhappy even when I had a bad day. – Until one day my little sister Sabrina called me and asked if she could speak with me and only me in private.

And I knew right then before I even hung up the phone with Sabrina that something was wrong. And on a day after having such a wonderful day of being pampered and loved on by Rico, for some reason, I just knew that once again my life was about to hit another big turning point after talking to her.

Especially after she began to go into the details of how she was feeling, because the whole time while she was talking. I was thinking about how I'd been feeling the exact same way as she was feeling, so I told her to meet me in the shed over Momma Bass' house around noon that next day. And I didn't tell Rico, Momma Bass, or anyone else that I would be meeting Sabrina in private.

And as soon as I saw Sabrina when I walked into the shed that next day, she immediately burst into tears before we could even sit down to talk. She caught me by surprise because she usually tells me all of her business, but she was starting to cry a little too hard. So I figured maybe we didn't have the same issues as I thought, but I couldn't image why she would be crying so hard like she was.

But then she looked at me and said. "Honey, I'm pregnant. And I don't know what to do because I know that Momma Bass is going to be so disappointed."

Stunned and confused, I was speechless and nervous after hearing her actually say those words to me. Although over the phone she had already explained her mood swings, sudden eating habits, laziness, and nausea. So I figured that's what it was, but I was in denial about it, just like I was in denial about myself. And the fact that every symptom that she was having, I was also having all of those exact same symptoms.

And that's why I was so nervous to even imagine the word pregnant being an issue in our lives, even with me feeling like Rico was thinking that I was pregnant also.

But he just never said anything to me about it, but I knew that he was figuring it out on his own by how he would act when I was sick.

Like he did one day after I was so sick that all I did was eat crackers, threw up, and slept all day. And he took care of me so well that I knew that he was thinking that I was possibly pregnant, but it seemed like he was just waiting for me to tell him from my own mouth.

But I knew that would never happen because I didn't want to be pregnant, so I decided to strictly deal with Sabrina. So I asked her how did she know for sure that she was pregnant, because even with those symptoms. I told her that it could've just been stress, but that's when she said that she had already been to the doctor and they confirmed it.

So at that point, I had no choice but to just sit there and stare at her and at the walls because I literally didn't know what to say or do for her or myself at that moment. I just knew that neither one of us was ready for a baby.

CHAPTER
3

A month had passed, and Sabrina had finally agreed to let me tell Don and Deon that she was pregnant. Since things were moving so much faster than she expected. But after that she had no other choice but to tell Momma Bass about it, as she was accompanied with the help of Don and Deon because I wasn't of much help to her at all during that time. Because I knew that I still had to face Rico, Don, Deon, and Momma Bass about my own issues.

Although none of them would've been upset or disappointed about me being pregnant, but I never had any plans on revealing anything to them because I wasn't planning on staying pregnant for long.

And with the thought of how upset they all would be at me for having an abortion was ravaging, and although I loved Rico, I knew how evil dads could be. And I refused to chance bringing a daughter into this world for him, his dad, or any other daddy to abuse her in private.

Although for the life of me, as I could feel it in my soul that Rico would never touch his child inappropriately in any way. I just couldn't risk it, and I knew that Rico wouldn't have understood how much a pregnancy would have pulled us apart. Especially if I had the baby and it was a girl.

Touching her in the wrong places and making her endure unnecessary pain was intangible in my mind, and I would've completely stopped our lives to protect her by any means necessary. And since we didn't need that kind of drama in our relationship, I just kept things to myself and didn't tell him about the pregnancy, or about how my uncle Snap had already told me the secrets about dads.

And by then, I had personally taken several home pregnancy tests and they all said pregnant, so I knew that I was going to go to the doctor to end everything before I started showing. I was just nervous because I also knew that me having an abortion would've hurt Rico worse than anything in this world, because he was always talking about how much he wanted to marry me and have kids together one day.

And that maybe could've came true one day, because I really did love him, but I just didn't want to have a kid at that time only to have to always worry about someone mistreating him or her. While I also knew that I should have been more upfront, open and honest with him in the beginning about my true feelings of not having kids and why.

But I think that I was just too afraid to tell him, or maybe just too embarrassed to tell him the truth about my past. However, regardless of what it was, I knew that having an abortion would've seriously pulled us apart as a couple. So I didn't say anything to anybody. But the saying of what's in secret will eventually come to light was starting to sprout, because the day that I called to schedule the appointment to terminate the pregnancy. I was questioned by both Rico and Don.

Rico had invited Don to dinner with us, and they both simultaneously asked me if I was pregnant after hearing how much food that I'd ordered from the menu. But I nervously laughed it off hoping that they were joking, because I knew that Don really didn't have a clue about me being pregnant for real. So I told them no, and that I ordered so much food because I hadn't eaten anything at all that day.

But then Rico looked at Don and said. "Look at her rubbing her fingertips together, she always rubs her fingers together when she's nervous." And that's when I realized that I was rubbing my fingers together really fast in front of them, although Don still didn't seem to quite understand what was happening.

He said that he was just joking when he'd asked me if I was pregnant, but Rico on the other hand was serious about wanting to know the answer to the question, so I looked at him and asked if he was serious, and he said yes. He said that he was super serious because lately it did seem like I was pregnant.

But I looked at him and Don both and told a bold faced lie by saying. "Hell nah, I'm not pregnant!"

Rico then raised an eyebrow and told me that it really did seem like I was pregnant for the past few weeks. And right then I could immediately see the disappointment in his eyes when I told him that I was just sick because I thought the same thing, until I took a pregnancy test and it said not pregnant. – And he really was disappointed to hear that, because he said that he had his hopes up in thinking that I was pregnant. And that he guessed that his hopes were a little too high, so he was just going to be patient and let it happen whenever it's supposed to happen in God's timing.

And that's when Don said that he didn't even know that we were trying to have a baby, but he would've been happy for us if I was pregnant. While he also added how he wasn't all that happy for Sabrina, but he wasn't going to tell her that to her face because the pregnancy was already hurting her enough as it was. — Don said that he'd spent so much time schooling me due to the environment that we were in, that he felt like he had just let her slip right through the cracks.

But in my opinion, that wasn't just his fault because we all agreed that we wouldn't let Sabrina grow up dancing, tricking, or anything else that wasn't concerning her growing up and staying a virgin forever.

Sabrina couldn't come to any of us about boys or anything that drew her away from staying innocent, because she was like our baby. Even Momma Bass knew how we all felt about Sabrina, and how much her becoming a big success in life meant to all of us.

That's why we eventually sent her to her room that day when I was thirteen years old and talking to them about my past, because she was like a little scientist already at the age of eight. She always kept her head stuck in a book, and they weren't always just simple little children's books. But as she continued to grow up, Sabrina was experiencing things and needed someone that she could confide in just like any other teenager needs.

But she had no one, so she ended up sneaking around with some guy that she went to school with. While we all knew that she was old enough to be doing things, but we honestly didn't believe that she was doing anything in a sexual manner. Not even kissing anyone, so sex wasn't even a thought in our heads at all.

I didn't even know that she was sexually active, and she used to tell me everything, especially after she had turned fourteen years old. She had come to me and told me how she didn't like how we all treated her like she was still five years old, and she was very serious as she damn near begged me to talk to Momma Bass, Don, and Deon for her.

And although I was just as bad as they were, she knew that I understood where she was coming from, so I did have a talk with each one of them individually. – But after receiving that pregnancy news, I knew that we had all failed her because none of us never really changed the way we saw her, nor did we change the way we treated her even after our talk.

Including myself because although she could come to me more than she could to them, she knew that she was still my baby, so sometimes she held things from me also. And since abortions were not popular with Momma Bass at all, Sabrina ended up having one of the most beautiful nephews that I couldn't have ever imagined that I would love so much.

And we all stepped up to help take care of him and Sabrina, and she has maintained things in her life quite well with our help. Unlike myself, because upon going to the abortion clinic for that consultation on terminating my pregnancy.

I decided to move forward with the abortion and got it done, then a couple of weeks after my abortion, when everything was finally back to normal.

Autry and I had a great day of shopping one day after we went to send out her wedding invitations, since Deon had finally proposed to her in front of the world because they went live on the internet and shared it with everyone.

But upon walking into Rico's house after having such a wonderful day out wedding planning. – Rico had thrown an envelope and a piece of paper in my face, and knocked the bags that I was holding out of my hands. And Autry and I both yelled and asked him what in the hell was wrong with him, because neither of us had ever seen Rico that angry before. And as you can imagine it caught us both off guard, but especially me because of how upset he was with me in particular.

And when I reached down and picked up the paper from the floor, I saw that the abortion clinic had sent me some information when they weren't even supposed to have his address. So I was extremely angry and completely beyond upset when I later found out that they had my friends address in their computers like I'd given them.

But their new receptionist had used the address that was on my driver's license when she sent out the mail. And Rico's address was on my license because when I was at the DMV to renew my driver's license, the mailing information with my name on it that was required had only his address on it. Therefore, I simply used his address instead of my own, since we were already practically living together anyway. But things went completely downhill for us after he'd found out about the abortion.

Autry had taken the paper from out of my hand and seemed a little upset with me as well after reading what the paper said, and she had a look of shock on her face after finding out that I'd been pregnant and didn't tell anyone. Because she knew just as well as everyone else knew how bad Rico wanted to marry me and raise a family together, so she couldn't hide her feelings because as I looked at her face I could tell exactly what she was thinking.

But regardless of her feelings, she still jumped in front of me to protect me when Rico started acting like he was going to hurt me bad. I started crying and told him that I would never have kids, and that I was so sorry for hurting him. While I also obnoxiously begged for his forgiveness and was really pleading and hoping that he would somehow let me explain myself. But that only made him angrier, so angry that Autry had to push me completely outside to get me out of his site to calm him down.

And I was so devastated and hurt because I knew that he would never forgive me for what I'd done. He kept yelling for me to get away from him and telling me how much he just couldn't believe that I would do that to him or our child. – While Autry called Deon, and was trying to get Rico to take her phone so that Deon could try to calm him down because he just kept telling me to get out of his face. But the whole time while he was yelling for me to get out of his face, he kept trying to come outside while asking me how could I kill his child like that?

It was horrible, and I felt even worse than I felt on the day that I had the procedure done. And that's saying a lot because out of all that I've been through, that day of my abortion was one of the absolute worst days of my life. But I felt even worse that day because I could see their heartbreak, even Autry was disappointed with me because I could tell that she was just trying to stay neutral. I could hear it in her voice and it was written all over her face that she 100% agreed with Rico.

And while Rico was expecting company that day, they'd showed up just in time to see me run to my car, start the engine and wait for Autry to come out of the house. Because by then, Rico was only getting madder and madder at me by the minute.

Although I knew that crying and begging him not to be mad at me wasn't making things any better, but I just kept crying and begging for forgiveness because I honestly loved him so much, and even had a ton of regret at that moment. And I wanted him to know that I was truly sorry for doing it, but I also knew that I was going to have to get completely away from him until he was ready to listen to what I had to say.

Unfortunately for me, after Rico's three friends had ran into the house to help Autry with him. I knew that it was all about to be over for he and I. – Autry eventually came to my car and said that we had to wait until Rico was done with her phone before we could leave.

While she also explained how she was in the house talking to his friends about what was happening, while Rico was still on her phone with Deon. And right then, I knew even more that things between Rico and I would never be the same. And I would be lying if I said that I didn't know that Don and Deon, as well as the rest of my family were going to be just as upset with me as Rico was after hearing about 'my' abortion.

But after everything had calmed down, Deon was especially mad at me. He came at me hard verbally, and damn near physically every time I would say "my" abortion because in his mind, it wasn't just "my" abortion since I didn't make the baby by myself.

He says that it wasn't a decision that I should have made without Rico being involved because it was his baby too. But I already knew that he and Rico both viewed abortions as murder whether it was still an embryo or not, so they never wanted to hear or understand my point when I would say that it was "my" body and "my" decision.

However, everybody seemed to have had an opinion about "my" abortion, and it seemed like no one ever saw my point of view. And it was very hurtful to me until I eventually talked to Momma Bass about it, and she helped me to see how they were all mad because I'd taken away a potential loved one of theirs whom they will now never get to know. And I kind of understood that as I tried to explain to them and to Rico how sorry I was for being so selfish, but eventually Rico and I permanently split forever.

Meaning no more phone calls, emails, texting, or not even a hello if we saw each other in the streets. We were completely done, and there was nothing that I could do about it at all at that point. And I tried everything to try and fix my mistake, but when nothing worked. I just stopped trying and eventually moved on.

I was so hurt and never found true love like Rico's again, until now, *eight years later*.

I have two men living in my house with me that I own mentally, physically, and financially.

And that's why I'm seeking therapy, because I just realized that after all of these years. I really do need to once again start taking Don's advice like I used to when I was a kid.

By first believing him when he says that I need some professional counseling from a real therapist about my daddy issues. He would always say that I need to go and talk to someone about my issues with fathers who are close to their daughters, especially after I had my abortion. – He said that my thoughts were toxic and untrue, and that I'll never know true happiness as far as that part of my life, if I keep going in the direction that I was going in.

And now that he has kids of his own, I guess he was trying to show me how happy I could be with a kid of my own, but it still scared me. While I knew that Don or Deon would never touch my nieces, I still felt weird about one day having a child and something bad happening to him or her, and they not tell me about it. So I just choose not to think about that part of my life for a while. But, Don, Deon, and Sabrina all have kids, and they always tell me how they wish that I would just settle down and one day experience having a child of my own.

And that brings me back to knowing that getting some therapy right now is the right thing to do at this point, because I'm all out of options now that I've placed myself in such a very strange situation.

I just couldn't seem to find my way in life anymore after Rico and I continued to go through so much until we could barely even look at each other, because he never truly forgave me.

And that's why I eventually left town and bought a house miles and miles away from everyone. I'd danced and continued to work for my boss, Brock, until I'd made enough money to move away and not have to worry about having money problems even if I didn't have a job when I left. I was sure to save enough money to be okay for the rest of my life.

Then after I'd bought my house, moved in, and was comfortable. I told everyone who didn't know me that I made most of my money through selling my paintings if the subject ever came up. While I had also taken the advice of my boss starting around two years before I'd left regarding buying and selling stocks. – Along with making a few other investments that ended up turning a few thousand dollars into several thousand dollars within only a year or so of investing.

And that also means that I started following Brock's advice on what to do and who to work with as far as my investments, and just being in the loop with good stock leads and business investments. And now I receive unbelievable amounts of money through my investments, and I still only work with whomever Brock works with during the good times and the bad.

I saved as much cash as I could before I stopped dancing and working as Brock's Secretary/Assistant. And I'd told Don and Deon that we could continue to split the money that was being made at our club three ways as usual, because although I was moving. I was still planning to come back home quite often, since I would only be four hours away.

But Don and Deon eventually agreed to pay me a lump sum of money to buy me out, because they wanted to make some changes between the two of them that I just wouldn't allow as a business partner, or as their sister.

Although they would all still call me, and I would still help as if I was still part owner every time I went home to visit, and I didn't mind because even when I wasn't at home visiting. I was still helping them out from four hours away.

So not too much had really changed after I'd moved, as far as the phones calls and my guidance on how things should be managed at the club.

But now days, things have gotten a little crazy for me, although I knew that changes were going to eventually come one day.

And some serious decisions were going to have to be made, but I'm not ready for any big changes just yet. Because the two men that I have living with me are men that I personally sought after. And now after all that we've been through together, I find myself back in a similar situation as I did with Rico eight years-ago.

When this all started anyway, because after I'd moved on from being so hurt. I took my money and went and found some unfortunate men whom I knew where at a point in their lives to where they didn't care if I took ownership over them or not.

I knew that I would be able to get them to work for me and sign papers and do just about anything else that I would ask of them. But I would first take care of them financially, then get into their mental and physical space while I helped them out like an angel. And as everything did work out just as I'd planned, I now have some serious decisions to make that I'm just not ready to make. But since I'm maturing, I can see that a person can't do what I've done to these men and not attach any love to them.

Therefore, I guess now is the best time to explain how I've successfully taken the money from my investments; and my stock profits. My club buy out money, the money from working at my regular job, my savings from dancing, along with my casino winnings that I stacked. – Because the casino was me and Autry's most favorite spot to visit on our off days, where often-times. I would take a risk at losing damn near all of my tips from the night before and bet super big with the high rollers. And I've had my share of ups and downs with winning and losing there also.

But I would sometimes actually win, and receive thousands at a time and I never said a word to Autry or anyone else about it. But I did slowly but surely take a lot of that money and separated it into a few separate accounts when I moved.

Then after that I moved forward with my plan to find some unfortunate men who had nothing to live for, and who would be willing to completely give in to me and everything that I wanted. – While I eventually did a background check on each one of them right after meeting and having a conversation with each individual as I secretly watched his every move.

I decided to get to work right away after I'd moved into my new home. – I went into the city area where I'd previously saw a lot of homeless people, every time I would drive by certain areas as I shopped to decorate my house. I saw several male and females that seemed to be homeless and had nowhere to go outside of the city streets.

So one day I dressed down, unlike how I would normally dress. But I maintained a cute yet proper look for what I was in search of, while all along staying strapped with my gun like Don and Deon have always taught me to do ever since I was sixteen years old. – Because I've carried my own semiautomatic pistol that was given to me as a gift from my brothers as a sweet sixteen gift.

It's cute and clean with no bodies on it, so I've always liked to have my gun with me. Since it's so small but carries a lot of power, just like me. Especially on days like that when I was dressed down and was on the prowl for my first Boyfriend-And-Man-Tool. – So I was sure to never leave my gun at home, as I've always kept my guard up consistently since day one. The day that I lurked in the streets until I'd officially found my first *BAMT*. – He's from Africa, and he's very-unique.

I'd went into a donut shop by myself and ordered me a blueberry scone with a lemon glaze, and a small coffee. Then I sat and watched my first *BAMT* (Boyfriend-And-Man-Tool), as he sat outside and watched the citizens with money walk around eating and throwing away food like it was nothing.

He'd sat in the same spot for about an hour just looking at everybody pass him by, while I sat in the donut shop across the street and watched him as he stood out like a sore thumb when I first noticed him hanging around the restaurant that's in front of the donut shop.

I had watched him for about three days in a row before I decided to go to the donut shop to watch him some more before saying anything to him. – But he was looking exactly, yet even better than how I imagined my first *BAMT* would look.

So I'd watched him for about an hour before I decided to get up and order him something to eat, so that I could take it to him. But then I decided that it would be better for him to just get up and come and order what he wanted for himself.

So after waiting and watching his every move for a little while longer, I got up and threw my things away. And I eventually left the donut shop and walked across the street to go and talk to him.

And when I spoke to him, at first, he just looked at me like he was extremely surprised to hear me talking to him at all. And even more surprised to hear me ask him if he would like to go across the street with me and have a scone and a cup of coffee.

CHAPTER

4

Confused, but eager, my future *BAMT* sat down with me and quickly took a few bites of his monkey bread that he'd ordered. Along with a turkey and cheese croissant, and some orange juice. Because he had immediately, and without a question took advantage of his free meal before he'd even asked me my name.

Although he never stopped looking confused and curious ever since I approached him, so he just sat at the table and ate his food without saying anything to me at the donut shop. And I stared back at him while he stared at me, then I eventually asked him to stop eating and stand up and take off his jacket.

Then he finally spoke and said "OK", while he also asked me why did I want him to take off his jacket? But I politely asked him did it really matter to him why I wanted him to take it off, and he said no, then he followed my request and took off his jacket. I then told him to sit back down and finish eating his food, and he immediately sat down without any hesitation and dug right back into his food like any other unfed homeless person would do.

But then after he finished eating, I asked him what was his name and where was he from because he spoke with and accent.

And he said that his name was Isaiah, and that he was from Senegal, Africa, and that he's been in America for four years.

And as my round of questions continued, he'd told me that he felt like he had become a failure after leaving his mother in Senegal, only to come to America and end up just like her. Strung out on drugs and stuck on empty with no way out of his drug infested life, until he had no choice and was forced to stop using drugs out of fear of over dosing and being just like his family.

He said that he and two of his cousins came to the United States to find good jobs so that they could earn more money. But they were all so excited about coming to America that they got lost in their purpose of doing the right things, because they all eventually ended up going in the wrong directions when they finally moved and got settled in.

And that led them to getting fired from their good paying jobs that wasn't easy to get, but now one of his cousins has an ill baby. But he'd lost contact with her after seeing the child only one time, and his other cousin died of a drug over dose. And that's what made him get clean because he said that he knew that he was going to die next if he didn't stop.

So I just continued to dig more and more into him and his personal life as far as I could, while at the same time I was also consistently looking at him and his body features. Just like I'd been doing for the past three days before I had decided to finally make my move from the donut shop.

While during those moments, I was also thinking of how I could repair him and make him over into being exactly how I wanted him to be from that day forward.

Because fortunately for me, I could clearly hear and see that he was at the end of having any hope in anything anymore.

But he didn't necessarily want to just give up and die, and that opened the door for me to proposition him. But by that time it was time for the donut shop to close before I could really mention to him why I was so interested in him.

So I held off on telling him why I cared to know so much, and I just let him continue to fill me in as much as he wanted to, because he could see that he had my full and undivided attention. Even after we'd left the donut shop and went back across the street to the restaurant where I usually saw him sitting outside until they closed.

He told me that it felt good to be able to actually go inside of the restaurant to sit down, instead of always having to sit outside. He said that there was a cook who worked there that always looked out for him and gave him whatever food the employees were allowed to take home or throw away at the end of the night. – And I just let him go on and on about how he sleeps anywhere, as long as it's clean. Because he seemed to think that finding his unusual homeless people hideouts were actually cleaner than just lying under any old viaduct like a lot of people do.

Above all, I told him that I could see why he was feeling the way that he was feeling, and that I could also see why he would rather be homeless in the United States. Rather than to go back to Senegal just as poor.

He said that he would be living damn near the same way, but a little worse if he went back home, especially with his family being all so messed up like they were.

He said that he loves Africa and its many traditions, because there's so much beauty in so many people and in so many different things and places. As he explained how it has its beautiful places just as it has its bad throughout the continent, but he said that he would never go back to his country so empty handed like he was.

And that's where I came in at, because in my mind the whole time while he talked, I was thinking that he was uniquely handsome. And too smart to be homeless, but he was just used to successfully living with nothing and surviving; because that's what he had been doing his entire life.

But I knew that with a little maintenance he could potentially become exactly what I needed him to be, since his personality was perfectly open for everything that I had in mind. – All the way down to his respect for me even stopping to talk to him at all.

Although I could hear and see that he was a bit of a pushover, and that he had too many soft spots in his heart that was left open to allow people to use him. And that was good and bad because soft spots are good and useful, but they can also be very deadly and very unnecessary.

Therefore, I intended to show him how to use those soft spots in a way that he wouldn't be such a pushover.

Yet and still he wouldn't be too mean and cruel to follow what I had in store for him. – Substantially, after letting time catch up to us once again, Isaiah had finally decided to ask me my name. And I smiled at him then started laughing because we had spent so much time together by then.

And he had been telling me all of his business, but he never even thought to ask me my name. So when I told him that my name was Tristan, and that it was funny how he had waited for so many hours to ask me my name. But he said that he wanted to ask me my name earlier, but he was just so shocked that I was talking to him. Let alone listening to him, and buying him food that he just didn't ask.

Nevertheless, I introduced myself to him by using my real name. But that was as far as it went in terms of me giving him anymore information about me during that time. I then offered to purchase him a hotel room to sleep in for the night.

Because I wanted to spend more time with him outside of those restaurants.

And I also wanted to see him cleaned up a lot better than he was, so I called a car service to come and pick us up and take us to the nearest Target or Walmart.

Whichever was closet, because I knew that either one of those stores would have everything that he would need to get cleaned up. And when we arrived at the store, I had given Isaiah five hundred dollars, and told him to take the money and go directly into the store and get whatever he needed.

And as he was about to open the car door to step out and go into the store. I had grabbed his arm and told him that he could fuck me over if he wanted to for five hundred dollars, but I advised him not to do that. I told him that he could have a lot more than just five hundred dollars coming to him if he did exactly what I told him to do.

I also told him that he could take as much time as he needed inside of the store, because I would let the driver leave us and just call another one whenever he was done shopping if he took too long. Then I told him that I wanted to stay outside and just wait for him in the car at that point, because I wanted to see if I could trust him.

And the reality was to test him, but also because I didn't want to walk into the store with a loaded weapon on me at that location. So I had to take a risk and trust him as I instructed him to go into the store and buy himself some new clothes and underwear. Along with a pair of shoes, a pack of socks, as well as a tooth brush, tooth paste, mouthwash, soap, and whatever else that the five hundred dollars could purchase for his clean up.

I also told him that I would give him another five hundred dollars, but only if his receipt showed me that he'd completely used all of the money strictly for what I'd told him to use it for. Then after he'd followed my instructions.

He came back to the car with all of his bags, and I asked the driver to drop us off at a hotel.

And Isaiah was just so happy, and seemed to be very grateful that he had found himself shopping and preparing to sleep comfortably in a hotel room.

Versus sitting around outside of some restaurant and waiting for leftovers for him to take with him where ever he would've found to lay his head for the night. – Then after I paid the driver, and checked us into the hotel. Isaiah got cleaned up and allowed me to throw away everything that he owned, and it wasn't very much. So it was easy for me to discard him of everything, including his shoes and his belt that he liked. While during this time, he stated how he also had a few more items stashed away in his secret spot in the city. For when he needed to brush his teeth, change clothes, and things like that.

But I told him that if everything worked out between us, then he should from that day forward view those items as trash as well. Unless he surprisingly had something of financial value, or something sentimental that he just needed to go back and get. But other than that, he would never see those items ever again while dealing with me.

I told him that I knew that he couldn't be changed and made into a new man overnight, nor by the end of the week. But I did want him to understand that I wasn't being nice to him for free, and that the only reason that I was showing so much interest in him was because I could see something in him that could help the both of us.

And with his personality being like it was, versus having a homeless hustling dope fen type of mentality. I immediately knew that things could get even better for us than I expected, because his actions showed me even more that he was perfect for what I was looking for. Because he stayed in the shower for so long that I had to knock on the bathroom door to make sure that he was okay. And when he answered "yeah", and told me that he didn't want to take away all of the hot water, so he was about to come out anyway. – He still wasn't done cleaning himself because after he'd opened the bathroom door. He came out and stood at the other sink for a long time with a towel wrapped around his waist as he brushed his hair and his teeth, flossed, and used his mouthwash.

And I could see that he was a guy that kept himself clean whenever he could afford to do so, because he was way too focused on getting himself together without me having to ask him to make sure that he takes his time and clean his whole body properly without rushing.

And he used everything that he'd purchased including his face astringent, his two in one conditioning shampoo, his finger and toenail clippers, and whatever else that he had to get himself together. But when he was finally done, he had come over and sat down on the bed across from me. While I sat up straight and uncrossed my legs, then I stuck my hands into my jacket where my gun was. Although I knew that he wasn't a threat. But my brothers taught me to always stay on guard no matter how it seems, especially when I'm handling business, regardless of who or what it is.

But Isaiah looked at me with a serious face and asked me why was I really doing all of that for him for real. But again, instead of me answering him, I asked him did he trust me so far with only knowing what he knew about me at that point. And he said that he only knew my name, but yes, he trusted me. So I told him that I promised to answer any of his questions to help him further understand who I was. But only after we finished our conversation that we were having at the restaurant. He simply agreed, then proceeded to fill me in more and more about his history. And I felt like we were really starting to get to know each other better within that short time, because after a while we found ourselves laughing, and even damn near crying at times as we talked.

Although I didn't tell him much about me personally, but we still ended up laughing and just having a good time. While still in the corners of my mind I knew that I was going to do an intense background check from as far back as I could on him.

Especially when he would get emotional about a few things that has happened to him in his past. And I didn't care how much I was going to have to pay to get his information, because I was intrigued by how he's had to live his life ever since he was a child.

While his English was good at the time, I could tell that his preferred language was French due to how some of his English words were coming out incorrectly. Nonetheless, he was fluent enough with his English to be understood, so ultimately I was still receiving a good understanding of who he was and how he was feeling.

Even the once or twice when I could barely understand what he was saying. I knew that all he's ever wanted was to be able to take care of himself enough to have a nice house, car, and other things. Especially since his mom was so messed up, and he never really knew his dad. So he didn't have a steady home foundation that he could always go back to when things got hard.

But I told him that I was there to help him, and that I could totally relate to him and how he was feeling.

Although he's never really had any long-term goals, or anybody in his life to teach him to want more out of life than to just have a nice house, car, and a lot of money. So I told him that wanting to have all of those material things out of life was very good and very necessary, but having someone to genuinely love you and to share what little you already have is even better.

And since he didn't have anything else to do, I stated how I wanted to try and bring him into my family if he wanted to be in it; but only under certain circumstances. Then I asked him how did he feel about one day being my boyfriend, and he just stared at me really hard without saying anything.

Then he eventually said that he could never see somebody like him having a girlfriend like me. So I explained to him how he was not only going to have me as his girlfriend, whom he would eventually be having sex with in a few months. After he's been seen and tested by a few doctors, but as his girlfriend. I would also be allowing him to sleep with other women that were similar to me. – But I needed to know how he felt about that.

Because at that point, I felt like since he didn't have a job, and of course he was homeless. So he probably hadn't had sex in a while, and was probably more STD free than an average guy who has a job and probably having sex with multiple women. – But without any knowledge of how Isaiah felt about having sex with multiple women. I went ahead and seriously, yet thoroughly explained to him how he would only be allowed to sleep with someone else with my permission only.

And he agreed by nodding his head back and forth like he was saying yes, while he listened to me talk.

Not knowing that it would not be as easy as it seemed, although our process would be fun. But I let him know that it could possibly get very challenging for him in the future, and I wasn't particularly worried about that personally. – Because I had already prepared myself for if or when any *BAMT* that I had planned on finding ever felt the urge to want to leave me and start back thinking for himself.

Then and only then would they really get to see the real Tristan, and really find out how much experience I have in the legal field after working for years as a personal assistant/secretary for one of the most respected and highest paid lawyers to ever walk into a court room.

Because they would have to sign documents that would be presented to them, visibly and fine printed with me having complete control over their finances. Along with everything else that they would ever own besides their own physical bodies for the remaining of their lifetime, they would always belong to me. Unless they could hire a good lawyer to one day fight the documents after they would sign and be video recorded doing it, just as I'd planned it to be. But even if they did find a way to afford a lawyer, there would be clauses inside of the documents that actually even gives me control of their bodies during specific situations. It would all be just so complicated for them to fight me over having so much control of their lives.

However, as we began our process. I asked Isaiah about his feelings toward me taking him to a health clinic that next morning to get a physical. As well as me setting him up to go and get checked for any and every sexually transmitted disease possible.

I told him that I wanted him to then go to a totally different clinic. And have them to test him for any STD's again, as if he's never been tested before. – Even if every test came back negative from the first doctor, I wanted a second test done on everything.

Along with him also getting as many tests as he could get for any nonsexual diseases that he could potentially have as well. While I would also schedule him a dentist appointment and pay to have his teeth fixed, since I didn't like how he was missing a tooth that was toward the back of his mouth. – And although it was barely visible due to it being towards the back of his mouth, in my eyes, it was still noticeably missing every time he talked.

And seeing how he did care about his mouth when he was able to do so, I wanted to ask the dentist to give him a good cleaning, plus whatever else that he would need to have a healthy mouth in general. And not just fix his smile only.

But thankfully, Isaiah's mouth wasn't as bad as I thought it would be. And I knew that if he made sure that he kept flossing, brushing his teeth, and using his mouthwash every day. Then he would be fine, the only thing that was left for me to explain to him was that I would need for him to sign some papers for me. Saying that he was willing to share his earnings with me whenever he started to receive any forms of income from anywhere in the world from that day forward.

And when I eventually told him about the papers, and how I would be presenting them to him for us to sign and get them government approved, sealed, and whatever else that would be needed to make the documents completely legal. He stopped me and said that he already trusted me even before I could finish explaining to him the details of the contract outside of just controlling his finances, and why I even wanted him to sign the papers at all.

We were able to just move right along without any problems concerning that, and I didn't even have to explain the extra fine print that would be included in the documents or anything. He was just ready for whatever.

And as our night continued while I explained everything to him that would be happening that next day, even before going to the health clinic. I told him that we would start with me taking him to the department of social services, the DMV, and wherever else that he would need to go to get some updated identification to start putting his life back together.

Therefore, as you can image, before morning came. I'd gotten to know Isaiah way better mentally and physically, and I was so overjoyed that those few long days of stalking him before I'd approached him were not in vain.

Including me getting to know how shy he was or wasn't when it came to his penis, and I needed to see it as soon as possible before I could continue to invest in him without even getting a good glimpse of how it even looked or anything.

Because regardless of his personality, I needed to know if I could seriously use his sex as my boyfriend when it came to his penis. So I asked him to stand up and unwrap his towel, since he had already been sitting down talking to me that whole time damn near naked anyway, ever since he'd gotten out of the shower he only wore a towel.

And at first he hesitated and asked me why did I want him to do that? And at that point, I did feel like it was time for me to start answering more of his questions.

So I told him that I wanted to see him because he was going to eventually be my boyfriend. And that if I had already saw him as dirty as he was, then why not show it to me, because I would eventually see it anyway.

Then I added that I also needed to see it to know if I was willing to deal with it or not, regardless of how it looked as far as him being hairy or anything like that. I told him that it would just be hard to invest in something or someone that I couldn't use.

And I knew that even with a glimpse of seeing it, I would immediately be able to decide if I wanted to deal with him or not judging from whatever I would see.

Then he eventually decided to stand up and slowly let the towel unravel, and his penis hung in good length without it being hard. Although it was much hairier than I pictured it would be, but nevertheless, it looked good enough to satisfy. With the head of it looking really weird as it was shaped like a really huge mushroom, not a normal mushroom, but one like I've never seen before. And that made him more attractive because I didn't know if it was some sort of African thing or what, I just knew that it could only get better when he was erect.

So I told him that I wanted him to keep himself shaved because I liked my man with little to no hair down there. And then I told him that it may be inappropriate, but I really wanted to see him touch on his penis to get it harder. So that I could really see what I would be completely getting.

And although I was very serious, I hinted around about how he didn't really have to do it if he didn't want to.

Because honestly in the back of my head, I had already seen all that I needed to see, even though it was limp and soft at the moment. But I just wanted to see how shy he was, and what would be his reaction when I asked him to play with himself, or do whatever it was that he needed to do so that I could watch it grow.

And while I could tell that he was very nervous, he didn't seem too bothered by any of my requests or questions as I attempted to see just how long it would take him to get hard without any help, or how much work would it take for him to get as hard as he could get without anyone's help other than his own hands. – So he positioned himself on the bed as he nervously began to squeeze, pull, and massage himself in front of me.

And while he did begin to grow bigger after about two minutes or so, he was still clearly nervous. But I could see that he was still growing and making me prouder already. And I could also clearly see that I wasn't going to see him at his best without giving him a boost to get him at least a little horny, since I'd just put him on the spot like that. – And while he was thinking the same thing, because he said that it was hard for him to really get into it with me just sitting there looking at him.

I laughed because it was a little weird of me to be sitting there just watching him, so I asked him what did he need for me to do other than physically touch on him in order to make him more comfortable?

And he said that me sitting there watching him was actually enough, because he was so attracted to me.

He said what stood in his way was not really my staring, but it was him thinking that I wouldn't be pleased with him.

So I then stood up and finally took off my jacket because I was still fully dressed. And I wasn't ready to part from my gun due to him still being a stranger, regardless of what we were doing.

But feeling completely safe at that point, I did take off my jacket, and just kept it near me with no plans of letting it leave my side whatsoever.

I then took off my shoes and asked him to sit back further onto the bed that he was sitting on, while I sat back further onto the bcd that I was sitting on.

I asked him would it help if I turned on the music app that was on my phone, so that it wouldn't be so quiet, and he said that it didn't matter. He said that all he was concerned about was me not liking him. But again, after having to explain to him that if I didn't like him, he surely wouldn't be there with me like he was. So to take my mission a step further, instead of me turning on any music. I unbuttoned my shirt and revealed my boobs while wearing just a regular purple and black bra, it didn't have any lace or sexy designs on it. But I sat in front of him and revealed my chest with my legs spread open and told him to relax and know that I was already comfortable and satisfied with him.

He was then able to relax a little more and let his penis rise and stand at attention for me. While my eyes also got bigger as I was truly able to see that he was definitely ready and good enough for me to choose after watching him present himself in the ways that he did.

And when he was done, and had ejaculated heavily into his hands and onto his belly. He laid there for a few seconds before telling me that he couldn't believe that he had just done that in front of me like that.

Then he got up and cleaned himself as the night was getting later. – But Isaiah and I seemed to have literally become great friends over night. Even with me keeping in mind that he was homeless, and was probably willing to say and do whatever he had to, to not be homeless anymore.

So with that in mind, I barely slept. I basically stayed up and watched television all night, no matter how close we had become. I knew that it was dangerous to place myself in such a situation, so I was sure to keep my guards up while remaining happy with our progress and sudden friendship.

CHAPTER

5

Waking up to the breakfast that the hotel provides every morning for their guests, Isaiah and I had a semi healthy breakfast while I explained to him how the rest of his day would be. And I also informed him of how I was going to pay for him to live there at the hotel for the next seven days.

But first, I wanted to take him to get a good shave and a hair cut from Ali, one of Deon's friends who lived in the city who's a barber. – Ali used to come out and spend a lot of money at our club every time he and his friends would drive out and visit us.

But I let Isaiah know that after he received a haircut, then we would take another trip to the store to get him some more clothes, shoes, and whatever else that he would need to live comfortably for the next few days. – Including buying some razors and clippers to shave his midsection, where he had allowed hair to grow in profusely.

I told him that I would be making his dentist appointment a few weeks out, to give us enough time to get his ID and everything else that he would need to rebuild his life. – And I was already acting like his girlfriend by making phone calls for him, while only having him to make calls to the places that I knew would strictly want to speak with him directly, as we sorted through all of his personal information.

And as I was already feeling like I was lucky and had found the perfect *BAMT*, Isaiah was proving me right every minute we'd spent together because he really was a smart guy that had more than just common sense. He just needed help with why and how to use his good sense to keep himself and me taken care of.

Meanwhile, as we sat and was finishing our breakfast after making phone calls and writing down all of the information that we'd gathered so far. – I did just as I said I would do, I went to the front desk of the hotel to arrange for him a longer stay.

I then called a car service to come and take us shopping until Ali was ready for us, because when I called him he had too many clients, so he wasn't ready for Isaiah yet. So we went shopping and I let him get whatever he wanted to get within the budget that I'd given him, and I could tell that he was just so grateful and submissive.

And as we finished shopping, I had the driver to take us back to the hotel so that we could drop off Isaiah's belongings. Then I asked the driver to go ahead and drop us off at the barbershop because I figured by then, Ali should've been ready for him after such a long wait.

But when we got to the barbershop, there was a woman that came in and later started complaining about how late she would be getting to work due to her son having to wait so long to get his haircut. So we offered to allow her son to get his haircut before Isaiah, so that she wouldn't be late for work. And that's when Isaiah asked me to come with him to the smoothie shop that was next door, while we waited for Ali to finish cutting the little boy's hair. And when we went next door, Isaiah and I sat down while he told me that he still just couldn't believe what was happening to him. And that it all just seemed too good to be true, but he said that he still wanted me to know how much he really appreciated me and what I was doing for him, regardless of what was actually happening.

He said that he would repay me however he could, and that all he wanted at that point was for me to be as happy as I was making him. Because I didn't just walk over him like he was nothing, like everyone else was doing. But then after I told him that he was welcome, and that I could already see that he was thankful anyway.

I let him know that the only reason why anyone ever walked over him in the first place, was because he allowed them to do it. And that he should never allow that to happen again, because that's nobody's fault but his own.

And as he was taking heed to what I was saying, he continued to tell me how he was feeling about me and what I was doing for him without even knowing him. He said that things like that usually doesn't happen to him, so he was just happy to see humanity at its best.

Then after he was done talking, and it was time for us to go back to the barbershop to keep our spot in line. I told him to tell everyone that he was just a close friend of mine from high school, and that we were just now catching back up to each other after being apart for so many years. If anyone would ever ask us anything about our friendship that would always be our story.

And as things were moving along quite well as I'd walked with him back to the barbershop. I told him that I had to make a quick run across the street, and that I would be back before he was done getting cleaned up.

Then I immediately went across the street from the barbershop and into the Real Estate office after seeing Abigail Mackie pull into her usual parking spot, for whenever she felt like working. Abigail was another one of the main reasons for me moving four hours away from home back then, aside from me and Rico splitting up.

She and her husband Kip owns a great amount of land and all kinds of real estate throughout the city together, while Kip is also the President of a National Credit Union. – And while Abigail has her own money that she inherited from her parents after they'd passed away, she still don't have nearly as much money as Kip and his family.

But together they are perfect for each other and would never leave each other no matter how insane they both are. And that brings me to how Don and Deon were champions in getting the right highfalutin business men to come out to our club on nights when we would shut it down early. Then step up our entertainment for them and produce the type of shows that were to never be spoken of again.

Because our corporate customers really didn't mind paying us thousands of dollars to do all kinds of crazy things to them without us even having to have sex with them. And Kip was one of our best customers because he did pay our set aside girls for sex every now and then, when my brothers and I would allow it. And when Kip was able to rise to the occasion, because sometimes he just couldn't do as much as he wanted to sexually. But my point is that Deon had already hooked Kip to our club after developing a relationship with him concerning some real estate business in their area.

And he's been hooked ever since his first visit, but as far as his wife Abigail, one night Kip came into the club and had paid me for a private dance. And he began to tell me about him and his wife, and how they were some swingers.

He said that they weren't allowed to sleep with anyone without them both being present, then he elaborated on how they were new to the swinging world, so they'd only done it twice. And it was with the same couple, but he said that he was recently starting to have some heart problems.

And that he couldn't perform in the bedroom like he used to, due to being on so much medication.

So Abigail suggested to him that they pay some guy on a regular basis to sleep with her while he watched, since they couldn't really swing anymore in his condition.

But then as he went on and on, and his point ended up being about how much he didn't know how he really felt about paying some guy on a regular basis to sleep with his wife. Although he didn't want Abigail to have to suffer sexually due to him not being able to give her that sexual release that she loved.

But after feeding me so much information about her and their relationship, and now fast forwarding to how I'd gotten to know Abigail for myself. — It was through me and my girls taking a few trips back and forth with Don and Deon to visit Ali.

Autry, Mia, and I would often leave the guys and go and do our own things to get to know the city better without them.

And one day when we were about to leave and go back home, we all met Ali at his shop before we were set to get back on the highway. But before we left, I'd bumped into Abigail at a store in the same strip mall as the barbershop. And we'd recognized each other from me coming into their office a few times to discuss and view some properties that Don and Deon were interested in.

And she was the one who'd began to ask me about our club, and how everything was going because Kip had already told her that we were doing well enough to purchase an even bigger building from one of their friends. If for some reason our deal with them couldn't go through due to any licensing or permit issues, they had friends of power who could help us in many ways. But still I was very limited with my words concerning the club at all, because I knew that although she and Kip didn't really have many secrets. I also knew that there was a flaw within the information that they would share, because I was certain that he didn't inform her of every single time that he would come four hours away just to throw me and my girls thousands of dollars. Because he'd told me a few times that she thought that he was gone on a business trip, and he just didn't tell her the truth.

Nevertheless, she had a few secrets of her own that I had to bait her into finding them out during our conversation that day at the store. But I ended up informing her of how I was looking to purchase a house in their area, because I wanted to open a massage Parlor there. While my boyfriend wanted to go back to school so that he could help me with my business.

And while I knew that I didn't have a boyfriend at the time, I just wanted to purposely tell her that my boyfriend wanted to become a Massage Therapist. Now after he's decided to retire from working as a Gigolo, as he'd change his profession to help me. I lied and explained to her how he talks about being a Masseur or a licensed Massage Therapist all the time after constantly being told how good he is with his hands.

And that was why I wanted to know if they had any properties available that I could look at when I was ready to move, because he was going to be ready to work. And before answering any of my questions concerning buying a house, Abigail immediately asked me about me and my boyfriend. And how on earth did our relationship survive with him being a gigolo. I told her that it was because he knew that I was an exotic dancer when he met me, just as I knew that he was a gigolo for women who he didn't love when I'd met him.

Then I added how it never affected us because no matter what or who we did, we both vowed to be extremely safe. And to always be completely honest with each other even if it hurts.

I then let her know that I was a little embarrassed to be talking to her about that kind of stuff, but I really could use her help when it was time for us to relocate. As well as use her help if she had any friends or family to send our way when they needed a good rub down whenever we got settled and ready to open. And at that point the door was open because she said that I shouldn't be embarrassed. And that she would definitely help by coming to get a rub down from my gigolo boyfriend, and that she would also help me with finding a house in their best locations.

I told her thanks, then joked around about how my boyfriend probably wouldn't mind providing her or her friends with a few extra squeezes to their private parts every now and then. If their money is right, and if it will help them with their stress.

Then after she laughed with me, I told her that she would first have to help me find a house and get settled in before I could bring him with me to do anything. And from there we joked, laughed, and just talked enough for her to share her thoughts and secrets of which some I'd already known, and some I was surprised to hear.

But ever since that day she and I became friends, and she did more than just assist me in my move. But she's the reason that my house had a huge hair salon already built onto it, thanks to the previous owner who lost the house in a big divorce battle two years after paying so much money to have it built somewhat connected to their home. Abigail said that she knew that it would be the perfect spot for me to turn into a massage Parlor as soon as she heard about how spacious it was, and she ended up helping me to negotiate an offer on the place.

While I ultimately purchased the house and the land that it's sitting on, thanks to her and someone's messy divorce. – But she was sure to let me know that whenever we were situated and ready to open for business, she and her friends would surely pay us a few visits.

But on that day when I saw her as Isaiah and I were about to walk back into the barbershop, I was just happy that I actually kind of had a boyfriend for real at that point.

One of whom I would be sending to school for about nine months to get his certification to come and work for me as a Massage Therapist for real. So I just wanted to let her know that I would be staying in contact with her about my business that I knew would take me about nine months to a year to open anyway. While I also thanked her for all of the help that she'd given me already. And she told me that she was just happy that everything was going well, and that she was excited to see how the Parlor would eventually turn out to be. Then after we chatted for a little while longer, I lied and told her how my boyfriend was just so excited to be going back to school soon after all of these years. – Then after more time passed, I informed her that I had to leave and go back across the street; while she had to leave as well to go back to work.

And as soon as I'd walked through the barbershop doors after leaving Abigail, I saw and heard everyone laughing so loud and just having fun. – So I had to ask them what was going on and they said that Isaiah had been teaching them how to speak Wolof, while also teaching them how to say bad words in French. They were all trying to speak French but no one sounded like they were saying anything right, so they told Isaiah that he was going to have to keep coming to the shop and teaching them French.

When at that moment, Ali turned his chair around and was dusting the extra hair off of Isaiah so that he could get up, and I yelled. "Oh my God, what in the world do we have here?"

And it was like the entire shop burst into laughter again, while Ali explained to me how everyone was laughing because they had just said how shocked I was going to be to see how different Isaiah looked with so much hair gone.

And they were right because I knew that he would look differently cleaned up, and earlier they all heard me say that we didn't want the lady to be late for work, but I made sure they knew that Isaiah was next in line because I really couldn't wait to see what he was going to look like without so much hair.

But Isaiah really did look like a totally different person when Ali turned that chair around, I even had to look at what he was wearing to make sure that it was him.

And the women that were there kept telling him that he should never let his hair grow all wild like that ever again, because he looked so much better with a low haircut and just that little bit of trimmed facial hair that was left on his face was all that he needed.

When honestly, he probably would've kept himself properly groomed like that if he had the equipment or the money to do so.

But of course, they had no idea that he was a homeless guy that I'd picked up from the street and just got lucky. Because he really could potentially become a forever friend due to not only his looks, but his overall character as a person.

But I walked over to Isaiah and told him that I guess he truly was my African diamond in the rough, he laughed, then looked at me and said thank you.

Then after that everyone started back asking him how to say a few more bad words in French, then he and I eventually left the shop to go back to the hotel.

And when we returned to the hotel, I ordered us a pizza then told Isaiah that I would be leaving soon to go home until that next day.

I let him know that the hotel had a room that had three or four computers in it, and that he should go downstairs and get on the computers and do some research in massage therapy. Even if he didn't know anything about computers, or massaging. I told him to take that opportunity to get on the internet to find out more about them both.

But thankfully he already knew enough about computers to do some research, so he said that he would go downstairs and see what he could find out about massage therapy.

Then after we ate, he walked me downstairs, where I suggested that he stay and take advantage of the happy hour specials that was at the bar. Since everyone staying at the hotel could drink a certain amount of liquor for free until a certain time.

And he could even take the drinks back upstairs to his room if he wanted to, but he reminded me of him telling me that he wasn't a big drinker of alcohol.

Although he said that he still may think about staying to have one glass of something small to celebrate his new start, before going into the computer room or back upstairs.

CHAPTER
6

While stepping over the few small boxes that still needed to be unpacked in my foyer. – I ran over to my phone charger so that I could call my former boss back, because he had called to tell me that I was going to hit the roof when he tells me how well one of our recent investments was doing. But I couldn't hear his entire message because my phone battery died right in the middle of listening to my voicemail. And he didn't answer his phone when I called him back, so I was left to leave a message as we played phone tag.

But feeling glad to be home, I got comfortable then poured me a glass of wine before turning on my lap top and going onto the internet to get as much free information as I could on Isaiah. Because I knew that he would be eventually coming to my house to live with me whenever I felt comfortable enough for him to do so.

But I still eventually bought locks and whatever spy equipment that I could get my hands on to place secret cameras throughout my house, even in my attic. I hid cameras in the attic that he wouldn't recognize even if he did decide to one day go up there snooping around for whatever reasons.

And as the days and weeks went by, Isaiah stayed a man of his word and kept himself clean by getting in the shower and brushing his teeth twice a day without me having to ask him to do it.

He was catching on and learning everything that I needed him to learn, and the day that his insurance plan finally started. He and I both immediately scheduled doctor's appointments, and stayed on top of his dentist appointment so that we could get his smile to how I preferred it to be. Even if I had to pay the dentist a little extra cash to get him together, then that's what I was going to do now that he had insurance to help me with a big portion of the cost to get him checked out by a more preferred dentist. And more preferred doctors in general, instead of continuing to go to the free clinics for everything.

And while his test results were always negative for everything sexual and non-sexual diseases, he remained in great health as I watched him grow daily. I also saw that one of the unique things that I liked about Isaiah besides his accent, was his demeanor toward women, and how appreciative he was of everything that I was doing for him.

He showed not just me, but all women a lot of respect. And he had a captivating look about him that made a woman want to look at him and stare. But he was poor and never really had any good financial guidance to get and keep nice things such as himself consistently groomed and looking good. Because other than his nice sized penis, he had plenty of sex appeal that he wasn't even aware of.

Especially with such a good haircut and face trim, because it was not hard to see that he wasn't from America, even before he would open his mouth to say anything. – And I would be sure to capitalize off of that within itself, while everything that he was becoming as he settled into his new look and wardrobe were becoming more and more unique every day.

And I couldn't wait to get him home and ready to work after having to live in a hotel for over six months by that time.

But I became anxious when his last day of living in the hotel was about to be over.

And it was time for him to officially move in with me as we ran into a problem that day. – Don and Deon had called me the night before it was set for Isaiah to move in, because they wanted to surprise me with a late house warming gift.

They said that they knew that I had been there for almost a year, but they still wanted to surprise me with a gift.

And they also didn't want to let me know that they were coming until they were almost at my house, so needless to say that I got a little nervous when I received that call. Because I didn't want them to scare Isaiah away, but with them not knowing anything about Isaiah at all. Let alone my plans with him or any of my other *BAMT's* that I was planning to get in the future, I had to make some quick changes because Isaiah didn't really know about them either.

And I wasn't going to let them know anything about one another until the timing was right. So basically, Isaiah ended up staying three extra nights at the hotel. After I lied and told him that I needed to suddenly go out of town for a few days to visit a family member, and I didn't want his first few days at the house to be him there alone.

And he was cool with whatever I said anyway, his only concerns were always to want me as happy as he was. And I could tell that by his actions in everything that he did anyway, and it wasn't because he'd graduated from buying his clothes from Walmart and Target, to now shopping at more expensive name brand stores by that time.

But he genuinely would have my back even when I would do slick things behind his back within those months of him being in the hotel, because I wanted to see what his choices would be when it came to looking out for us while I tested him.

I really wanted to know if he would choose to only look out for himself after we'd gotten to know each other better as the months passed.

Especially if he knew for a fact that I would never find out certain things. But my number one *BAMT* has never let me down even years later when it comes to how loyal he is to me.

And that's why sometimes I say that I'm so fortunate to have him in my life, although I can say the same great things about my other *BAMT*.

And you'll be able to see and judge him for yourself as I continue to explain how even in the beginning.

I knew that by helping each *BAMT* in their own individual ways, my actions would grant me their loyalty.

But grooming Isaiah to be my number one was a top priority for me back then, before I'd even went out and found my other *BAMT*. – And the good thing is that it all just worked out even with a rocky start of having to constantly hide things from my brothers. Nonetheless, when Don and Deon came to visit me, they'd brought me more than just one house warming gift that day.

And you would've thought that they were the ones who paid the bills at my house because of how much they made themselves at home, and was trying to get all in my business. While they also informed me of how they were finally about to open another spot, and it was only about ten minutes away from my house, but it wasn't going to be a strip club. Deon said that it wouldn't be our normal club setup, although there will be a dance floor in front of the stage for when people are invited to come and perform their poetry or music.

And I knew right then when they started talking about it being more so like a poetry lounge, it was mostly Deon's idea, because he's the one who writes poetry and stuff. But I immediately let them both know that I would not be able to help them like I usually do, because I was too busy trying to build my own business that would keep my bank account just as loaded as theirs, if not more.

But of course, with me not wanting to jump in head first with them and their plans of opening the lounge, it had them suddenly extremely interested in my business and in my personal life.

Although I did originally mention to them that I was going to start some type of business after I found a house and got settled in, I just didn't tell them exactly what I was planning to open.

And as Don, Deon, and Autry knew that I was good at braiding hair, painting, and successfully running a club, and just being a good leader. They still weren't sure of what kind of moves that I was about to make as far as my future plans for after I'd moved. All they knew was that I would be perfect for them as a business partner mentally and financially.

Especially since I loved to make money just as much as they did, but I also knew that they weren't expecting me to just say yes to their partnership right up front, knowing that I was mysteriously working on something of my own.

So I knew that they had something up their sleeves, and that something was that they'd already arranged for Autry to pop up at my house a day after they'd popped up. For just in case I did say no to their offer because fortunately for them, Autry could usually talk me into changing my mind on certain things. But unfortunately for us all, this time just wasn't one of those times.

Although she was quite convincing as she couldn't even get through the door good that next day before she started raving about how cool it would be if I would help them, stating how it also just wouldn't be right without me. And that's when I found out that the lounge would be partnered by the four of us, while Autry continued with how much she would need my help.

Not knowing that they were really going to have to find someone else to help them for real this time, because I truly had other plans that I was already committed to. – Not saying that I wouldn't help them with whatever they would need as much as I could, because I was definitely planning to help no matter what I had going on. And they knew that I was always willing and would help them just as much as I knew that they would do the same for me.

And that's why at that point I had to inform them of my plans of turning that big salon into a Spa Massage Parlor, and I knew that it would take up too much of my time from the lounge. While I even took it a step further and told them that I already had an employee who was currently in school for massage therapy and everything.

I told them that I just wasn't going to tell them anything about him until it was time for him to graduate, and that's when they offered to help me with setting up my Parlor.

While at the same time I could join them in opening the lounge so that we would be helping each other. But I just couldn't because I knew that I had other plans in motion for my Parlor that I didn't want them having any parts of, so I continued to decline their offer. But eventually out of guilt, I suggested that I go ahead and partner with them financially and accept their offer. But only if we could hire someone like me who's already been in the business long enough to help manage the place properly, since I wouldn't physically be there to do very much myself.

And although Autry was cool with my idea of hiring someone to help us run the place, while the three of them would rotate traveling back and forth from home every now and then to help maintain the lounge. My brothers just wasn't feeling my sudden change of heart, even if it was to help them. Nor were they feeling me declining their offer to help me open my Parlor.

So I had to let them know that I would always be visiting and keeping my eyes completely open to what's going on with the lounge no matter what, because the manager would have to personally send me his or her daily reports for me to routinely keep a check on everything every day. – Yet and still Don nor Deon was interested in my ideas on how I was planning to help them with the lounge regardless of how much sense I was making.

All they wanted to know was why couldn't they help me with my Parlor, so I lied and told them that I just wanted to be independent and open it on my own to prove to myself that I could do it strictly by myself.

And I did eventually convince them to let me handle my business on my own, while we moved forward with hiring someone to help us with the lounge as I suggested.

And things worked out smoothly as I'd also escaped from having to explain who Isaiah really was due to him still being at the hotel.

While overall, my brothers and Autry enjoyed their visit just as much as I enjoyed them and their gifts. But when the visit was over, and it was time for Isaiah to come home. He moved in with me and our relationship as him being my boyfriend was officially about to begin. And I made sure to reassure that he completely understood that he wouldn't be my only boyfriend, and in true salutation he told me that all he wanted was to hold his title as my number one.

Therefore, he didn't care how many boyfriends that I end up with, he just didn't want us to ever let go of our friendship.

As he continued to mention how he's never had a friend like me before, so he was down for whatever, even if he hadn't already signed those papers that I'd had him to sign. Because by that time Isaiah had already been seen by not just two free clinics, but also by his own primary care physician under his insurance, as well as a good dentist. And he was completely ready to continue with his new life at my house, but as far as school, there were a couple of things that became hard for us when it was time for him to enroll in school and apply for financial aid.

And it seemed like the process took forever before he was finally accepted into a financial aid program, right before I was about to say forget it, and just go ahead and write a check for him to get it done. But when he was finally accepted, and everything was put into place, we continued to move on.

And one day when we were in the Parlor painting, as I showed off my painting skills, and continued to go over everything with him concerning him being my *Boyfriend and Man Tool*.

He told me that he already knew his position, and at that point his allegiance to me was very clear judging from his past actions within those several months of knowing him.

Nonetheless, that day after we were done painting at the Parlor. I told him that I wanted us to continue our conversation while he practiced on his massages by massaging my body, while I also explained to him how and where I liked to be touched. Along with how much we women love for a man to devour us with his full libido when he's being intimate with us.

He then took off my shirt while I laid flat on my belly as he rubbed and massaged the back of my arms, neck, ears, back, booty, and my legs while he listened to me tell him a few dos and don'ts when it comes to being seductive and very intimate. But I quickly learned that most of my teachings would be of me teaching him how to manage his money, and just his life in general because he basically had the whole sexually seductive thing intact by just being himself. As he explained how a lot of African men automatically knows how to caress a woman in every way possible, including knowing how to put women into various sexual positions that could make them have multiple orgasms within three or four minutes. And naturally, I told him that I thought that was some bullshit because four minutes is not enough time to have multiple orgasms.

And we debated about it until he told me that he would just have to show me.

While I laughed thinking that he probably does have some good sex, but multiple orgasms within three or four minutes was most likely inaccurate.

Yet as he laughed along with me, he made sure that I understood how African men has a history of knowing how to satisfy a woman in bed.

Before it was just laughed off and overlooked as if he didn't warn me. But I told him that the warning was duly-noted within my head, along with his explaining of how authentically overprotective African men are of their women.

And we just moved forward with our conversation and with my massage. But we didn't have any oil for him to rub on my body, so he stopped and went and got some oil.

He then put the oil on me and started squeezing a little more while rubbing and gripping the backside of my body so well that I think my bones fell in love with him that night before he was even taught anything at school. – I told him that he wasn't lying about knowing how to use his hands, and that he had me curious and excited to see how much fun our first sexual intercourse would be.

He said that he was just as excited about how our first time would be too, but also nervous because he doesn't want to be too anxious when it happens. – He said that he knew that he wasn't going to have a problem with whatever woman that I would allow him to touch sexually, because he would do whatever he needed to do to make me happy. He said that as much as he could assure me that those women will be pleased, and will probably want more. But when it comes to us, he was still somewhat shy because he don't want to disappoint me.

And as he continued on about how in his heart there will always be a weakness for me with or without sex, he then turned me over to massage the front side of my body. And joked around by saying that my other *BAMT's*, boyfriends, as I referred to them at that point as my 'boyfriends'. – But he said that he knew who and whose he was, and that any other boyfriends after him would have to prove themselves to be worthy of my friendship.

And with my shirt being off, and me not having on a bra from the start, it was completely clear that I was on to something great with Isaiah. Because he was literally single handedly taking away my stress by slowly rubbing my bare chest with oil and saying all the right things about him making sure that any *BAMT* that comes after him having to prove themselves to be worthy of my friendship was exactly what I needed to hear.

Then he continued to massage my body from my neck all the way down to my toes as he took his time and gradually gripped, squeezed, and pulled on everything including my toes.

And I had been so tense and needed a massage much more than I thought, so I thanked him by placing a big kiss onto his lips as a payment.

Then I told him that our day was coming when we would be able to make sweet love like we'd been talking about doing for so long. Because his entire demeanor read sex every time he would touch me when we were alone, but I had to make him continue to wait for just a little while longer. Because little did he know, I was planning him a surprise congratulations/birthday party that following month. Because his birthday and his first day of school fell on the same day, so I felt that it would only be fitting that our first time full on sexual connection should also happen on that night after his party was over.

CHAPTER

7

I went through the process of registering my business and also receiving my license and doing whatever necessary so that I could continue to move forward as I ordered tables, robes, towels, oils, stones, aromatherapy agents, facial steamers, and so much more equipment.

With everything already designed with my logo and ready to be shelved at the Parlor as soon as the construction workers were finished with the saunas. Along with the Vichy spa showers that they were preparing on the other side of the hall, opposite of the sauna rooms. But it was taking the construction workers a little longer to finish than they expected.

And while Isaiah, along with my brothers. They were all going to be putting in my multifunction steamers, exfoliation and microdermabrasion machines. But before they could start setting up anything and permanently placing it where it belongs. Everything along the walls of where I needed for them to start was on hold until the saunas and the Vichy spa showers were fully completed.

Therefore, I had more time to prepare for Isaiah and my brothers to officially meet, before they would begin their work together thanks to the construction workers. So as my brothers were postponed, and their meeting also wouldn't be happening at Isaiah's party that was coming up. Because I purposely neglected to tell any family members back home about the party, although I did slowly but surely tell them things.

But all my brothers really knew was that Isaiah was a friend that I'd gotten close to, and he was going to school so that he could come and work for me. And they had definitely expressed how much they wanted to meet this mystery man who I trusted and viewed as a close friend, and I knew that I needed to make their introduction happen soon because Don and Deon will force themselves on us in order to check him out for themselves.

But until it was time for their meet and greet, I excluded them from the party while everyone from the barbershop. Along with about ten to fifteen other friends of whom Isaiah had gotten to know over time were all invited to come and help me celebrate him and his birthday. – And at that point it was bound to stick out that he and I were more than just old friends, and that's what I didn't want my brothers to know just yet. But it was okay even if Ali or anyone else informed them because I had done a great job with keeping things quiet that long.

And by the time his birthday came, I somewhat didn't care who knew whatever anyway, because I'd already schooled Isaiah on what to say to everyone including my family. And of course, he went with the flow of however I chose to wait or not when it came to him and my family and what they knew about him.

Ultimately, I knew that I would have to be the one to deal with my brothers and their concerns with my *BAMT* whenever they would eventually find out more about him and anyone else in the future, but I would just have to cross that overprotective bridge of theirs when I got to it.

In the meantime, after having Ali and two other guys from the shop to take Isaiah out for his birthday that Thursday evening of his first day of school. They had picked him up so that they could drink and keep him entertained at a nearby bar, until I'd made the call for them to bring him home after everyone that was invited had come over to surprise him.

And as I'd hidden their cars away from the house, and in the opposite direction of where they would be bringing him in from. Isaiah was completely shocked and unaware of everything when we all jumped out and yelled surprise. – I got him good, and he was very pleased because all of us who were there had gotten to know and genuinely love him as a person, and he could see it in our actions that night.

Although no one knew that he was previously homeless, and they probably wouldn't have believed it even if someone would have said that he used to do drugs and was homeless because he looked, dressed, smelled, and even talked with just as much sense, if not more sense than the guys who has never been homeless in their lives. – And I was determined to keep it hidden so that they wouldn't find out about that part of his life, and I stood proud and excited to see him so surprised and happy about how his birthday turned out.

Then after eating good and serving jello-shots, along with serving a variety of other intoxicating treats that were made and added to the counter top that was full of bottles of alcohol ready to be served. Isaiah still didn't drink very much of the hard liquor, maybe one glass, but he did have a few extra beers than he would normally have.

Therefore, he was just as tipsy as the rest of us, and that was perfect because he had even taken a few bites from the edibles that Ali brought. And the evening was getting later as we continued to party into the night, everyone kept getting full and having a great time. – That is until I started cleaning up and throwing out subliminal hints that it was time for them to leave. And I knew that I didn't need to be tipsy or completely drunk to dance or to have sex like I was planning to do with him after everyone left. But unlike Isaiah, I'd gotten a little beyond just tipsy strictly for the fun of it.

But I kept my composure because although I was intoxicated, I was not as sloppy drunk as I'd told myself that I would be by the end of the night. Especially after working so hard by then to get him together, I'd planned on being completely overwhelmed with food, liquor, sex, and whatever else that I felt like doing on his birthday. As if it was my birthday too.

And since he and I kept giving each other looks of seduction all night, he immediately knew exactly what time it was after the last person walked out of the house due to my unusual ways of touching on him. And the places on his body that I'd been touching on all night, so he wasn't really surprised when I asked him to go into the master bathroom and get into my shower.

But he did give me the biggest smile ever after I'd also instructed him to put on his towel and just wait for me to come into the bathroom with him after he was done. And after he'd went into his bathroom to get his own soap, after joking about how good my soap smelled on me. But he said that he didn't want to smell so soft and pretty. We both then smiled and laughed a little more as he said okay to everything that was being said, before I'd left him to go and get prepared to give him his last gift of the night.

And when I finally heard the shower stop. I waited a few minutes then I walked into the bathroom with a chair for him to sit on, because I wanted him to have a seat and watch me take a shower. Since my bathroom shower is designed mostly of fixed glass so that I can see the entire bathroom even from the shower. And just as I wanted, he watched my every movement from when I got in and washed my body. Until I was done.

And when I turned the water off, and was about to step out of the shower. He'd given me my towel and started helping me to dry off. – I then took him by his hand and led us into my bedroom where I already had soft music playing.

I told him to have a seat in the chair that I had already placed on top of several large trash bags that was scattered all over the floor in front of my bed. And he was looking very curious, yet excited to see that something was about to happen. He just didn't know what, especially with so many huge trash bags and towels placed everywhere. So he just smiled and went with the flow of everything.

And as the lights were already dimmed, I stood beside a stack of big towels while holding a bottle of oil. And still only wearing my bath towel, I told him to just sit back in the chair and relax so that we could finally share some intimate boyfriend and girlfriend time. I then walked onto the trash bags while holding the oil as I began to dance and put on a show for him as if he was one of my top paying customers. And it turned out great, although stripping down to nothing wasn't an adventure for me. But for Isaiah, seeing me rolling my bottom and flexing to the rhythm of the music while only having to take off a big towel seemed to be very much of an adventure for him.

My only concern was to be sure of not to use too much oil as I used it to slide around all over the trash bags doing what I do, especially when I'd dropped down to my knees and crawled away from him after he became antsy in his chair from watching me slowly pour a little more oil onto my body while standing directly in front of him. I danced around and on top of him while sitting on his lap and letting our oily bodies rub against each other as we did whatever we wanted to do.

But I had to crawl away in efforts to calm him down because I felt like our body contact was making his penis grow more and more before I was finished having fun with him.

But seeing how much I was sliding around dancing while tugging and rubbing on him, me crawling away from him didn't really help much for real because his penis. Along with both of our eager desires to have sex after waiting so long, it all somewhat stopped our foreplay anyway because by the time I'd turned around from crawling away from him.

He was completely erect and had gotten out of the chair and onto the floor with me. And from there we allowed our bodies to slip and slide all over each other's until I'd reached over and grabbed one of the big towels, where I had also had some condoms sitting next to the towels.

I grabbed a towel and a condom and handed it to him, then I told him that if there wasn't so much oil covering us, then I would've just grab his penis with my mouth and put the condom on for him. He laughed, then reached over me and picked up another big towel and said that he could easily wipe the oil off.

And as intoxicated as I was, I honestly didn't care about the oil or anything else if he really wanted me to suck on him that night. And he absolutely did want me to do that for him, especially after I'd told him that I didn't mind sucking on him for his birthday anyway. But he just needed to remember that in our relationship, I would be mainly receiving oral sex instead of giving it.

He then got up to sit back in the chair while I made my way over to him to remove the oil from his penis, although it wasn't just ridiculously oily anyway. But after wiping the oil off, I admired how clean shaved and robust he was, then I slid him in and out of my mouth while I was still on my knees in front of him. And I just willingly gave him whatever he wanted without being too dramatic, although he was quite excited as he watched me grip and deep throat, jack, tongue, and suck on his penis and caress his balls while he enjoyed his gift.

I eventually pulled him to the edge of the seat so that he could put both of his legs on top of my shoulders.

And I let him grab my hair and submerge into my mouth as hard, soft, or as slow as he wanted to. While I rocked my neck and head back and forth and listened to him speak in French a few times as he frequently did throughout the night, but as usual. I didn't understand anything that he was saying. – But he sounded very sexy and very into what he was receiving, so I liked it, and I kept going and eventually used both of my hands to handle his penis as my mouth was smacking on his balls.

And when I finally let his legs down from my shoulders, he showed no signs of shyness as he'd opened his legs wide and let his penis hang while freely letting me do whatever I wanted to do with him. Until he had swiftly reached down and grabbed me and lifted me above his head. And I was very surprised because I didn't expect for him to lift me above his head like I was a pillow. Although I am small compared to him, but still definitely not small enough for him to be handling me like he was, and especially with oil covering us.

But he held me up to his face while I was the one who became nervous because I thought that he was going to drop me.

But his truth stood out as he controlled the entire situation by not only holding me up to his mouth, but holding me up for so long that I made him put me down because I needed to feel his bigheaded penis inside of me immediately.

So I then picked the condom back up that I was previously holding.

I placed it on him by using my mouth like he wanted me to, then I picked up two more big towels and laid them on top of the trash bags that had little to no oil on them. Then I told him to lay on the towels while I stood over him and danced my way down to a split and onto his penis while I began to get more into him every second that I entertained him.

I had placed both of my hands where ever they needed to be as I rode him as best as I could without being too dramatic, especially before letting him put me into any of his so called "African" sex positions.

Although my reality did quickly become 'True to the Game', and that's exactly what I wanted to nickname him from that night forward. Because his words eventually held nothing but the truth, as he'd made me have orgasms stemming from deep inside of my vagina. All the way to the tip of my clit within more than three or four minutes of him getting on top of me as he claimed he could.

But nevertheless, regardless of it taking him longer than three or four minutes. It still didn't take away from his truth because it wasn't very long before I began to release and couldn't hold back my trembles or multiple orgasms throughout him holding me, gripping, and flipping me all over the floor.

While he kept taking his penis out of me and rubbing it against my clit every now and then, and he would slowly stick it back in to keep it doing whatever and hitting whatever spots that he was hitting inside of me.

And his words were truly no longer a myth, and I eventually had both of my hands placed flat on the towels. While he stood behind me and held me up like a wheelbarrow, and we both eventually finished with a bang. And I felt that Isaiah's actions were so real and unexpected that I needed to take a minute to figure some things out within myself, but first I paused and told him that I couldn't believe that his penis was still hard after I'd just experienced him cum the way that he came.

Then he said that he wanted to put on another condom because he wasn't done, and of course I wasn't going to stop him. Especially when he told me that his penis has never stayed hard like that before, and that he must have been just super excited.

Because when he pulled out of me the first time, we both saw how much he had released into that first condom.

And I knew that I could go all night if that's what he wanted to do, so the fun continued while my thoughts of how much more I could capitalize off of him was a consistent thought in my mind.

But more so, I was also thinking that his future customers would not be receiving his full throttle like that for two reasons.

Number one being because some of them will be older women whose bodies can't be taken through all of what he had did to me, and number two will be strictly because I'm saying that he just can't have that kind of sex with nobody but me, period. And as for the rest of his birthday night, he and I both treated one another to as much of each other as we could take, until we were exhausted.

So much so that neither of us got up to get back into the shower, or even really left the floor outside of disposing of the used condoms into the trash. Then that next morning, when we woke up to towels and condom wrappers scattered around us. We actually had sex one more time before we got up to get cleaned up and started with our day.

And from that day forward, I still referred to Isaiah by calling him Isaiah. But more times than not, his nickname Tru has taken ownership of being his name. Since 'True to The Game' was too long of a nickname for him.

Because as I judged him for his sex and his loyalty to me at that point. I just couldn't think of any other name more fitting for my number one, and he told me to my face that he would do anything for me to show me how much he loves and appreciate me.

Including hurting someone if he had to, and those were his exact words with me putting words into his mouth when he explained how he just wanted me to know that he had my back like I'd shown him that I had his. So from that day forward, Tru is what I call him, since true is all that he's proven to be in all areas of his life with me thus far.

CHAPTER

8

Now as all of the bills were paid, all I needed is for one more piece of paperwork to be signed, sealed, and officially delivered back to me before I could officially open the doors of the Relief Spa & Massage Therapy Parlor.

My entire project was a success so far, as I'd made it over every single stumbling block that presented itself.

Including Tru not having to meet Don and Deon because one of the construction workers that was working on the saunas was an instructor. And he wanted to use the building and installation of each sauna and the Vichy spa showers as some sort of onsite teaching course for his class, and that also made some of their labor free of charge.

So of course, I accepted their offer to do certain things for free. But they'd helped me in more ways than just financially because his students freely did their work, along with the work that I was going to have Tru and my brothers to do for me.

Although I could no longer hold Sabrina or Momma Bass back from coming to visit, and to help me get prepared for my grand opening. So I knew that I was going to have to officially introduce them to Tru.

As well as explain to them why he had been living with me for so long, and they had no idea, even though Sabrina and Momma Bass have both been to my house a few times.

But they hadn't been there as much since Tru left the hotel and comfortably moved in with me, and when they or my brothers did come to visit after he'd moved in. I would always put him in a hotel and just lock his bedroom door so that no one could go in there.

However, Sabrina and Momma Bass ended up meeting him first, while I still managed to keep the nature of our relationship private even after they'd met him. It wasn't until it was time for all of my family to come and visit—that's when I really had to sit down with Tru and explain to him that they were all coming. And that he needed to know how to respond to things as he did know more about my family by then, and he'd even talked to my brother's over the phone, so that they could get to know him better. But I needed for him to know more of how to be and how not to be upon physically meeting them.

I explained more of how close we are as a family, and how we rarely hold secrets from each other. And that he needed to know that they would all be coming to stay with us because no matter how much money we have. We never let family stay in a hotel, unless they just want to.

But without a doubt, I told him that I knew that they would all be coming straight to my house instead of a hotel.

And that they would probably be asking him a thousand questions to try and see more of who he is because he would no longer have to hide, so they were going to pry into what they don't know about him. While I also indicated that he could be honest and tell them where he's really from, just give them a different timeline of when he actually moved to America.

But I didn't care if he told them the truth about some of his history, aside from us knowing each other from our last year of high school. I wanted him to stick with that lie of how we were friends back then, but we just lost contact after graduation. Until we linked back up so that he could come and help me with my Parlor after losing his job and needing a place to stay, so I stepped up and let him live and work for me.

And that lie was just going to have to stick no matter how open we usually are with each other as a family. He knew not to tell them that he literally came from the streets, just as I knew not to give him too many details about my family. Other than the basic and obvious things that he would find out anyway, just from being around us.

Although ultimately, Tru was just happy to be a part of a family unit at all, so he was ecstatic about my family coming even if he wasn't allowed to ask a lot of questions. And I was very confident in my family liking him because he was always charming and easy to get along with anyway.

It wasn't until it was officially time for my family to show up when things got a little worrisome, because lo and behold after I'd dropped Tru off at school. And was headed to the grocery store so that I could stock my kitchen with groceries before everyone was set to arrive.

Traffic was almost completely still, and the police were trying to make everyone take a detour because there had been a bad car accident on the highway. So I drove slowly alongside everyone else, until I saw a grocery store. I then exited the highway and figured that if I did my shopping there. Then maybe the traffic would be better by the time I was done shopping, although I'd never been to that grocery store before. I'd only saw it in passing when I would drop Tru off at school, since at the time, I still didn't want him to have a car yet. But that day at the grocery store, I had no idea that it would soon become a regular shopping spot that I would be visiting more frequently within those following days and weeks to come.

Because I was approached by my next *BAMT* after I'd parked my car and was about to walk into the store. – Although the timing of me getting approached by Keenan couldn't have been worse, but when he had approached me and asked for seventy-five cents. So that he could dry his clothes that was in the dryer at the laundry mat that was horizontal of the grocery store.

I had to ask him his name because unlike Tru, he did look like he had a home. But I could look at him and tell that it was nowhere near what I could potentially offer him, while a part of me also felt like he just didn't look like the type of guy who would be out here begging. But his tan colored shoes looked like they were previously white, and his t-shirt and jeans looked clean. But overall he was still just as dingy as his shoes, so regardless of him being dressed a little better than Tru was when he was on the streets. Keenan still looked a mess.

Although he didn't have any facial hair, which was another reason why I was drawn to him because I'd noticed how his bare face and teeth appeared throughout the mess of him begging.

His clothes, as well as his body looked dingy, but I could immediately see within seconds that he had *BAMT* potential by his smile and his actions. He was poor and probably broken, but his dinginess wasn't so dingy that he couldn't be cleaned and fixed.

Therefore, while I did hesitate for a small moment because Tru would soon be graduating. My Parlor was about to open, the Lounge was about to open, and my family was just now about to officially get to know Tru better. So I wasn't quite ready to have another guy in the picture just yet, not with so many things going on already.

And training my next *BAMT* wasn't supposed to be until later, after everything was opened and operating for a little while before I would find my number two.

But as Tru was damn near perfect, and I had even recruited a legitimate classmate of his who would also be working in the Parlor full time, as I continued to look for one or two more. Because his classmates wouldn't be aware of any of the extracurricular activities that would be going on when they are not there.

So I knew that passing on helping Keenan would have been the easiest thing to do, until things were more situated. But everything in my body was telling me that Keenan was my next *BAMT*. As he stood in front of me begging for change, and looking just like the kind of person whom most people would call a bum.

But what I saw was his clothes and just his overall appearance was terrible, but his teeth and his body was still just as intact as any other guy without or with a job, and a comfortable home. He was just dingy and would still be going to the dentist and to see just as many doctors as Tru did, no matter how intact things were or were not.

My aim then was to immediately see where his mental state was, and to see if he could be tampered with if I didn't like something about him. So I told him that I would give him a fifty-dollar bill, along with the seventy-five cents that he'd asked for. But only if he was still standing there after I was done shopping.

He laughed and told me that I was lying, and then he said that he could just come with me into the store and help me shop, because he didn't believe that I would give him a fifty-dollar bill for no reason. – And that's when I looked at him and told him that if he followed me into the store, or if I just so happen to look around and see even a glimpse of him inside of the store at any time at all while I shopped. Then I wasn't going to give him anything at all, not even the seventy-five cents that he needed. He continued to laugh and thought that I was either lying, or I had something up my sleeve because he didn't know me at all, so I had no reason to just give him fifty dollars for no reason like that.

But after a few seconds, he could clearly see that I was serious. While I could clearly see that he didn't have much of anything, and could use that fifty dollars. Therefore, I knew that he would be waiting for me whenever I came out of that store, and since I didn't know anything about him or his background.

I didn't get too excited about him just yet, although everything about him seemed to be perfect for me and for what I needed. With the bonus of it all being that he really didn't seem like he was the drug addict type, or anything like that. Even though I was still planning to treat him like he was on drugs and had every sexually transmitted disease possible, until I would be able to investigate further.

And since he knew that I had at least fifty dollars on me that he could potentially try to rob me for, after my shopping was done. I made sure to keep my guard up and watched my back in case he or anyone else tried anything foolish.

But when I came out of the store, I saw him standing in the same area as I'd left him. He was smiling and talking to damn near everybody who came through the doors of the grocery store. Apparently, he was just a regular bystander that asks people for change on a regular basis, because as I was walking out to exit the store. I heard and saw a random guy look at him and say. "Bye Keenan", as if he knew him from coming up there so much. And that was kind of confusing because again, in my opinion he just didn't look like the type of guy that would be so thrown together and standing outside asking for money.

But that's why a part of me was thinking that something just wasn't adding up with him and how he was, because his face and his personality just didn't match up to his overall appearance.

Ultimately, I still wanted to know more about him and his situation. So when I walked up to him, I laughed and said. "It's pay day, huh?"

And he kept that same smile and laugh as he had before I went into the store, and with that smile he agreed to walk me to my car while I asked him his name. And he said that his name was Keenan Sims.

And that he washes cars and help the elderly people with their groceries, and he usually use their tips to take care of himself. And after he was done helping me with my groceries, I asked him how was it possible for him to live off of washing cars and making small tips from the shoppers?

He told me that he had a mobile water machine, so he usually washed the cars in front of the laundry mat, because the owner of the laundry mat also pays him to keep an eye on the place for him when he's not there.

He said that it all started because he'd gotten so used to hanging out at the laundry mat, that people just started giving him money to do things for them since he was always hanging around.

He said that he couldn't live off of the shopper's tips alone, so that's why he had so many jobs. Because once he'd lost his real job, he started waking up every day to go to the laundry mat and the grocery store in hopes of somebody paying him to help them with anything. And it's just been like that ever since then.

I then handed him a fifty-dollar bill and three quarters, along with some fabric softer sheets for his clothes.

Then I asked him if it was okay if I walked over to the laundry mat with him to dry his clothes. And of course with a huge smile on his face he agreed, and as we proceeded to the laundry mat. I asked him how did he lose his job and end up homeless and outside asking for change. Although I admired his hustle, because at least he did wake up every day to wash cars and try to help people with their groceries. While I also told him that he just looked like he should be doing something a little better than that with his life, since he seemed like such a good guy.

He then thanked me for the money, and the compliments of him getting up every day to make his living as best as he could. But he said that he wasn't homeless, he told me that he lived about a block away, inside of a two-bedroom duplex with his uncle.

He explained how the home used to be only his, until he lost his job. And his uncle had gotten put out of his house for using drugs and just being irresponsible with his money, so his wife ended up divorcing him. And since he could no longer afford his rent and his bills by himself, he allowed his uncle to move in with him so that they could share the bills.

But when he said that he was getting tired of his uncle, because he could do bad all by himself, that was all I needed to hear as I got happy and knew that I was on to something. Because in my eyes he truly didn't need his uncle and he didn't want his uncle anymore, as he explained how his uncle worked in the meat department at the grocery store. But he still never had any money due to his continuation of drug usage.

He even told me how much meat his uncle steals from the grocery store, on top of him receiving a regular paycheck every two weeks. But he still never had anything, so he wanted nothing more than to get away from his uncle, but he couldn't.

He said that he couldn't put him out just yet because with his uncle's help of being a Veteran, he's in some sort of program that dropped his rent all the way down to only a few hundred dollars a month.

So overall, I knew that he didn't like his life nor how things were going as he continued to talk. While I observed and took in as much as I could until I told him that I had to leave to get my groceries home.

Then I suggested that he follow me back to the grocery store so that I could purchase him a prepaid cell phone, because I wanted to call him later. And since I'd heard him mention that he had no phone, or he'd broken his phone or something like that. But I wanted him to follow me back to the store to get one.

And his mouth dropped in disbelief, then he asked me my name again, and who was I, and why was I doing all of that for him.

And of course, I only answered one question in full, and that was my name. I told him that my name was Tristan, and that there was a reason why I wanted to help him, but I had to get home. So we would have to just finish our conversation later concerning who I was and why I was so interested in him.

And as he kept smiling, he simply walked with me to get him a phone. While looking excited, as well as stunned by my generosity of giving him money, talking to him, and especially purchasing things for him.

So as we walked to the store, I clarified how much the phone would be his, and that he could do whatever he wanted to do with it. But I also expressed how much he needed to know how important it was for him to save most, if not all of the minutes provided strictly for me and him to talk. Because I would have his number and he would have mine to use at any time day or night. And after the purchase, before we parted he said some interesting things that continued to plug his spot in my life.

He told me that the only person that has ever really seemed to seriously care about him was his daughter's mother, and when she died of Sickle Cell Anemia, he almost lost his mind.

And with his daughter also being really sick, because she had Lupus. Things had gotten rough for him because he was losing everything and everyone that he ever loved all at once, so for me to suddenly show him so much love like I was showing. He was just amazed with my actions as a stranger, because it was odd but refreshing.

And as I could tell that he was a somewhat strong guy who has been through a lot of pain, especially only after a year in a half after losing his girlfriend/daughter's mother. He then lost his daughter, the only person who he felt that ever genuinely loved him besides his girlfriend. – So this was my plugging entry to him, as I intended to show him that he now would have me to love.

But after all of that, including losing his job all within a three-year period was just exhausting for him. And he wanted to tell me more, like how much he didn't used to look the way that he looked.

But I didn't care to hear about that part, because he could explain that later. I was more interested in how desperate he was to make a comeback or not. Because as sure as the sky was blue, he would have to live by my rules and completely sign and comply with every single document just as Tru had to do.

But after I'd programmed my number into his phone, and his into mine, he didn't want me to leave because he tried to keep talking. But I had a ton of things to do to prepare for my family to arrive, so I was done listening to him until later.

But when we eventually parted, and I had gotten back onto the highway headed home. My mind was swarming with thoughts of how unexpected meeting Keenan was, and how was I going to work him into my life so suddenly. Because I could definitely see me tampering with his mind and his actions, I just wasn't sure yet of how much.

And I knew that I didn't have any time or space to train him in anything concerning working for me while juggling Tru, my family, my Parlor, the Lounge, and everything else that I had going on.

But I also knew that I wasn't going to pass on him no matter what, at least not until I could find out if my gut instincts were right about him or not.

CHAPTER

9

I was feeling super excited, proud, and thankful for everything that had been done to bring out such a big crowd to my grand opening.

Because Ali and I ganged up and did a lot of marketing through the radio with him promoting free haircuts for the kids and discounts for the adults. While I promoted my grand opening with specials for the parents to come in and get some relief after seeing their children off to school, or after work and weekend specials.

I also had a great deal of solo promoting going on in plenty of other places without Ali, including Abigail holding up her end of promises as she'd sent several people, male and female to get massages and a lot of other treatments.

But the most special bonus was since my business was licensed, registered and had everything needed for it to qualify as a place for the massage therapy students to do their internships for free. I'd recruited a Nurse who was also a Masseuse who was pregnant. But she helped me because she had almost ten years of experience with working with massage therapy students. Although she had only a few more months to work before it was set for her to deliver her baby, and change her career into becoming a stay at home mom like she's always wanted.

But she still agreed to come in and help me open the Parlor until it was time for her to stop working and take care of her family.

And with her help in knowing an unsatisfied Masseur, who has managed Massage Therapy students with her in the past.

I met with him and made an agreement that if he came to work for me as a manager for a few months. Then I would match his salary plus give him a few dollars more, but only for a few months, because Tru would ultimately become the manager.

And when I guaranteed him that he could still work at the Parlor for a little while even after he'd trained Tru to become the head Masseur/Massage Therapist, he couldn't resist my offer so he joined our team. I told him that I wouldn't just kick him to the curb when I was done with him, although it was very important that he understood that in the long run. Tru, and two or three other guys that I'd already had in mind would end up being the only ones working for me in the future, so he should continue to look for another place to work.

And with that understanding we all got along great, my pregnant friend Cosewh assisted tremendously with the training of the three intern students from Tru's school. – And she would sign the papers that they all needed her signature on for them to pass that part of their schooling.

While Marlon, my head Masseur/Massage Therapist was teaching Tru and training him just as he'd agreed to do. And when the time came, Cosewh signed off on Tru's paperwork as well.

And if I should say so myself, they all deserved great praise because even until this day, none of the people who came to the grand opening knew that a lot of the staff were intern students.

I'd urged them to not tell the customers that they were students because I didn't want them to think that they wasn't getting our best services due to that.

And they all did great with the customers, so much so that some of them are still customers even until this day.

Because with the help of Cosewh, Marlon, Tru, and the three other intern students. Along with Sabrina, Momma Bass, Don, Deon, Autry, and plenty of others. I was truly blown away with how good things turned out with opening the Parlor.

And as time passed, and the Parlor had been opened for a while, I only kept one intern student to work with Tru after they graduated. As well as Marlon, and soon after Keenan would be joining them. But Cosewh did all that she could do before she was at nine months and had to stop working to deliver her son. But then she would still come in every now and then to help when she wanted to get out of the house, or if I called her and seriously needed her to come in sometimes to assist the guys.

I just had to take her off the payroll and start paying her under the table after the baby came, but other than that everything was great. And I couldn't have been happier with the progress of the Parlor and of the Lounge by that time. As well as my family knew about Tru, and that he and I were just close friends, just as they also knew that Keenan and I were also close friends by that time.

And my brothers were cool with the fact that Tru was paying me rent to stay with me, or at least that's what they thought after I had to eventually explain to them that Tru was an old friend that I'd previously slept with in the past. But at that point in our lives I was only helping him out as a friend, just like he was helping me out by working in the Parlor so much.

They also knew more about Keenan, and how he was also a close friend that used to work with me when I was a secretary/assistant to my former boss Brock, until he moved near me and now we've linked up to help each other as well, or so they thought that's how he and I met and became friends.

While I was sure to be clear to everyone that I wasn't sleeping with Tru or Keenan, no matter how close we were. But sometimes my family still had their concerns about a guy living with me whom they knew, but not really, regardless of how much we were helping each other out.

Just as they had their concerns with me telling them that Keenan would also be coming to pay rent to stay with me. – They'd voiced their concerns a few times because it was unlike me to allow employees to live with me, old friends or not.

But I simply stood on telling them that Keenan needed a stable place to live, just like Tru needed, and since I was cool with them both. And knew how much working in the Parlor would help us all out, I made the decision for them to stay and that was just that, and everything eventually worked itself out.

My family saw Tru a little more than they saw Keenan because Keenan had been staying at a hotel. But as time passed, and it was almost time for him to graduate as a Massage Therapist, I'd invited him on a few occasions to come and hangout with us while my family was in town during his stay at the hotel.

But again, as my family had their small concerns about my "close friends", I'm a grown woman so no one could stop anything whether they like it or not.

Yet I was still careful with how and why I introduced Tru and Keenan to my family at all, especially with their introductions being laced with a lot of lies anyway. But as everything was slowly but surely working in my favor, Keenan was preparing to graduate while Tru was running the Parlor. And the Lounge was also doing well, so everyone was happy.

Keenan had even signed his stack of papers giving me all of him and more, and he was also cool with the fine print, although he barely read any of it. But after several months of everyone getting to know Tru and loving him, they were eventually introduced to Keenan and had gotten to know him as well.

Don would even joke around about how hard I was on him, Storm, and Booby. While Tru and Keenan would both hold my hair and wipe my mouth when I sneezed if I let them. And he would always say that we were lying when we say that we don't have threesomes, because they are just too close to me.

And one time when it was just he and I, Don asked me do I have them to wipe my ass after I shit, because he honestly believe that they would wipe me if I told them to. And with the truth in the matter being that they probably would wipe my ass and do whatever else that I tell them to do, but they both knew that I would never ask them to do such a thing. – Although what Don didn't and still doesn't know is that my only issue in life back then had become between the two of my guys showing each other love.

Because they had a slight bit of a jealousy issue toward each other that I actually was having a hard time dealing with. Seeing how their jealousy towards each other was a lot different from the jealousy that Don and Deon eventually displayed to me every time we got together. They would always bash Tru and Keenan's need to always be around me, although they didn't have a doubt that they came first in my life because I always let that be known to them and everyone else by my actions.

But it was still funny to sometimes see and hear my brother's jealousy towards my "close friends". Whereas Tru and Keenan's jealousy reactions and words when we were in private weren't as funny to me. – And since I couldn't go to my brothers with any problems concerning Tru or Keenan's jealousy, because I'd sworn to them that I wasn't sleeping with neither of them, so I just did whatever I had to do on my own without my brothers finding out the truth of our relationships.

And I wasn't going to let Tru and Keenan's jealousy towards each other ruin our good thing, especially since the problem was mainly with how much Keenan was always with me. When in my mind Tru was around me just as much, if not more, but apparently Tru didn't see it that way.

He constantly had something to say about Keenan following me everywhere like he was my security guard or something. When at the end of the day they both had me equally because I communicated with them both all day every day. And with the small bonus about their arguments being that they wouldn't argue in front of people no matter how much they disagreed. They made me happy with that because they understood the concept of our relationships as far as our sacred trio.

They would only exchange their bad words in private because they never let others hear them being combative, but I still didn't like their jealousy even when they compromised.

And their words and actions truly were bonded to me even through their personal issues with each other, because they never took things too far as to jeopardize what they have, or at least they haven't so far. Seeing how I had someone to try and play them against one another if they had the chance to do so concerning me, as well as not concerning me.

And they both proved to be submissively loyal and official to me, and to each other when it came to their actions of how much they stood strong with the three of us having an unbreakable relationship. However, their issues really didn't bother me so much until after Keenan graduated, and no longer had to live in a hotel.

Keenan had stopped communicating with his uncle after he moved out of their home and left him to take care of himself, but before he left he was a good nephew. Because ever since the first day that we'd met on that grocery store parking lot, Keenan was upset with his uncle, but he was still willing to help him.

He even continued to stay at home with his uncle when he didn't have to after a while of us talking on the phone and meeting up, while I was getting his information and preparing for him to become my number two. I'd began to meet with him and help him and his uncle financially, but it didn't work because his uncle had eventually gotten fired from his job at the grocery store. And had become even more reckless than he was before his wife divorced him.

So Keenan was starting to hate him and his actions, he felt like his uncle was his only family no matter how messed up he was. But eventually he wanted to just disown him and never look back, he said that he was done with him because he knew that he was headed straight to jail or death. And that's why I eventually got him completely away from his uncle, because Keenan was always smiling. Even when he was serious, a person can see his seriousness through his smile, and can pick up on his vibe with or without a smile. But his uncle always knew just how to make that smile disappear, and since Keenan felt like he had hit the jackpot with me being in his life. He surely wasn't about to let a dope fen mess it all up for him, but I could see that he was letting his uncle get to him negatively sometimes way more often than he should have. So I took it upon myself to just remove him from that life completely.

As you can gather that I had eventually put him in a hotel as his *BAMT* training began immediately, and he started to want nothing more than to be away from his old life and closer to me. As things between he and I concerning him being my boyfriend was a lot different than how things went between Tru and I, although Tru doesn't know that.

Tru knew that Keenan came from nothing when I first told him about him, and he knew that Keenan had been at a hotel in training to be my *boyfriend and man tool*, just as he had to do. He just didn't know the reality was that I'd trained Keenan's mindset in a different thought pattern than his, because Keenan and I had sat down on several occasions, as he explained how not even his daughter's mom had ever done as much for him as

I'd done. While I was sure to give him plenty of material items to love me for, but during that time. I was also growing, molding, and maintaining how I wanted him to think and act from that point on. As he eagerly wanted to be my number two boyfriend with all strings attached.

And Tru really was accepting and happy that I'd found what I was looking for when I'd met Keenan. But again, their jealousy didn't really bother me until Keenan moved in with us, and became an official *BAMT*. While slowly but surely my small little weird family that I'd put together was working everything out, as we kept moving right along while working through our issues.

But when Keenan moved in, I wanted him to wait for about a week or two before letting him do anything. So that he could get more familiar with how I ran our household, as well as how the Parlor stayed so successful. But things moved along way quicker than I expected, so Keenan immediately started working at the Parlor while Marlon, Tru, nor Paxton; who was no longer a student, but an employee who was quite good with his hands.

But Paxton, nor any of the guys had a problem with training Keenan at the Parlor, and I loved them all so much for genuinely working together and doing their part as a team. – And while things weren't always so great with Tru and Keenan, they were also never so bad that they couldn't talk to each other or any none sense like that.

Because if we did nothing else together, we knew when to let things go before it got stupid, or just too unnecessary. And that's why we had so much fun at home with our unbreakable tactics, regardless of if it still didn't stop them from competing.

We still moved forward and helped each other as I had also eventually helped Marlon find another job, while keeping only Tru, Keenan, Paxton, and sometimes Cosewh working at the Parlor during that time.

While Abigail and her rich friends had become so regular, and so impatient that I could no longer hold back their eager urges to pay me whatever I wanted them to pay me. To allow my "boyfriend" to have protected sex with them during one of their massage therapy sessions.

And while Keenan and I hadn't officially had sex yet, I still knew that he was a winner in bed immediately. Even before I'd made him prove himself just as Tru had to do in the bedroom without me having to touch him. I saw early on how hard he could get, as well as how short or long it took for him to get hard and horny enough for him to ejaculate in front of me.

Because during my third-time meeting Keenan, before I would decide to help him and his uncle any further, he had to first pull out his penis and show it to me. And when he did it hung damn near the length of my forearm when it was hard, and it wasn't fat or big headed and round like Tru's. But it was slim and super long, and that was more than okay with me.

And as clean of any STD's as he was, while I had the documents to prove it, and as we stayed in contact with each other damn near at all-times day and night since day one of us meeting. – Abigail nor her friends would be getting the pleasures from his sex drive until after I'd had him first, especially knowing how much he was going to try to prove his sexual worth to me.

And that means that the time was nearing for Tru to be paid his first few thousand dollars in cash, cash that would first have to be placed in my hands before I would allow him to get Abigail together for me.

And while I knew of Tru's every movements, and knew how clean he was also, he and I had already been together more than just a few times sexually. So he would have to be the first one to rub her down and put on a condom and do her good. – And although there weren't any issues with Tru and Abigail after their first sexual hookup, I still knew that I was going to have to have sex with Keenan sooner than later. So that I could also start using him to get my training money back through Abigail and her three satisfied friends. Friends that Tru had also eventually had sex with after more time had passed.

And when I say more time had passed, I mean like two months had passed since Keenan left the hotel to move in with us, and Tru was the only one hitting up Abigail and her friends all by himself. And of course, Tru didn't complain about having to be the only one secretly having to pleasure the four rich women, especially since they had all been to the Parlor each on separate occasions, instead of him doing them all in one day.

But my point is that he'd been with all of them more than once all within two months. And there was no way that I was about to let them wear him out, no matter how much money they were paying us due to them not receiving any pleasure at home. Their rich asses still had to calm down, follow my rules and wait.

While I knew that Keenan was going to have to help Tru sooner than I wanted him to, with things moving as fast as they were, but I still wasn't willing to let them wear Tru out.

Sometimes I let him do whatever he wanted to do, as he was careful to follow my strict protocol with the women at all times.

And still, his only concern has always been with me being pleased with him in whatever he did, so he was usually cool with whatever I said and did.

Until within that two months when all of this was taking place.

He then suddenly had a complaint or two, but his complaints had nothing to do with what I was asking him to do or not do with Abigail and her friends.

It had become time for me and Keenan to share some sexually intimate boyfriend and girlfriend time, so that he could go ahead and share Tru's duties.

But just as I was geared up and ready to ride Keenan a few times for myself. Tru's complaints came when Keenan and I couldn't fight the urge to have sex any longer one night after watching a movie together as a family, like we always do.

Tru had fallen asleep laid back in the recliner, while Keenan and I was on the couch and had started touching on each other.

But then after the movie ended, I'd sent him into the other room to get a condom. And when he came back we'd began to get a little freaky on the couch, then we moved to the floor. But before Keenan even got a chance to open the condom or anything like that, Tru stood up from the recliner and said that he knew that I ran shit. And that he would never do anything to disrespect me, but he said that we needed to take that shit either into my room, or to Keenan's room because he was getting mad and wanted to seriously punch Keenan in his face. And while Keenan and I laughed, Tru was dead serious.

And that meant that I had to remind him right then and there that I was going to do whatever I wanted to do, including touch on them and kiss on them both separately, and together in front of each other and in private if that's what I felt like doing.

While I also informed him that I would respect his wishes for that night, because I did understand where he was coming from in his feelings. So I agreed that I wouldn't have that kind of sex in front of him that night, while I'd also made it clear to them both that I would still be receiving oral sex from them both in private. And in front of each other because they hadn't had a problem with it before, and Keenan still didn't have a problem with any of it.

Whereas Tru did, and that made me kind of irritated with him for being so serious, because he'd given me sex orally and in other ways a few times in front of Keenan. Before and after he'd moved in with us, and he had no hesitations at all about it. And he was usually in fact the main one who would initiated it, and was always doing it out and in the open in front of Keenan on purpose.

Sometimes without thinking about it, he would stop whatever he's doing and just begin to give me oral sex when I was just laying around, or just getting out of the shower or something. And we would all laugh because no one would be thinking about sex, until he would just start doing things.

And while I never stopped him, the fact is that he was the first person to take things as far as we have when he would pull out his penis and bend me over the table in front of Keenan.

And there was no anger, no complaints, or anything else until now, when it was finally time for me and Keenan to take things further.

However, the rule of no aggressive intercourse between us in front of each other was put into effect for that night, and it turned out to be a good idea because Keenan's penis stood up in my vagina so graciously. And I didn't want Tru to see that, while I also did my best to not let him hear us too much, because at times I knew that we were getting too loud.

But regardless of all of that, Tru knew that I had love for him and that I respected him and his request, because before I'd left the room to leave to go and be with Keenan. I'd turned around and walked over to the recliner and jumped into Tru's lap and kissed him long and hard enough for him to know that he was still my number one.

And ultimately, I understood him and he understood me. But I still think that Tru just liked things much better when he was the only one having intercourse with me, while I would only receive oral sex from Keenan, but nothing more. – Nevertheless, as things began to change with how we adjusted in making each other more comfortable. I still made Keenan wait for almost two more months before I decided to share him with my friends.

While all in all Tru was still making me proud to have him as my number one in managing things, as our finances continued to put a smile on my face and his.

And he knew not to discuss any type of finances without me being present under any circumstances.

And that was with Abigail or anyone else because they would only need to focus on having some great protected sex, without anything orally being given unless it was coming from them sucking on him.

I was cool with them sucking on him if that's what they wanted to do, and because of how much money they were paying us. But in my mind if they couldn't receive anything else at home, they should at least be able to get their oral sex from their husbands. Because my guys supplied no oral anything at all period, only finger and protected dick services was allowed.

And I made it very clear that they knew that any oral favors, or anyone discussing anything concerning money without me being present was a total violation of respect to me as far as I'm concerned.

And if I'm nothing else when it comes to handling my business. I was, am, and will always be very direct, arrogant, and extremely clear in how much I do not play about not just the welfare of my family. But also the welfare of my money, my businesses, and the loyal that has been established with my *BAMTs*.

CHAPTER 10

People were always talking about how much Keenan smiles, and how much of a gentleman he is because he never stopped helping people, or just being the same ole Keenan that he was when I'd met him looking straggly and homeless at that laundry mat and grocery store parking lot.

But as I'd gotten to know him as time passed when he was training, I began to understand his smile and why he did it so much. While others simply thought that he was just a nice guy, although he was and still is a nice guy, but there's a story behind his popular smile. And quite frankly, I wanted him to always have that helping spirit and to keep that nice smile no matter what, because I knew what was behind it when he wasn't smiling.

And with knowing as much as I knew about his smile, I still purposely committed myself to being with him anyway. Although the customers at the Parlor, my family, and everyone else didn't have any detailed information about him other than we used to work together. And that he'd lost his girlfriend to Sickle Cell Anemia, and his daughter to Lupus.

Tru knew a little bit more about Keenan than anyone else did, because he was my number one.

But he still didn't know a whole lot about him just as Keenan didn't know a whole lot about Tru.

But with Keenan always wanting to be around me and acting like my body guard. Tru wanted to sit down and have a talk with me about that, as well as talk to me about Keenan being able to even follow me to the Lounge. And it's supposed to be off limits to them because I needed them to focus strictly on our lives at the Parlor, while they could visit any other Lounge in the city if they wanted to. But PMF; Poets, Music & Fun lounge was off limits to them, and they had no other choice but to be cool with that.

That is until I found out how Tru really felt about Keenan being able to follow me there, when as my number one, he'd never been to PMF at all. And while it was yet another complaint from Tru, I understood his frustrations, so I told him that I almost didn't care if they started attending PMF or not.

But Tru said that he didn't care if he wasn't allowed at the lounge, if that's what I wanted. He said that he still wanted to talk to me about Keenan and his security guard ways of following me to the lounge and damn near everywhere else.

Then after a few days had passed of him informing me of his need to talk to me, Tru and I had gotten up one morning and went to the gym together. And then we went back home, took a shower then hit the golf course while Keenan managed the Parlor.

And we had one of the best days of our lives hanging out and enjoying each other's company like we used to do when it was just the two of us. Then he eventually began to tell me how he wanted to admit to being jealous. But he also wanted me to know that he felt like if a guy was going to be following me around everywhere, he felt like it should be him.

He said that he wanted that personal time with me to explain how much he wasn't trying to hate on Keenan, or even trying to block him from me. But he also didn't want to be holding in his feelings when he knew that he could simply just talk to me about it.

And at first, I was again a little irritated because he was always the one who had a complaint. But his complaints were never about anything besides Keenan, he never complained about the Parlor, money, us, or anything else. As he was damn near perfect in being my go to guy, and he seemed very happy fulfilling his part as my number one.

He just couldn't let go of how close Keenan and I were, since it seemed to him that Keenan was trying to take his spot. But as I'd listened to him, I knew for a fact that I needed to fix the situation a little more concerning the two of them, because my plan from day one has always been to have a total of three *BAMT's*. And I knew that I wouldn't be able to find, and successfully add my third and final *BAMT* to our little family without first fixing Tru's concerns. I just wasn't sure of exactly how to fix the problem, since I knew why Keenan followed me everywhere unless I told him not to.

But I just couldn't tell Tru the full reasons why, although I could see why he was feeling the way that he was feeling. So I didn't let us leave without explaining to him how Keenan did those things because he'd asked me if he could, due to a lot of reasons that I couldn't share with him right at that moment.

But I did assure him that I would somehow figure out how they could both be around me equally, without me having to tell him the real reasons of how Keenan shared things with me and showed me things that places him in a totally different category as Tru, in terms of him being my security *BAMT*.

And thankfully, without having to go into too many details. I'd smoothed things over by telling Tru that he wouldn't have to continue to always question me about Keenan, because I would deal with his concerns because I understood him.

Now Keenan on the other hand proved a background that stamped his place in my life way before Tru or anyone else even knew that he existed.

But regardless of any of that, I still needed another *BAMT*, or to simply hire another employee like Paxton. Who still didn't have a clue about anything sexual ever taking place at the Parlor, but I needed another MT as soon as possible, since my third *BAMT* quest had to be pushed back until I could get my first two on a steady pace of sharing.

Eventually, I just let Cosewh, Keenan, and Tru deal with hiring another MT to help them out.

While I personally worked on Tru and Keenan individually as if they were in training all over again.

I took it upon myself to allow them to run the Parlor without me, while my attention had to stay on PMF as always, because I kept a steady eye on it no matter what I was doing anyway.

But for the most part, I mainly focused on retraining my boyfriends at that time because I knew how much I'd taken them from a place of nothing to something, while completely infiltrating their brains in the process.

But it was time to enhance my guys as they were no longer in need of anything mentally, physically, or financially.

And I wanted to keep it that way because that's what would be needed to prepare them for my third and final *BAMT* to join us, as he would be my last but certainly not my least.

I'd told only a few people outside of my brothers, Sabrina, and Momma Bass about me taking a two-week vacation. As I'd began my journey of upgrading my boyfriend's away from everyone.

Although I would still be checking in on everybody during my absence, but I eventually left and took Tru with me for the first week.

Then Keenan would join me that following week after I send Tru back, because I knew that they both could use a relaxed vacation.

They had been massaging clients and providing great sex to the women that I'd ask them to do, so it was time for them to take a week off with all expenses paid. Where they would be receiving massages, enjoying the beach, a yacht, and plenty of food and fun with so many different options of activities to choose from. It was all about my *BAMT's* and their wants and needs while I also mentally prepared them to handle my wants and needs for when we got back home, and would prepare for my number three. And since Tru and I had been together for a long time by then, and he was the one with reasonable complaints after all that he'd been through with managing the Parlor, and helping us to keep a great looking home and so much more. I knew that it was the perfect time for me to thank him.

Although Tru nor Keenan seriously had a hard job, because I was sure to rotate the one hand full of women who they did do sexually. Especially after I'd talked to the ladies about Keenan being just as much of my boyfriend as Tru, and I was willing to share him as well, if they didn't mind dealing with him. And of course, Abigail and her friends agreed to keep coming in to cheat on their rich husbands by getting sex from them whenever I would schedule them to be with either of my boyfriends. While neither of their rich over paid husbands had a clue of how much cash I was receiving from them to get laid by my guys.

And although I only gave them a small portion of what they made from having sex, they were still getting paid heavily for their services.

While they also received a decent percentage of their salaries from being therapists at the Parlor professionally like any other employee.

At any rate, compared to their past life they were happy. Especially Tru, although he always had so much more on his shoulders to manage than Keenan or my third *BAMT* would, but he also made more money than they did.

And I was sure to not add any new women to our little tag team sex gang, because my goals of keeping only the women whom I had already rotating would remain the same, even when I got my number three. Because I wasn't interested in expanding anything since I was already pocketing a lot of cash from the women I had.

And I wasn't going to be greedy, since the Parlor paid for itself and its employees, and the Lounge was in a great location and always doing good business, so overall I was happy. And was planning to keep things that way long term, so I was glad that everything went according to my plans during our vacation.

Tru was happy and was king on how he would never question his position ever again, no matter who or what.

While my mission to get Keenan to back down, but not necessarily back off from me went over with him well enough for him to understand that some changes were about to take place with he and I. Changes that I knew would bother him because he and I made a pact that he would always be my safeguard.

Especially after he broke down a few weeks after we'd met, when everything was happening so fast, and I wasn't expecting to bring on another *BAMT* so quickly after leaving that grocery store parking lot. But as I've said before, I was intrigued, so I couldn't just ignore him because just as I was sure about Tru when I first met him. I was just as sure, if not even more sure that Keenan would be my number two in that parking lot even before his break down.

We had been talking daily as I'd become his top priority after I'd bought him that cell phone that day, and just like Tru, he was just as shocked and grateful. And I know this because I'd called him when I got back onto the highway that day when I left the grocery store to go home. He'd said those exact words to me of how shocked and grateful he was. And while I told him very little about me, I had eventually gotten his entire life history as he knew it.

Then I immediately began to take care of him financially and mentally, even when I'd threatened to leave him alone completely that day when he surprisingly hesitated to talk to me at the hotel when he broke down. Although I knew that I wasn't going to seriously turn my back on him. But he didn't know that, so he ended up telling me how he believed that I was an angel that had come to give him another chance to do what he did best.

And at the time he wasn't wearing his familiar smile when he said it, and his facial expressions were very still, but also visibly strong when he finally decided to open-up and inform me that killing is what he did best.

And as you can imagine, me keeping my hands hidden in my pockets while I kept a tight grip on my gun was all that I could think about, because I didn't see that in him at all. But I never left home without my gun every time we would met, no matter how much information that I'd gather on him by that time.

I was ready to shoot him and call it self-defense if I had to, and while I actually did become a little fearful of his demeanor during his break down. I didn't show him any fear at that time, I acted cool because I knew that he had been hiding a few things from me anyway. But I had no idea that was his secret, because I'd checked his background, and he'd already showed me his penis and had ejaculated and everything by that time in our relationship.

I mean we'd talked about his life even as far back as when he was a baby, and I'd gotten on the phone and called my connect, and paid to get as much of his background as I could immediately after meeting him.

Therefore, his break down truly did come by surprise as he didn't cry or anything like that, while I listened to him and his confessions.

But he wasn't the same ole poor homeless looking Keenan who was out here working for coins. He had rocked back and forth and was acting strange before he completely blocked me out, as if he was tired of trying to dodge my questions. He had completely shut down until he realized that my threats were about to become a reality, when I acted like I was about to seriously walk out on him and never look back. And it was all so weird because I knew that my very accurate connection didn't find anything too harsh in his background, so I was certainly curious and wanted to hear more about these killings and why.

But with his behavior being so different from the Keenan that I'd gotten to know, I told him that I needed some distance from him because he couldn't be my *boyfriend and man tool*, or anything else if he held secrets like him being a killer from me.

And that's what finally made him talk to me, right before I was seconds away from walking out and leaving him by himself in that hotel room.

Because the only thing that I knew in terms of Keenan's criminal background was that he'd only been arrested one time. And it was for a petty theft that they ended up letting him go for, after dropping the charges when they found out that it wasn't him who committed the theft. He was damn near clean as a whistle as far as my knowledge when it came to him doing anything illegal, but as I kept that piece of information to myself, he did end up telling me about that arrest.

But that night when he stopped me from leaving, I began to talk to him and told him that anything that he shared with me while we were alone belonged to us and only us, and nothing would ever be repeated.

And I could tell as he began to talk about the terrible and fearless actions that he'd committed. – He himself had then become the scared and fearful one, because he didn't know where his confessions to me would lead, it was like he'd turned into a helpless little boy who was about to get in trouble. And I could tell that he was afraid that his past actions would possibly turn me away from him.

But me prying too much into his past worked in both of our favor because I told him on that night that his honesty and his personality had already granted him a solid place in my life. Then I eventually stayed just as honest with him by pulling out my gun and telling him that I understood why he did what he did, because I myself stayed ready to pull the trigger on anyone who I thought would pull it on me without a hesitation.

And when he saw my gun, he started smiling again, then he shook his head and said that I was a masterpiece in his eyes. And while I was extremely happy to see that smile back on his face, I laughed and told him that I was flattered because his masterpiece is always ready for whatever. Even if things would have turned out badly for he and I right then, such as him trying to take my gun from me or something worse.

I told him that I always have a plan B for any situation, and that I wasn't afraid to pull the trigger at any time if I had to, although unlike him, killing wasn't what I personally liked to do.

I then explained how a person like him would be considered dangerous in some people's eyes if they knew what he has done. But I was thinking that I on the other hand felt like everybody has a weak spot, even a skilled killer, and that's where my talent is. I'm skilled at taking control of that weak spot and doing whatever I want to do with it.

However, as he continued to express himself. I'd stopped him and asked him how did he expect for me to believe that he had to kill people, or he would be killed if he didn't?

And how was I supposed to believe that his uncle was ever sane enough to harm anyone and not have snitched to anyone by now with his drug infested brain. – He then rationalized his facts, then offered to take me places to see things and to prove things to me while he ran down the details of his movements, and just his overall whereabouts as he committed these crimes. While I curiously drove around the city with him and mentally took in everything that he was saying and eventually showing me.

But in those moments as I could see how precise and dangerous he was, I could also see where he was lacking by providing me with such sensitive information. Therefore, I knew exactly what his first lesson would be, after I would officially bring him aboard my journey to protect me. Especially since I felt confident that he wasn't opening-up to me only to kill me after releasing such information.

He'd suggested how good he would be at watching my back and making sure that no one does me any harm. While he laughed and said how much he could see that I can protect myself, but still that's what he would love to do. As he also clarified how he didn't like to just go around killing people for fun.

I told him that I understood him, but still some things just shouldn't be shown or ever repeated, but he said that with my many requests of the truth. And my words of how much loyalty is the key to my heart, his point in giving me so much of his criminal information like he did was because he thought that by telling me absolutely everything. Then that would help me to see that he was giving me all of him, including his killing skills while he wanted nothing more than to be my boyfriend.

Especially after seeing how much I didn't care about his past as much as he thought I would. Since I'd told him that we could still move forward, although I don't condone killing. But I did understand that if he didn't do as his "Boss" asked him to do, then he could've potentially been killed also. – And that's why I felt a little sad for him at first, because his choices in life was made by a lost little boy who didn't have anyone to turn to.

Just like I didn't have anyone until Momma Bass took me in as her own child, but Keenan didn't have a mother like Momma Bass. His mom's boyfriend and her brother were working together for a while, but after some time had passed, he said that he saw just how bad of a guy his mom's boyfriend was.

And he knew that the results of his mom's choices got her killed, just as her choices left him to be raised by her boyfriend after she was murdered. While he also believes that his mom's boyfriend had something to do with her being murdered.

And his uncle wasn't of much help to him at all after his mom died, but that was still his mother's brother, so he forgave him for not protecting him. And he felt like his uncle was all the family that he had left besides her boyfriend.

And that's when he had described how his uncle had accidently killed someone, and his mother's boyfriend had it on video, so he had started blackmailing him into doing a lot of bad things as he'd threatened to give the video to the police. – But even through all of that while as terrible and as violent as his mom's boyfriend was, Keenan said that he knew not to ever act like him. Even one day when his mom's boyfriend had gotten high on drugs and told Keenan that he had to stab some guy in the head because the guy wouldn't come and work for him.

And Keenan had to call him Boss instead of calling him dad or calling him by his first name.

He was just a scared little boy back then who did what he was told to do. Although when he couldn't bring himself to hurt the guy whom he was told to stab, his mom's boyfriend beat him very badly after he was too afraid to even pick up the knife.

126

His "Boss" then had one of his friends to stab the guy several times in his face right in front of Keenan, then he told him that real men do whatever they have to do to get their point across. And without going to much further into the details, his Boss's words eventually came back and bit him in his ass because after suffering from years of abuse, without turning into a permanent demon.

Keenan was the one who did what a lot of people wanted to do, but they didn't have the balls to do it, and that was to kill the "Boss".

Keenan said that he had a point to prove, so he did what he was taught to do as a man when he'd finally looked his Boss in his eyes while he killed him. But no one knows that he's the one who did it, even until this day not even his uncle knows that he's the one who killed him.

He kept saying how he just couldn't take it anymore, but then after their Boss was dead, his uncle still just couldn't get himself together for himself or his wife and kids or nobody. So he just tried to save them both from eventually going to prison or being killed.

And that's why he didn't have a problem with eventually completely letting go of caring anything about his uncle, because even before meeting me he felt like he was getting worse instead of better. So with his mother, girlfriend, daughter, and his uncle being out of his life, me being in his ear about strengthening my little faithful family sounded like heaven to his ears.

And he was fully committed to his love for me, and had already damn near signed his life over to me early on anyway. – But as our lives continued after that, bringing us to even after our vacation was over, when I needed to see some upgraded changes in Keenan and Tru both. Before I could bring someone else into our lives like I was planning to do.

They knew that I seriously didn't need any kinks in our chain at the end of the day as we'd come so far in our lives. Because regardless of their backgrounds, they both knew how I wanted it to be as we ended up going back home feeling refreshed and ready for an even greater life together.

Keenan fully understood my expectations, although it was going to be hard for him to grasp the fact that he wasn't the only guy who would be watching my back like he did. But we understood each other, and so did Tru and I.

CHAPTER
11

After months of sitting around looking and bouncing from shelter to shelter, and just being on the streets and hanging out in places that I knew that Don, Deon, Tru, nor Keenan would be pleased that I went without either of them being with me.

But I had a mission to complete, and just as I needed to be on my own when I found Tru and Keenan.

I needed to be solo when I found my number three, as I stayed alert and always strapped with weapons after dealing with Keenan and his secrets. I felt like I needed to be carrying a lot more than just my gun for people like Keenan, especially after he told me that even when I dressed down, I still look like a beautiful flower.

While he also said that my looks are also very deceiving, because he can see evil in me when I'm angry, but his comments about me looking like a beautiful flower stuck to me. So I made a few changes in my approach on how I now handle my *BAMT* quests.

Although after seeing how hard it was to find my number three, I wouldn't need to use any weapons because no matter what I did or where I went. I just didn't see any guys that caught my attention, not even the ones that had somewhere to live, but was still very poor and would appreciate my help.

So after I had continued to find absolutely nothing, one day after thinking long and hard about giving up on finding my number three. Because by then it had been almost a year of searching, and I still didn't see anyone on the streets or beyond of whom I felt comfortable enough even talking to, let alone to be my boyfriend or man tool.

From laundry mats, grocery stores, restaurants, pool halls, and damn near anywhere else where there's usually a lot of loitering happening amongst those who are less fortunate, and could use a person like me in their lives. I kept coming up empty handed, and it became frustrating until I figured that so much time had passed. And Tru, Keenan, and I were doing so good financially, that maybe I should just stop my search and stay focused on just the three of us until further notice.

Because I was making thousands of dollars each month from them both, and no one was unhappy with anything. Even our regular customers became so permanent in coming in for legit therapy treatments that we had to hire not one but two extra employees to accommodate everyone. Especially since we were known to have great customer service, and I really wanted to keep it that way.

And on the sexual side of things, my guys used their health insurance regularly to make sure they stayed as healthy and as safe as they could be, because we wanted no mishaps in any areas. Even if they did make sure to always use protection. We all liked to stay cautious and careful while I consistently requested doctor's visits and paperwork to keep a check on Abigail and her friend's sexual health as well.

And they understood that. Therefore, I did have a change of heart and decided to only work and live with what I had. And the three of us loved each other and had a lot of fun together as a family, and as coworkers because even at the Parlor our friendships grew at work and outside of work.

Along with all six of my employees who respected me as their boss and it showed by their actions, and that made it easy for us to all hang out together outside of work.

Like we did one perfect fall evening when my life once again changed forever, and brought me to this point. Where I should explain how Cosewh's husband has a regular job to pay their bills, but he also promotes parties and other big events on the side.

But on that fall evening when we all hung out together, there was this huge concert that some other big promoters had, and they'd hooked her husband Gerald up with nine free tickets and four backstage passes. And the entire night was just wonderful as we received VIP treatment everywhere we went, thanks to Gerald and his connections.

People owed him a favor for him helping them, or he would just owe them a favor for helping us. So no matter where we went, we didn't have to pullout any money at all that night, because Gerald and Cosewh really knows how to party. And although it wasn't unusual that Cosewh, Tru, Keenan, Paxton, David, Turtle, and I would all sometimes hangout after work.

But I would never let them go into my house regardless of how connected it was to the Parlor. But we would however go out to eat at restaurants, or to a bar, or even to PMF every now and then.

But my house was off limits, although that still never stopped them from asking me if they could come over sometimes. But I would never allow them into my home like that, especially after spending so much money on having construction done to somewhat separate my Parlor from my home. I did all of that for a reason, and the contractors did a great job in making my house look like a home, and my business look like a professional business, with its own parking lot and everything.

And while everything was so big and spacious that I had to pay extra for so much space, it was well worth it.

So that's where I ultimately always drew a line in the sand on how close I got with my employees, and I never had a problem with anyone disrespecting my privacy. And we all just loved hanging out as a team, and Paxton would even bring his girlfriend along to join us sometimes.

But on this particular fall evening when me, Cosewh, Gerald, Tru, Keenan, Paxton, David, Turtle, and Gerald's brother Roman went to the concert together, we had a blast.

And after the concert was over, Cosewh, Gerald, Roman, and I went back stage. While everyone else left to go and get something to eat, as we all agreed to just meet at the after party later, after Gerald finished making his rounds with everyone backstage.

Then as we took our passes, Cosewh and I basically just stayed low in the background. While Gerald and Roman made their rounds in speaking to everyone and making future connections with everyone like most promoters do. Since Roman helped Gerald out sometimes, and he would receive a percentage of whatever money he brought Gerald's way, so they both were in work mode backstage.

While Cosewh and I didn't say very much to anyone, we just stood in the background judging people and their clothes, hair, and just their eagerness to be seen and etc.

And we had so much fun cracking jokes and following people around backstage, while trying to see who was who and what was what and where were they going. Until we'd completely gotten separated from Gerald and Roman. And when we began to look for the guys, we knew that it was going to be hard to find them because our phones had no signal, and we had been following people all over the place backstage. So we didn't even know where to begin our search to find them.

Then voila, as soon as we'd turned our first corner, we saw Gerald and Roman walking with a large group of people in our direction. And they told us that they had been looking for us because we had to leave immediately, to catch some guy that Gerald was trying to get with about an upcoming event.

And as they were rushing us to leave, Roman was shaking hands with a guy whom I've never seen before.

And I heard him telling Roman that it was nice to see him again, and that he looked forward to reading his proposal. Then the guy looked up at me after I'd already gotten onto the elevator to leave, while he and Roman were saying goodbye. And right then our eyes connected with each other's as soon as he looked up and saw me looking at him.

But everything was moving too fast, he even yelled. "Hey!"

As if he was about to say something to me or to Roman or to the both of us.

But the elevator was so crowded, and the doors closed as soon as Roman got on. Then Roman looked over at me and said that it was kind of weird, but he thought that Snow was yelling something at me instead of him, so that prompted him to ask me if I knew Snow.

But I looked at him and said, "Snow, who is Snow?" and he said. "Hamilton Snow."

He said that it seemed that when Snow looked up and saw me, it was as though he was yelling for me, but since I didn't know who he was. Then he was probably yelling something at him instead of me, but I immediately told him that he was right the first time.

I said that I didn't know the guy at all, but I felt like he was definitely yelling for me too, because I couldn't wait for him to raise his head up and look at me before they said their goodbyes.

I told Roman that I'd noticed Snow as soon as we walked up on them, but he just never looked up from swapping information from their phones until after I was already on the elevator.

Therefore, in my mind him yelling when he saw me is exactly how I felt when I saw him, I just didn't yell.

But with the question remaining of who was he yelling at, I asked Roman who was Hamilton Snow? But he couldn't tell me much because the elevator doors was opening to let us off.

And we were once again on the move so that Gerald could get with some guy, and I became frustrated because I really wanted to know more about Snow, but we'd spent our entire elevator time discussing if he was yelling for me or him.

So that means that I didn't get any information about who he was or why did he have so many passes around his neck, along with a few other questions that I had for Roman. But when we'd gotten off the elevator, Roman told us that he would meet us at the after party since he'd driven his own car and needed to make an extra stop before going to the party.

We then had to separate from him until later, so I just couldn't wait until Gerald was done handling his business. So that we could leave and go and meet back up with everyone, especially with Roman.

I really wanted to talk to him about this guy, since I couldn't stop thinking about him. And it was all too familiar, weird, and just so scary because I hadn't felt like that about a guy since Rico. – I mean I love my *BAMT's*, but the feeling of a totally different connection came over my body within a matter of seconds of seeing him, and I still didn't know anything about the guy other than his name at that point.

And as sure as the weather stayed perfect, and we were treated very well everywhere we went, Roman soon ended my fun by not showing up to the after party at all.

Gerald said that he had to go and pick up his girlfriend and do some other stuff that he was trying to explain to me, but I didn't care to listen because all I wanted was for him to show up so that we could talk.

But then since I finally had Gerald's attention, because Cosewh nor I could keep his attention long enough to hold a decent conversation with him, because he was all about work that night. Although he made sure that we all had everything we needed, and was being taken care of, but I took that time to ask him a few questions about Snow.

But I actually knew more about him than Gerald did because when I asked him who Snow was, he kept saying. "Snow who?" And when I said Roman's friend Hamilton Snow, he said that he would ask Roman about him because he didn't really know the guy. But I told him that I could do that for myself, and since I saw that he didn't know anything about him, I eventually just let it go.

I had to tell myself to either leave the whole Snow sighting alone all together, or to just get Roman's phone number from Gerald or Cosewh, and call him later about him. But I wasn't sure of what I wanted to do, so as the night went on. I decided to just let the whole Hamilton Snow elevator meeting pass, and just have fun with my guys.

And when I did let it go, the night became fun again thanks to my crew, and I even ran into an old friend that I'd previously saw coming out of the bank a few weeks prior.

During the time when I was in the city and on the prowl for my third *BAMT*, I'd saw her on my very last day of even trying to look for my number three. Although he probably wouldn't have been in that area anyway, because there were a few stragglers here and there in that part of the city. But not very many, but when I saw my friend coming out of the bank that day, we gave each other a big hug.

Then I told her that I had no idea that she had moved four hours away from her momma, because she was a momma's baby for real, but she was also a little hot box.

And that's how I'd known her in the first place, because Storm and Booby introduced her to me when she was interested in dancing at our club.

But when we saw that she just wasn't cut out to be the kind of dancer that we hired for our club, we told her that we couldn't let her dance. But the fact that she had a great looking body, we eventually decided to work with her anyway, because she really was one hell of an entertainer.

She kept us laughing every time she would come around, so we offered to have her come and keep everybody entertained with her beautiful body and outgoing personality. By mingling with the crowd and helping the girls with whatever they needed.

But that didn't last long because her mom was very over protective, and she eventually just disappeared on us. Not even Storm and Booby knew where she was, because she and her mom had moved away. But I heard that they didn't move very far from where they used to live, although I don't know how true that was because we still never saw her again.

And when I saw her at the bank that day, she said that she had gotten pregnant and her baby's father was a married man. Along with a lot of other drama that was going on with him, her, and the man's wife back then. But she said that since then she had gotten married, and had two more children with her own husband. – I told her that I still had a hard time believing that her mom would allow her to get married because even at the age of eighteen years old, she could barely leave the house without her mom lecturing her about stuff.

And I think that she ended up trying to come and dance with us because she wanted some wild excitement in her life because she was constantly sneaking around trying to get away from her mom's tight grip on her. And she must have finally snuck around a little too much since she ended up getting pregnant by a married man.

But everything still turned out good for her because she looked great, and she loved her kids and her husband from what I can tell from listening to her talk about them.

She said that her mom was always visiting her and her family, and that she was still just as over protective as she's always been. But by that time her mom had eventually found herself a boyfriend and was now also married. – And although I'd saw her a few weeks prior at the bank, imagine my surprise to see her again when she had walked over to me at the after party and changed everything that was going on in my head about wanting to know more about Snow.

And she was just as sociable and as funny as she'd always been, with the bonus of it all being that she had been drinking. Therefore, she was even funnier because she always has something to say about everything. No matter who's talking or what they're talking about, she has something to say about it, and sometimes her statements and comments are so off the wall that even if you are mad or agitated about the things that she says. You just can't do anything but laugh at her because she's going to say how she's feeling and when she's feeling it.

Even if it has nothing to do with her, and she has no idea what's really happening. She may still speak on it when she knows that she shouldn't, and it's usually very awkward and hilarious.

But when she approached me at the after party, we greeted each other and reminisced for a moment.

Then I introduced her to everyone while we caught up and enjoyed the rest of our night with her and her cousin joining us, and that's how I really forgot about seeing Snow by the time the night was over. – On top of Tru and Keenan being completely drama free, and making little jokes amongst the three of us about having a threesome without any jealousy.

While they also kept saying that they didn't know what was going to happen to me when we got back home.

And although I knew that they were tipsy and feeling good, they weren't heavy drinkers, so they weren't drunk. They were very serious, horny, and ready to let bygones be bygones, so that we could do things that we've never done before.

But I tried to stay out as late as we could due to their unusual behaviors, because it was clear what they wanted, and I wanted to be a lot drunker than usual if I was going to do a threesome. While I knew that I didn't have to do it if I didn't want to, nor did I have to be drunk to have great sex with them, but I wanted a little more to drink because the night was just too unusual. Notwithstanding the fact that I never get too tipsy, drunk, or anything else when I'm out with my staff like that, and they have all witnessed that I don't need to be drunk to have fun.

However, on this night, Tru and Keenan knew that something was up with me by the way that I was downing drink after drink towards the end of the night, and I could see that they were alarmed by my unusual drinking around everyone.

But I eventually didn't care, and neither did they as we ended up going home with me being the drunkest of us all. After I'd drank as much as I could while also getting Gabrielle and her cousin so messed up that I later found out that instead of driving them home.

Tru had called a car service to pick them up at the end of the night, right after Gabrielle and I had made plans to meet again in front of her bank that next day.

And while I was as intoxicated as I wanted to be, I wasn't sloppy drunk enough to embarrass myself in front of everyone, and neither was Gabrielle or her cousin.

Although Tru still didn't take them home or allow them to drive themselves home, because he said that they were not sloppy drunk but still drunk.

And while my memory was foggier than it should've been by the end of the night, I could still remember me and Gabrielle making sure that we had each other's numbers, so that we could meet on familiar ground, and that would be in front of her bank. Where we would decide where to eat from there, since we knew that there were several restaurants in that area.

But after we made those plans, I have no idea how they got home, or how I got home myself. The only reason that I can recall some of these details is because Tru and Keenan had to help me clear the fogginess of my memory of everything that next morning, after they made sure that Gabrielle's cousins car was returned to her safely.

And although they said that I wasn't sloppy drunk, and I can remember not being embarrassing or sloppy. Because I remember just doing a lot of laughing at Gabrielle, and a lot of playing with my guys about really doing a threesome. But I still ended up watching my home video footage later that morning, after they'd left the house.

Because as I do trust my guys with my life, and I usually give them their privacy because I don't really view any footage of my spy cameras, unless I'm curious about something. And since I could only remember a few bits and pieces of what happened, I wanted to watch the footage to see how things really went, and surely enough I saw us having a little too much fun.

And it was okay because by the time I saw what we did, the three of us had already had a good laugh about everything before they'd left. Then after I was done watching the videos, and just trying to recuperate from everything so that I could take a shower and get dressed to go and meet up with Gabrielle.

I called her to see how she was feeling, and just as I thought, she was just as hung over as I was.

But not so much that she couldn't move around, because she said that she was about to get up and start getting herself together when I called her.

She said that her husband was working, and her kids were with her husband's parents for two more days, so she was ready to hang out regardless of how hungover she was.

She even suggested that we go shopping after we finish eating, but at that point I knew that the alcohol didn't affect her as much as it did me. Because I was planning to eat, then go back home and lay around the house all day to recuperate.

CHAPTER

12

With my hair pulled up and into a bun, I wore a trefoil lady's jumpsuit, my new sneakers, and a pair of sunglasses that I'd purchased from the mall two days before that big concert.

I went to the bank, parked, and walked around to the front entrance of the bank where there was a bench on each side of its entrance.

I sat down on one of the benches to wait for Gabrielle to arrive, and in only a few seconds of me sitting down. I could not believe who stood near me, I mean I literally couldn't believe my own eyes. – Nor did I want to believe my ears when I looked up from my phone after quickly checking the time.

To my left I saw Snow going off on some guy that was standing several feet away from me.

He was telling him that he was getting on his nerves about having to talk to him about the same shit every day, he was yelling at the guy saying that he was too smart to be out here begging. And that if he kept on then he was going to kick his ass and he was serious.

But the guy was apparently used to arguing with Snow, because he kept saying yeah, yeah, yeah, I'll be out here all day today until I get what I need.

I then rushed to turn my body away from them and to put my head down as they began to walk in my direction, although I had huge sunglasses on my face.

I still knew that they weren't big enough to cover my entire face from Snow noticing me, if he would've looked more in my direction. So I crossed my legs then continued to hold my head down while acting like I was texting.

And I heard Snow telling the guy that he was about to go back to work, but when he comes back outside he better not see him again, because everybody has offered him money and a job. So there was no need for him to keep hanging around and asking everybody for money.

Then Snow walked away from the guy still without noticing me as people were helping to cover me by walking in front and on the side of me as he went into the bank.

He was dressed in some slacks and a nice shirt and tie set, and as I was relieved that he didn't see me at that moment. I also wanted to immediately approach the homeless looking guy because I'd been to that bank and in that area at least two or three times, and I didn't see many stragglers or just any type of homeless people in that part of the city like I thought I would.

But I knew that I had to talk to that guy, but I didn't want Snow to see me, nor did I want Gabrielle to see me. But everything from the way that he talked to Snow, and the things that he was saying to him, along with how he was dressed made him look like he could potentially be my number three.

So I swiftly paid attention to his whole appearance all together, and I knew that I wanted to meet him even if it wasn't to do anything more than just talk to him and leave him where he was without going any further.

I just sat there and watched him as best as I could to see what he was about to do after his spat with Snow was over, then after about five minutes, I was about to chance Snow coming back and noticing me talking to the guy because Gabrielle still hadn't shown up yet. And the guy had already looked over at me twice, but he just didn't approach me as it all seemed too good to be true that another *BAMT* would just suddenly fall into my lap like that.

But that's why I felt a little uneasy and confused, because sometimes if it looks too good to be true, then it probably is. But that hasn't been the case when it came to my *BAMT's*.

So just as I was about to stand up to risk Snow possibly coming back out and seeing me talk to the guy, Gabrielle showed up just in time to stop me. But when she finally arrived, she told me that she needed to go inside of the bank to the ATM to get some money out.

And that was great because that would give me time to go over and still have a word with the guy while she was gone.

So I told her that I would sit there until she was done, but instead. I immediately took off my sunglasses then rushed over to the guy and asked him his name.

And he had looked at me with a look of surprise and said. "Huh?" I then repeated the question and said. "What's your name?" Then when he said that his name was Uniray Ford, I almost passed out while looking at him like damn, even your name sounds homeless.

But I told him that I couldn't talk to him long, but I wanted to give him my phone number because I wanted him to call me in about two or three hours. And he just continued to look surprised as he took the number from my hand, after I'd written it down and watched him put it into his pocket. Then he asked me if I wanted him to call me for real? He said that he bet that was a fake number that I'd just given him, but he would still call me anyway. I told him to just call me, and if I didn't answer then he should just leave a message. As well as try calling me back again later if he didn't hear back from me, because I would like to talk to him about something.

I then lied and told him that I was about to go into the bank and talk to my friend Snow, while also telling him that I heard him and Snow arguing.

He laughed and said that they argue all the time, and that he was going to be calling me in a few hours. I said okay, then I turned around and walked away from him and into the bank to go and find Gabrielle, not Snow. And as soon as I walked into the building, I saw Gabrielle leaving the Tellers counter instead of the ATM machine.

And I also saw some chairs placed against the wall, so I asked her if we could go over and have a seat in the chairs before we left. And even though she had no problem with sitting down, she was confused and didn't understand why I wanted to have a seat. When I saw that she was done and ready to leave, but after we'd sat there for a few seconds I began to talk.

I told her that I was just sitting outside and saw a guy that I liked walk into the building, but I didn't know where he went. I also told her that I didn't want to leave the bank without first deciding if I wanted to go and look for him or not, so I just sat down to think.

But as unsure as I was about going to find Snow, I knew for a fact that I didn't want Uniray to say anything to me after Gabrielle and I was finished, and would go back outside to leave. But at the same time, I would know how to handle that if he did approach us, so I just sat there strictly thinking about if I should go and find Snow or not. Because I knew that there was something special about him that none of my *BAMT's* had.

So I just continued to sit there until I could figure out what I wanted to do. And judging from how nice Snow was dressed, and hearing him tell Uniray that he better not be there when he got off.

That let me know that he worked there, so I knew that I could just take my time to think over things a little more, and just come back to his job after I figured out what I wanted to do with him and why.

Because I knew that I wasn't ready for a guy like him, but I also knew that it had only been twice, but I felt something every time I saw him.

And he really didn't look like the type of guy who would be cool with me having a couple of boyfriends at home already, so I knew that I needed to seriously ponder on wanting to connect with him any further. Then when I finally told Gabrielle that we could just leave, because I could just come back some other time to deal with the guy when I'm ready to deal with him.

But when we got up and was about to leave, she had looked down at her bank receipt and said that her balance wasn't right, she told me to hold on for a minute so that she could go back to the Teller and check her account.

And since I suddenly didn't want to talk to Snow or Uniray, at least not until I could figure some things out first. So I told her where I was parked, and that I would be waiting for her outside in my car. – Because there were just too many thoughts moving around in my head, so I didn't want to chance being seen by anyone.

And that's why I was going to exit out of the banks side doors, opposite of where I last saw Uniray.

Gabrielle then proceeded to leave to go and handle her business, while I had turned around and walked right into the arms of Snow. I think I may have even pissed on myself a little bit because my nerves ran wild, and I couldn't control my body movements or anything. I'd turned to walk away from Gabrielle and there he stood, reaching out to me as if he was about to touch me on my shoulder before I'd turned around.

But I had literally turned around quickly and walked straight into his arms, and when I looked up at him he said. "I knew that my eyes weren't playing tricks on me when I saw you get up from that chair!"

I then nervously smiled and said. "Where did you come from?"

He smiled back and said. "From William and Aretha Snow!"

I laughed, then asked him who was William and Aretha Snow, and he said that they were his parents.

Then he stretched out his arm as if he was gesturing to shake my hand, so I shook his hand and just continued to smile when he actually grabbed my hand and introduced himself.

He told me that his name was Hamilton Snow, but everybody calls him Snow, then he immediately brought up how he'd saw me on the elevator last night. As well as how he'd saw me a few weeks-ago at the bank, but when he tried to find me I had disappeared, just like I did on the elevator.

He said that's why he wasn't about to let me get away from him again, because it all seemed too coincidental ever since he saw me at the bank weeks-ago.

As he explained how he had been keeping an opened eye out hoping to see me again, that's why he was so surprised and yelled out at me when he saw me on the elevator. He said that he couldn't believe that it was me again, and that he'd missed me again.

And as he continued, he even explained how he had ran after me that day at the bank, and on the elevator. And how he was willing to run after me this time as well, if I would've tried to disappear on him again.

But I honestly had no idea that he had saw me prior to being on the elevator, so at that point I knew for a fact that he and I had something special brewing. Because on top of all of that, I just wasn't myself the entire time in his presence.

I stayed nervous the whole time, and I was shocked that he had been chasing after me just as much as I was pondering about chasing after him. – I just had too many things going on in my life at the time to just give in, so it was very possible that I was willing to fall back and just let him go if I hadn't bumped into him like that.

I told him that I had no idea that he'd saw me before last night, then he interrupted me and said that he's seen me at least five times before seeing me on the elevator. – He began to smile and laugh while saying that his first sighting of me was at the bank, but the other four times have been in his dreams.

He said that's why he yelled, "Bae!" as the elevator doors were closing.

I told him that I thought that he yelled. "Hey!"

But he said nope, he yelled, "Bae!" because he and I had such a good time in his dreams about two days prior, that I'll always be his "Bae" forever.

As he continued to talk about how he couldn't believe that he was really standing there talking to me for real, because I had become just a figment of his imagination before that moment.

And I literally laughed the entire time as he was talking because he seemed to have had a whole relationship with me in his head, and I was just stunned.

But then he asked me my name, and if we could go out sometimes as I continued to laugh at him.

But I said. "Dang, so you're not going to ask me if I'm married, have a boyfriend, or anything?"

He then told me that he had already looked at my ring finger and he didn't see a ring.

He said that I had been showing up around him so much lately that he just assumed that I would automatically be with him. And I just laughed myself right into a big ole mess, because he was just so funny with how he just knew that I was supposed to be with him, and I liked it because I knew that I wanted him in a way that I've never wanted anyone other than Rico.

But again, since he didn't look like a guy who would approve of the real me, or my lifestyle of how I am with my *BAMT's*.

I was kind of afraid because things felt so weird, as if I knew that my life was about to change. So I went ahead and told him that my name was Tristan Bass, and that I would love to go out with him.

Then I asked him when he saw me a few weeks-ago at the bank, where exactly did he see me because I remember being at the bank, but I never went inside.

He said that he was in his office and was standing by the window when he had looked down and saw me walking across the street in his direction.

He explained how he had stopped what he was doing and ran out of his office and down to the lobby to find me, but I was gone by the time he'd made it to the lobby.

And I knew exactly when he was talking about because I wasn't walking to the bank, I was walking across the street to get to my car that was parked next to the bank. Just as it was parked in the same parking lot that it was currently parked in that day also. Then I asked him what did he do there at the bank, and he said that he was a Financial Analysts, and a Personal Financial Advisor that hopes to be the Vice President of his branch one day.

And I was very impressed, but also a bit more nervous than before because he just seemed very down to earth and lovable, and he liked me a lot. But he was just so professional and different from everyone else that my nerves just kept getting the best of me because I really liked him too. But our timing was bad because I also couldn't forget about my *BAMT's*, so I was just a mess. Then thankfully Gabrielle was done taking care of her business and had walked over to us. And that helped me to take my mind away from all of that because when I introduced them, I told her that his name was Hamilton.

And he was like. "Yeah, but my friends call me Snow."

I told him that I was now his friend, but I wanted to call him Hamilton. And he said that he was cool with whatever I called him, just as long as I called him.

I laughed then introduced him again as Hamilton, then I told her that she could call him Snow if she wanted to.

Then after the introductions and everything, I told him that it was nice to meet him 'again'. And that I was happy to now be the real thing, instead of some figment of his imagination.

He said that he was happy about that too, as he pulled out his phone and asked me if I would save my number in his phone.

I then locked my number into his phone, and we eventually said our goodbyes as Gabrielle and I proceeded to leave.

He then said that he already knew that I was about to be on his mind for the rest of the day, and that he probably wasn't going to get any more work done.

And I was all giggly and smiling because he was just so sweet and perfect for me.

Regardless of our timing being bad under the circumstances, but I didn't care because I was feeling him just as much as he was feeling me. But I told him that he would be okay after I was gone, and that I looked forward to hearing from him later as we continued to walk away from him.

Then as Gabrielle and I left the bank with me leading us through a side door to avoid possibly running into Uniray, whom I was then having second thoughts about at that point. Because now I was suddenly back to not wanting another *BAMT* added to what I already had.

And I knew that I wasn't going to give up Tru or Keenan for Hamilton, because I loved my guys, and they are both mine forever regardless of how I felt about Hamilton. But I also knew that Hamilton and I had something different, so different that I knew that I would definitely be watching my phone for his call to come through.

Gabrielle then suggested that we leave our cars parked and just go and eat at a nearby restaurant that was about two doors down from the bank.

Because she still felt a little drunk and was ready to eat some greasy food right away, but I on the other hand was ready to leave the area and just go somewhere else.

Even shopping at that point because I felt anxious and no longer wanted to eat, nor did I want to go home and lay down.

Consequently, due to our shenanigans the night before. I knew that Gabrielle seriously did need to eat something, so I suggested that she leave her car parked. While I drove us to a restaurant further down the street. She agreed, but when we got into my car to leave, my phone rang. And I hadn't even had time to start my car yet, and guess who it was?

Hamilton, he must have felt my vibe because he had called me immediately to say that he really enjoyed talking to me.

And I wasn't irritated that he was calling me too soon, as if he was desperate and already being over bearing.

Instead, I started smiling and kept that smile on my face the whole time while we were on the phone. He had basically just called to tell me that he enjoyed meeting me, and that he couldn't wait for us to link up again. And I told him that I was looking forward to spending more time with him as well.

Then after all of that, Gabrielle and I went to lunch and discussed a lot during our meal, especially me telling her how much I liked Hamilton.

But as she already knew from hanging out with us from the night before, Tru and Keenan were my guys.

And she could see that they were just as protective of me as her mom is of her, she even joked around about how my best friends were already two handsome guys that treats me like a Queen. – As she began singing the wedding song from the movie, Coming to America.

Every time I said that I'm not sure of how my guys are going to feel about Hamilton, she would change the words and sing. "They're your King's to be, your King's to be forever, your Kings who would do whatever her highness desire's."

And as we had a few laughs, she did say that she was happy for me, and that she thought that I would be more worried about how Don and Deon would feel about Hamilton.

Versus how my best friend's Tru and Keenan felt about him. Because anyone who knows anything about me or my family, knows that my brothers are always in me and Sabrina's business, especially when it comes to who we're dating.

But my family had gotten so used to only Tru and Keenan being around that I did begin to think that she may have had a valid point, because I hadn't dealt with any other men besides those two for years by that time.

So I truly didn't know how my brothers would feel about this new guy, but I figured that when they saw how professional, and the caliber of the type of guy Hamilton is.

I didn't think that they would have a problem with him, especially if I was happy.

Although at that time, I didn't know if Hamilton had a lot of women on his trail, or if he had any kids, or has he ever been married or anything.

I just knew that he was special, and that I wanted to be with him.

So in my mind, my brothers, my *BAMT's*, and everyone else was just going to have to deal with him and how I felt about him. If anything ever became an issue.

But as Gabrielle and I spent that time together having lunch, I decided to invite her to Sabrina's birthday party that Autry and I was throwing for her back home, and it would be happening in about four weeks or so.

And she said that she would love to come, and that she wanted to know if she could bring her husband to the party.

She said that her mom would have the kids, and that would give her and her husband some adult time away from everything. And I told her that would be great, and that I couldn't wait to see the man that ended up with her crazy self, and I also wanted to meet her children.

CHAPTER 13

Almost two weeks had passed and I'd accomplished two things, I stopped Uniray from calling my phone by telling him that I was married. And that I'd given him my phone number because I was going to hook him up with a job, but it was too late because the position had been filled.

And he eventually stopped calling me, while Hamilton and I have managed to talk every day since I fell into his arms at the bank.

I had successfully managed to keep my *BAMT's* on track, while also keeping Hamilton at a distance, yet very close to me as we talked very often over the phone. But then we soon set a date to meet again and had gotten together and haven't spent one day apart since our first date.

Although he didn't come to my house or my businesses, and I didn't go to his because we would meet at restaurants, movie theaters, art galleries, and where ever else that was suggested. While he did invite me to his home, his job, and everywhere else that I would be able to find him at any time, so that I would know that he had nothing to hide.

But I was the one who kept requesting that we take things slow, as far as us visiting each other at home or at our places of employment.

But other than that, we had gotten to know a lot about each other even with me hiding so much from him, because I had also truthfully opened-up and honestly told him a lot about myself for real. – I had even told him that I had two male best friends living with me that I loved dearly, and that we were completely platonic.

But he still didn't know very much about them other than I love them a lot because they're like my family.

And I knew that the three of them would eventually have to meet, but I just wasn't sure of when that would be.

And I didn't care to worry about it at that time because it was soon time for me to go back home to help Sabrina have a great birthday, so I put my focus more into that than I did on what I was going to do about the three of them.

Autry had called me and told me that she wanted to put me on speaker phone so that she and Deon could explain to me how Brandon had contacted Momma Bass, and asked her for Sabrina's hand in marriage, because he wanted to propose to her at her party.

And since Sabrina and Brandon had been dating on and off for so many years, we had even stopped getting into their little relationship spats. Because Brandon was always around even when they broke up, so he was like family anyway.

Even when Rico and I had our big breakup, Brandon and Sabrina didn't get involved as they continued to date, because Brandon is Rico's first cousin. And he and Sabrina met at one of our cookouts that Rico and I would have and just invite both sides of our families over to have fun.

And their love just continued throughout the years of thick and thin no matter what, although we all still take care of my nephew like we are the ones who gave birth to him.

Just as we do with all of our nieces and nephews, but I can honestly say that I trust that Brandon doesn't have anything but good intentions for both Sabrina and my nephew.

And as I agreed and approved of everything that they were suggesting that we do for Sabrina, since she knew about us throwing her the birthday party.

But she had no idea about Brandon's big proposal, so that would be the highlight of the night. And we all knew that she was going to say yes to him, and that's why I made sure to complete my part in her surprise because I wanted it to be one of the best days of her life.

While I was also plotting on how I would invite Hamilton as my date to the party, so that I could see how my family would respond to him during that time.

Even though I knew that my brothers would probably have a lot to say about Tru and Keenan trying to block anyone from coming my way, especially a guy like Hamilton.

So I figured that they'll probably be looking forward to seeing how my guys are going to respond to him versus their own responses.

And while Tru and Keenan would just have to eventually accept that they will still be in my life no matter what, but just in a few different ways. I figured that I could maybe propose some sort of freedom for them to possibly even date another woman if Hamilton and I got more serious.

But that was the furthest thing from my mind at that point, because they would continue to keep Abigail and her friends happy, and that was about all that I was going to allow as far as them concerning other women during that time.

Subsequently, my guys didn't want to go to Sabrina's party with me because they already knew that I needed them at the Parlor working, and I didn't always take them back home with me anyway.

Therefore, I was hoping that Hamilton would accept my offer in taking that Thursday and Friday off from work to go with me, since he was already off on Saturday's and Sunday's anyway. And when I asked him to go with me for four days he was more than obliged.

While at the same time he had me laughing so hard when he started telling me how crazy it was that I wouldn't let him come to my house or my places of business. But I wanted to take him all the way to my mom's house to visit my close friends and family.

He said that it was too weird that I was willing to take him and show him where my mom and my other loved ones reside, but my local family and residence seemed to never be an option of visitation for him.

And that's how I knew that he knew that I was hiding something, although he knew that I wasn't married, and that it wasn't something so bad that we couldn't work through it.

But since we'd only known each other for a little over a month by then, he had told me that he was willing to take things however slow as I wanted it to be.

Yet I knew that he was getting more curious about why I didn't want him around my house or my businesses.

As well as why I made him wait almost four weeks to even give him a real hug and kiss that lasted longer than just a quick peck on the cheek, because I always pulled back from him when we would hug or get close physically.

And since he had already agreed with my suggestion that we wait ninety days before having sex, he asked me if we could at least sleep in the same bed during those four days, if he vowed to behave.

And I agreed that we could sleep in the same bed if we stuck to our ninety-day agreement, but I knew that I was still going to have to confess a few things to him as we moved forward in our relationship with or without sex.

While I also figured that if we were truly getting as close as it felt like we were getting, then as my friend he would take me as I was after finding out that I had danced my way into a comfortable lifestyle.

While I would also inform him that I wasn't dumb or stupid because I chose not to go to college, especially since I had successfully ran not just my companies, but I had helped other companies as well without a degree.

And since he had already told me damn near everything about his life just like my *BAMT's* did.

I was ready to open-up a little bit more to him, although I would never tell anyone absolutely everything about me no matter who they are. But I was prepared to tell him a lot, still not giving away too many details, but I would definitely be more open.

And as close as I was making Hamilton, I knew that he would have to just take me or leave me because I was no longer ashamed of where I came from or who I am, because he and I came from two totally different backgrounds.

He had graduated from two colleges, and his biological parents have been together his entire life.

His brother played professional basketball in a country that I could barely pronounce, his older sister is a Veterinarian, and his youngest sister was currently in college.

And more than that I found out that he used to be married to a girl that graduated from the same college as he did, and he said that she used to complain about his parents not liking her because she used to date women.

So I could only imagine what they were going to think about me and where I came from, because after listening to his life story, he and his brother and sisters had a very good life starting from their birth. And it was the same way with his ex-wife, because it sounded like she came from a privileged life as well.

He explained how his family really did like his ex for the most part, they just didn't like how she acted and did things sometimes. – He said that she was beautiful on the outside but she was spoiled rotten on the inside, so his mom didn't like how arrogant she was. He said regardless of his ex's beliefs, his mom really didn't care about her past relationships with women.

Because they all knew that she was in love with him, so his mom and everyone else just accepted her and her arrogant behavior, since that's just who she was. He told me that he'd been divorced for two years, and that he was looking forward to introducing me to his parents.

Whereas I had been nervous, and was planning to prolong meeting his parents for as long as I could, because although I know that I am an attractive woman. And I've independently made my own money, but I just couldn't get over how beautiful his ex-wife is, and that she was raised much differently than I was. Because after doing my own background search on her and Hamilton, I had found a few family pictures of them online. And I knew not to keep pondering too much on her looks or her background, as well as to keep hiding things from Hamilton.

But that's why Sabrina's birthday weekend was the weekend to release it all, while I continued to help carry out hopefully one of the most memorable birthday's that Sabrina has ever had.

Also, during that entire time Autry knew that Deon was hiding something from her, and we later found out the secret was that Brandon had invited Rico and a lot of their family members to the party to come and celebrate with us.

She told me that Deon knew that Rico was going to be there and participating in Brandon's proposal setup, but he just didn't want to tell us because he didn't want any drama.

However, at the party, I was extremely surprised by how things were.

And a little nervous when I saw Rico there, but I didn't panic or feel too weird for long, because I was still more attracted to Hamilton than I was to Rico.

And that was just another reason for me to acknowledge how much interest I really had in Hamilton. So I happily introduced him to everyone during the party, and they all loved him just as I thought they would.

He was so handsome and so smart and educated, but still very down to earth and fun to talk to.

While in the meantime, Rico and I did say hello to each other, but that was as far as we went concerning conversation after so many years had passed since we'd seen each other. – While through it all Sabrina was completely surprised, overwhelmed, and just genuinely happy with how everything went as she said yes to Brandon.

And we all had a wonderful time enjoying each other, although I did see Rico looking at Hamilton a few times as we made our rounds when I was introducing him to everyone. But there was no drama before, during, or after the party.

So Hamilton and I ended the night by going back to his hotel room, because staying at Momma Bass' house wasn't an option for him during that time, although I didn't care if he knew where we lived.

But he was still a stranger to them, and I didn't want anyone to feel uncomfortable. And everyone understood that so it all worked out, and when we had returned to the hotel, and had gotten comfortable after such a long day.

I then admitted to Hamilton how I had been hiding a few things from him due to my embarrassment. And that I wanted to seriously talk to him because I was no longer embarrassed, and I didn't want to go any further into our relationship without clearing up a few things.

I told him that my guys Tru and Keenan were my best friends like I'd told him from the beginning, but I admitted that our relationships was a bit more than just best friends as I had claimed.

Although I would never tell him about Abigail and her friends, or about any of that kind of sex business at all. But I did tell him that they were more like my boyfriends who did whatever I told them to do, while I'm allowed to go out and date and do whatever I want to do, but they are not.

He then stopped me and asked me was I having sex with them, along with what kind of guys would allow me to date someone else, but they can't date anyone else?

I told him that in our past I have had sex with each one of them individually, but never together. And that we no longer did things like that anymore because our sexual relationships had been over a long time ago, even before he and I bumped into each other that day at the bank.

I told him that Keenan and I had a sexual relationship after Tru and I was over.

But even with all of that we just never let that part of our lives affect our business relationships. And since they were single and free to do whatever they wanted to do, I told him that I decided to just let them both stay with me in my home and work for me, since I was single and free to do whatever I wanted to do as well.

I explained how I knew that it was weird for me to eventually put such a rule in place that if they were going to live under my roof, then they can't date, but they agreed to it regardless of how single and free they were. And it all just worked out for us, so ultimately to Hamilton's knowledge. I wasn't having sex with anyone at that time, because my guys had truly become like my business family and my personal family

And I let him know that they were very protective of me, and looked out for me so he should be prepared for that.

And if he was cool with all of that, then at that point he was invited to come to my house and my places of business at any time whenever we returned home, as long as he understood their feelings towards me and the way we lived our lives.

Overall, Hamilton's thing was that I didn't have a ring on my finger, so he was ready to stick around.

He said that the only thing that could've kept him away from me was a wedding ring, while also stating how he wanted to be the one to give me a ring, just like we had witnessed Brandon doing for Sabrina.

And that made me very happy because I just knew that he would potentially look at me a little differently after finding out that I had slept with my best friends in the past.

Along with my unnecessary thoughts of how my family didn't have as much money as he and his family had, although that was never a real factor because he saw that we lived almost just as good as he and his family lived.

But none of that mattered anyway, because he was accepting to everything. Even when I told him about my regrets of having an abortion due to the fears that I had at the time.

He told me that we shared the mourning of a child together because he also wished that he could've met the baby that his ex was pregnant with, but he never got to meet the baby because she unfortunately had a miscarriage.

He had also expressed how he felt like my guys would have to eventually move out, because he would eventually want to be the only male lover and protector in my life, after being together for a while. And he continued on by saying how he felt like after meeting me, he'd finally met his forever lady, and he really didn't want to share his lady with two other men.

And while he stayed consistent with his feelings of me being it for him forever, and how he wanted me to feel the same way about him.

I did feel super close to him, and I knew that he was something special to me and for me. But there was no way that I was going to be getting rid of my guys completely at any time, no matter how close he and I would become in the future.

But I felt like our feelings were real, but I also felt like he and I were moving too fast, and I wanted to continue to take things slow.

Just not so slow to leave room for us to have irritating problems, especially with him trying to get rid of my guys because that would become a problem for us. – And although sex wasn't the most important part of a relationship like ours, I wasn't about to make any commitments concerning my guys without first seeing how and what he was working with sexually anyway.

Because I was truly building a relationship with Hamilton off of pure hope as far as our sex life, although his body was amazing, so I just couldn't imagine something so fine and built like that being terrible in bed.

Even though you never know, he could very well be horrible and not worth teaching, but I doubted it because he could kiss like he knew exactly what to do if he had the chance to go farther. And I would always stop him from kissing me because I myself didn't want to take things farther than our original plan, judging by how aggressive he could be. So I knew that our sex life wouldn't be an issue.

Our only real challenge appeared to be that I'm a person who loves to have control and so is he. But I have had plenty of experience with corporate guys such as Hamilton in public and in private, so I was confident that I could maneuver my way right into his already opened heart and get my way.

My only task from that point was what was I going to tell Tru and Keenan regarding my feelings for Hamilton, and how would they receive him.

But I, in true Honey fashion chose not to deal with that part of our situation until the time came for it, so I just laid and cuddled with Hamilton and enjoyed him for the rest of the night.

Then that next day, Hamilton and I joined Sabrina, Brandon, Deon, Autry, Don and his girlfriend Elaine for breakfast at Momma Bass' house.

She had cooked us a big breakfast and we all talked, laughed, and just had fun as they all loved Hamilton. And Momma Bass was impressed that he was a Financial Analyst, and a Personal Financial Advisor. Because I'd noticed how she was smiling at us while they bombarded him with financial questions.

But then just as I thought.

Don couldn't wait until we had a moment alone to ask me where were my submissive servants, and how did they feel about Hamilton. – I told him that they haven't met him yet, but they did know that I was spending a lot of time with some guy that I really liked.

I informed him that I wasn't going to let them know too much about him until after my family had gotten a chance to meet him first, but now since they had met him. I would be telling them how he really wants a serious one on one relationship with me. And I knew that they would accept it because personally in my mind, regardless of how Hamilton felt, I still wasn't going to give up my guys anyway.

Along with them not really having a choice but to also accept Hamilton and our relationship, and probably a few disappointing changes in our lives.

But nonetheless, they would be okay because I would let them know how important they are and will always be to me.

While aside from sex, we would pretty much stay the same. – We would just have another member added to our little bonded family like I was planning to have anyway.

He just wouldn't be quite a *BAMT*, so he wouldn't need to know anything about how I manage to make thousands of dollars from them each month aside from massage therapy.

Therefore, keeping some of our business antics strictly between us will need to be enforced under every circumstance, with a clear understanding that there are a few things that Hamilton just doesn't need to know regardless of how close we become.

So they would need to send him directly to me if he ever starts asking too many questions concerning us.

Because as submissively fond of me as he was, I knew that Hamilton was still controlling and would try and command that he's the master of our family.

But I would never let him come in and dominate our situation that we had worked so hard to establish.

Although I knew that he was taught by his father to be a man, and the man is the leader of his household no matter how submissive to me that he was willing to be at times.

I knew that he would eventually try and take charge over how I interacted with my guys, but by then I'm sure he knew just as well as anyone else knew that I wasn't a pushover.

And allowing him to come in and just take over my home was a long shot, but I knew that we were still in for a challenge.

However, our trip was still an overall success, as my family was happy. And so was I, since Hamilton decided to somewhat accept me and my flaws that I was willing to tell him about.

I even got a chance to get a good feel of his penis through his shorts while we spooned in bed the night before we left, and neither of us wanted the trip to ever end because we felt so much closer to each other after our chat.

But the good news continued because Autry, Deon, Don and Elaine all made plans to come and visit me and the lounge because there were a few groups that wanted to perform live at PMF.

And the groups would be coming to meet with us that following week, or either the week after that to go over the music line up and other show ideas with me and the manager. But they all wanted to attend the meeting to see the groups as well.

And I couldn't be happier because I needed Autry and Elaine to come so that we could have at least one day of girl time with just the three of us, since Sabrina wasn't going to make the trip. Because it's clear that they are my sister-in-law's, although Don hasn't married Elaine yet, but we've bonded as sisters because my brothers have been in a serious relationship and have only had kids with them.

And it's not a secret that they have dealt with more than enough drama from Don and Deon, especially Autry.

Although before Deon married her we knew how much he loved her since he was a teenager, but he was still terrible at times. But they both had to deal with so many other females that they deserve the respect that my brothers now show them after so many years of being disrespected, used, and abused.

I even had to curse my brothers out a few times in regards to how blatant they could be. But now things have gotten a lot better because they, along with my nieces and nephews are always happy when I see them. And while Autry has always been the oldest of all of us, even when people really couldn't see it. But eventually she even stepped up and matured a lot after she had her first child.

Because now she and Elaine both are very family oriented, and they both do a great job with the kids and with taking care of my brothers. Although in my opinion, they are sometimes still slaves to my brothers just like Don says that my guys are to me.

But that's why I don't listen to Don when he meddles with me about how at my feet Tru and Keenan are.

Because sometimes he's even worse than me, and I would tell him that all the time because I felt like my guys were no more slaves to me than Elaine was to him. Even though Elaine knew how to step up and set his ass straight at times, but it all seemed to just work out in a way that we were all happy with how our lives went.

And that was just that on that, as our sister-in-law pact always stayed strong no matter what they went through.

Although I was still always limited with my personal business, but Autry and Elaine knew a lot more than I was telling my brothers because I knew that I could trust them to a certain extent.

They are two loyal females that love hard on our family and it showed, so they have my respect just as much as I have theirs. And they knew that Tru and Keenan meant more to me than just some old best friends that I was strictly helping like my brothers thought, but they still didn't know that my guys used to be homeless. Nor did they know anything about Abigail or her friends.

But they knew that my guys felt things beyond a normal friendship, because I told them that I was having sex with them both whenever I felt like it. – Except I led them on in believing whatever they wanted to believe at some points as far as that, because I really would let Tru and Keenan both rest their penis's. While I would only use their tongues, because I was mainly letting Abigail and her friends enjoy what their penis's had to offer.

But when my sisters visit, I did want to hear what they have to say about my sudden need to only want Hamilton mentally, physically, and spiritually. Even though I still wasn't at all willing to stop my relationships with Tru or Keenan.

Because I'm sure that they could already see, hear, and could feel free to assume that Hamilton was a man who was all about it being strictly he and I only, without my guys.

And he made that clear to my family and his family as well, although I would continue to stay a mystery to his family for as long as I could, no matter how much they knew about me and wanted to meet me.

But usually after talking to Autry and Elaine, they always help me to sort through my difficult decision making a little better, although this situation happens to be a bit more difficult. Because I really was falling for Hamilton, yet they knew that I would never let go of my guys because like my family, I wouldn't just throw Tru or Keenan away when I know the genuine love that we have for each other is real and everlasting.

But everything was moving so fast from every angle, and I knew that Hamilton's family really wanted to see who had come along and stolen his heart so quickly.

So with my sister's help, my plan was to fix any possible dilemmas with my guys concerning Hamilton first, before seeing how I would tackle having to meet his family.

CHAPTER
14

It was back to business as usual when I invited Cosewh to lunch, then later I met with the manager of PMF, since I was going to need for both locations to stay on top of keeping things in order. Because I didn't know what was about to take place when my *BAMT's* found out that things were about to change, so I set my two strongest employees up to have my back as a precaution for just in case things go differently than I expected.

Tru, Keenan, and Cosewh were my go to employees when I knew that I wouldn't be around to open and close the Parlor. But they still had to transfer our daily reports to me each day no matter what I was doing or where I was, and so did PMF.

And although they didn't know a lot of details about my personal life, they knew that I had a new boyfriend. And that we were becoming exclusive, and that my two guys may not mix well with him due to some of the comments that they had been making.

But we all usually just laugh, and could understand their jealous comments due to everyone always seeing only the three of us together.

Whereas now everyone knew that I had been spending a lot of time with this new guy. Therefore, I needed their attention to be on having my back.

Especially Cosewh, even though in my heart my guys weren't really a true threat to me or my businesses. – But staying prepared for anything was necessary, while Cosewh didn't need to eyeball my guys too much, or treat anyone or anything any differently than usual. I just needed extra eyes to be aware of any possible drama.

Because depending on how my personal life would meet my business life, I didn't know what was in store for us, especially with Hamilton's eagerness to be around me and for us to become closer.

And as his wants heightened when we returned home, after only two days of returning from our trip.

I waited until it was almost bedtime to get with Tru and Keenan about what was about to happen. I explained to them how a few things would change, along with how much a lot of things would remain the same.

Even with me and Hamilton trying to be exclusive in our relationship, I made it extremely clear that my bond with them wouldn't be tampered with outside of who we would have sex with. And under no circumstances would I allow Hamilton, or our relationship to end my relationships with them.

While I also expressed how I would need for them to be open and understanding to why I chose to have such a relationship with him. And Hamilton would also need to be the same way, instead of being pushy and gung ho to show them his power.

Because he already knew that I wasn't going to get rid of them no matter how he felt, but with Hamilton's strong personality of taking the lead. I intended to warn him not to challenge Tru or Keenan's place in my life with his urge to be my one and only.

And while my guys were always accepting of whomever I loved, on this night of our conversation they weren't as accepting of the fact that I liked him so much that I would let him have a say so in anything. Because they both expressed to be okay with him being in my life, even supposing that they didn't really have a choice in the matter at the end of the day. But they still expressed their concerns as they listened to me talk, while I could see from their facial expressions and from their comments that they felt some type of irritable way about him becoming closer to me than they thought he was.

Therefore, they both were adamant about wanting to meet him. So as time went on, and the moment eventually came for them to meet, after I'd talked to Hamilton about how I needed for him to be just as accepting of them as they were of him.

And eventually, for as good as their meeting could have went, it went okay considering the circumstances.

Tru and Hamilton got along pretty good, while at some point Hamilton seemed to have rubbed Keenan the wrong way.

Because he felt like Hamilton was too demanding over me, so for the most part their interactions were timid, and Keenan just couldn't shake his feelings of why I would let Hamilton have a say so in anything concerning our lives.

Regardless of how much I kept telling him that Hamilton had no say so in anything, he was just going to be present sometimes because I was the one who wanted to make some changes in our lives, not Hamilton. – But like the true friend that he is, Keenan tried his best to swallow his uneasiness and just accept things for what they were.

But after a few months had passed, and we were still adjusting to my best friends coinciding with my now real boyfriend.

You can only imagine how we've had a few ups and downs during those months, but things were still okay for the most parts. And I was even finally about to meet Hamilton's family, since I couldn't put it off any longer after staying overnight at Hamilton's house so much.

And we were becoming closer each day, even with the real problems or issues that we had been having consistently with me not wanting to meet his family that whole time.

Along with his control versus my control at times, combined with him and Keenan having their mini spats that could get very uncomfortable.

But that's why I decided to stay at Hamilton's house more so than he stayed at mine. Because Hamilton is the type of man that's not going to back down from anyone no matter what his background is, as he truly is his father's son judging from the things that I've learned about his father.

But Keenan was dangerous, and of course he would love to show his hands if he had to because he didn't mind challenging any guy for his position in my life.

No matter what their takedown tactics were, Keenan was always ready for anything and anyone. And when it comes to Hamilton, he would turn things up a notch as if he wanted Hamilton to do something wrong so that he could step in and do something to him.

So that's why we mainly stayed at Hamilton's house all the time, while I still never made it a bad habit to stay away from my own house for too long.

I would often call and check in and stop by to help them work, while making sure to keep Tru and Keenan busy sexually with my old buddies. While they also continued to work as successful therapists, and as they enjoyed my house and had the options to go out and have fun together without me on their off days. But Tru and Keenan were both home bodies because they always preferred to stay at home, even on the holidays they would rather eat and drink at home; instead of going out. Unless we were going home to Momma Bass' house for the holidays, they loved that, but other than that they liked to be at home.

Hamilton on the other hand eventually proved Keenan to be right, seeing that he did ultimately gain more control over me than I'd realized.

Because for a moment, I had temporarily turned into everything that Don taught me not to be, no matter how he treated Elaine or any other woman. He had always taught me and Sabrina to stand for something or we'd fall for anything, especially if we were in love.

He would always say to love the person as hard as we wanted to, but we should never ever lose ourselves and let any man completely take over our lives.

And in view of the predicament that I had put myself in, I couldn't believe that I had done just that by eventually letting Hamilton use my love for him against me; stemming from his birthday party.

Where I was so happy to be celebrating with him and mingling amongst so many high-classed people who knew me by name, but they had never saw my face until the day of his party. I truly felt like a celebrity amongst his friends and family due to how much he'd told them about me.

No one treated me like I was less than them, because everyone was coming up to me and introducing themselves, hugging on me and talking about PMF and my Parlor. I was even given business cards and invitations to things that would help grow my businesses, because there were so many bankers and financially successful people there who worked with Hamilton or either someone in his family. – And they were all advising me on how opening another lounge like PMF would benefit us and benefit certain areas in the city, and how we wouldn't have to pay a lot of money for a building that was being foreclosed on that they could help us to get.

So I was very grateful for their cards and the advice that I was given thanks to Hamilton.

And more than that, his family was genuinely into me and kept trying to pull me away from everyone all night, but then we all ended up sitting together and eating together before we sung happy birthday to Hamilton. 'Snow' as they all called him, even his family members called him that, as if they all didn't have the same last name.

But the night was grand, and I knew that Hamilton couldn't be happier, and neither could I. Until that next day following his party, and he was informed that it was time for me to return home like I usually do when I'd been away for too long.

Hamilton decided that he didn't want me to go back home for a full week like I told him that I was planning to do before I would return to his house, since I'd been staying with him for two full weeks and only went to visit my home twice during that time.

And I never stay away from home that long, but celebrating his birthday and meeting his family and friends was important to me. And I wanted to give him and his entire birthday event my undivided attention, because by then I'd fallen in love with him.

And I really thought that we were in a good place in our lives, so his sudden need to only want me to strictly visit my home. Versus staying there overnight was bothersome to me, because he knew that I had a business to run, and that I had already been away from my home and my business for too long as it was.

But his main concerns were about me missing my guys, and how I wanted to give them some consistent time with me, because they were like my family. And that's how it has always been as we've continued to move forward because by then, he knew that there wasn't anything sexual going on between us for sure. Because I would always invite him over to my house whenever I was away from him for too long as well.

Especially when things were good, and he and Keenan weren't disagreeing about anything major.

Hamilton was free to come over and hangout at any time during good times and bad times, because he and Tru got along great, so regardless of his feelings.

I had *BAMT's* and businesses that I had to tend to, and I wasn't going to neglect anymore of my responsibilities due to his controlling issues.

Plus, I had been at his beck and call mentally and physically during his entire birthday month, so I needed for him to be more understanding of how I felt about him and our relationship due to how I'd stopped everything for him.

But he didn't seem to care about my businesses, or my unusual sacrifices of neglecting everything and everyone for him. Because the morning after his party, when our lives were so perfect. He ended it all with his macho need to claim ownership and take control over my life when he demanded that I finally stop going back and forth between homes, and just move in with him since I'd met his family and friends.

He said that they all loved me and I loved them, so he didn't understand why I was still taking things so slowly after meeting everyone.

Although in reality, I wasn't moving slow at all because I'd finally met almost everyone. And I figured we had our whole lives to spend together, so the need to rush moving in together and getting married and everything that comes with that whole movement didn't need to be rushed. But I was still showing him that I was moving in that direction of us becoming more every day, because I truly did love him.

But Hamilton just refused to understand my words of telling him that marriage and kids between us could potentially happen one day. But it just wouldn't be happening during that time, and those words pissed him off. Along with me reiterating how my guys would always have a place in my life, and I had always been clear to him about that.

Just as I'd been clear about no one being as special to me as he was as far as a mate for me, so he really had no reason to flip out on me that morning and prove Keenan to be right.

Because when I'd gathered my things and was about to walk out of the door to go home for a while, after having to argue with him like we'd never argued before.

He had blocked the door and wouldn't allow me to leave, so I invited him to come and go home with me, but he was just too angry and felt like he wanted me there with him period.

And he'd began to yell and talk about how my guys were going to have to learn how to live without me, because he didn't like sharing. And before I started yelling back at him and requesting that the old Hamilton come back, because somehow overnight he must have left and become someone else because he was no longer himself.

Ever since that day that I'd bumped into him at his job, it's been all about he and I connecting our love regardless of my guys, and he knew that because I'd shown him every day how I felt about him.

So my anger quickly escalated along with his because he started talking crazy to me and getting all in my face like he wasn't my sweetheart anymore. All because he didn't want to share anymore, and I was just so mad, lost, and confused because none of my behavior was new to him or our relationship in terms of sharing.

But things got bad when he had pushed me away from the door and continued to block my way out, because I'd began to curse him out about trying to control my life and getting in my face all because I just wanted to go home. – While things had been that way for months without any of that type of rage and anger over me packing to leave, so for him to display such negative behavior the day after everything had went so well between me and his family and friends was extremely hurtful.

Because he was extremely mad for no reason, and I didn't like him at all for that, so my request for him to get away from the door and let me leave heightened.

But it was like some sort of switch had flipped in his brain that told him that meeting his family and friends meant that my life with my own family and friends wasn't as important anymore, because he wanted me to live with him and just continue to work from home.

And that was upsetting because he knew that wasn't possible at that time, but he continued to block my path and wouldn't let me leave, so I told him that I was going to leave whether he liked it or not. And that I would try to communicate with him later after he'd had a chance to calm down.

But then he literally grabbed my arm with one hand, and grabbed the bags that I was holding with his other hand and slammed me to the floor.

And I just laid there because I was so surprised and stunned that as feisty as I was known to be, I really couldn't move. I was in shock as if my spirit had left my body or something, so I just laid there waiting for him to apologize and help me up from the floor, but that didn't happen. But still I just knew that there was no way that the Hamilton whom I thought that I'd gotten to know so well had just slammed me to the floor.

And this Hamilton was serious about me not leaving his house, so I got up from the floor without his help and watched him pick up my bags from the floor and hand them to me. Then he told me to go back into the other room and just relax, because he didn't want us to have to fight over me trying to go back home. Although by that time I was over his frustrations and his stupidity.

So again, I told him that I was going to leave and not come back until he could fix his sudden anger problem that was totally unnecessary, no matter how he felt.

And I told him that I wasn't a woman that was going to allow him to violently put his hands on me.

Although in my heart, I did love him, and I don't think that I would've even used my gun on him even if I would've had it with me due to my feelings toward him, and that's what really scared me.

But I told him that he was starting to show me everything that he said that he didn't like about his father behind closed doors. Because he seemed to have transformed into everything that we'd talked about in the past that would prevent him from turning into his father, who was so controlling that when Hamilton left home to go to college.

He said that he would strictly visit their family home after he'd moved out for college, because he would never live under his father's roof ever again due to his violent behaviors.

While his father was very successful in the banking industry also, and was a great father and husband when he wasn't drinking alcohol. But controlling his family by any means necessary was always present in their home is what he told me, no matter how successful they were.

Hamilton said that no one knew that his father even cursed, but he and his brother and his sisters knew to go into their rooms and close their doors after a certain point when they were kids. Because his father would become reckless after drinking, and his mom would always fight him back. But in my mind, regardless of how much of his mom's strength that he saw in me, I wasn't going to be fighting him.

And while my brothers did teach me to fight back, and that if I allow anyone to put their hands on me once, then it would happen again. But instead of following my brother's advice, I stayed for a few minutes and tried to talk to Hamilton because I knew that he was only acting out due to his family's history. Considering that he'd never put his hands on me before, and that we have had some good conversations regarding his temper when things didn't go exactly the way that he wanted it to go.

And since he had only slammed me to the floor, and he didn't use his fist or anything like that, then maybe he really wasn't trying to hurt me.

Because I knew that he didn't want to be like his father in that aspect for real. However, it was during the morning so he couldn't blame his temper on alcohol, but then I figured that he did take the day off from work thinking that we would spend it together, so I decided to stay.

While also considering that he had always been at my feet just like my *BAMT's* were, so for a moment I honestly did think that he had only gotten so angry with me because he genuinely just didn't want me to leave, and I understood that part.

What I didn't understand was that he just wasn't relating to any of my logical ways of thinking.

Even after I decided to calm down and just stay with him, I told him that I felt like he was only acting out because of his genuine love for me, mixed with him and his father's past.

But he still just didn't seem to grasp certain things like he normally do when we discuss his father, even when he started to get emotional and told me that he was sorry for slamming me. He said that he felt like he had to slam me to the floor to stop me from leaving, but I told him that hasn't been how we operate in the past when we disagreed.

And that it wasn't how we would operate in our future either, because we were better than that.

And it wasn't until the moment came when I again told him how I would soon still be leaving until he's had time to really think about what he had done to me, and how bad things could get in the future due to that kind of behavior. And that's when it seemed like his tears just suddenly disappeared.

Especially when I eventually tried to leave again after we'd had time to gather ourselves, he ended up blocking the front door again. Then he followed me to the back door when I tried to leave that second time, because after a while of talking to him about what had just happened.

I was starting to feel like he just wasn't as sorry as I thought he was even when he'd gotten all emotional and apologetic, and he proved me right because he'd hit me twice in my face with a closed fist when I tried to leave during that second time.

And as I'd hit him back and started crying, because I was blown away and just astonished. It felt like I was bleeding but I didn't see any blood, so I just kept punching him back, and scratching him while I shoved as hard as I could to try and push my way out of the door.

But with my back being pressed so hard against the wall, I couldn't hold onto anything but my keys as I managed to escape the madness when I'd ran back toward the front door, and I nearly made it out before Hamilton picked me up and held me against the wall yet again. And no matter how much I tried to hit, kick, bite, and scratch him to get away from him.

His final punch was in my eye, and I surely felt it.

Along with the opened hand slap across my face before I fell to the floor without getting up that time, because that time I had no choice but to lay there holding my face while I thought about my brothers and my *BAMT's*, although they couldn't help me. But I didn't want him to hit me again, so I just laid there feeling so overwhelmed with heartache and pain from how Hamilton's love had turned on me over night. And I also felt so stupid for not being able to protect myself, and I hated myself for still feeling sorry for him because I knew that just wasn't who he really was as a person.

He soon picked me up from the floor and carried me into his bedroom and brought me a warm towel while wearing a face of shame because he could barely look me in my eyes after that. But then when he gave me the towel he began to cry, and he later tried to hug and kiss me while apologizing.

But I'd pushed him away and refused his hugs and kisses because he had just apologized moments earlier the first time, right before he had started punching on me.

But after his apology attempts, and his reasoning for acting out, I just threw my keys to the floor and took off my shoes while I kept my clothes on and just got underneath his bed comforter.

I laid there holding the wet towel against my battered face because I knew that his plan to keep me there had succeeded, because there was no way that I was going to keep trying to leave and risk my face, or any other body parts getting any more bruises.

Along with my fears of what would happen if Tru or Keenan saw my face, while I also couldn't allow anyone else to see me and risk rumors getting back to my brothers of me being seen injured due to looking like I'd been in a fight. Because there was nothing that I could've said to anyone to convince them that I hadn't been in a fight due to my appearance, even if I could've covered up the bruises that I knew would be on my back and on my legs.

Hiding my face would've been impossible, so in my mind at the time staying inside was the only option that I had to avoid anyone getting in trouble over my injuries, or over the injuries that he also received that would let people know that it was him who I fought. And that's why I just laid there in his bed crying until I fell asleep.

Then later after resting for a few hours, I was awaken by the smell of some food that Hamilton had ordered. So I got up and took some pain medicine, and I couldn't believe my eyes when I looked in the mirror and saw how swollen my face was. I became upset all over again because I immediately started to realize that I was in a terrible situation. – One that I would definitely be removing myself from, but not until my face healed because there wasn't a doubt in my mind that Keenan would literally kill Hamilton if he knew how he had violated me. Just as much as Tru would also rise to ruin Hamilton's life with the knowledge of how he'd taken his kindness for weakness on my behalf. Therefore, no matter how bad the decision was.

I chose to stay in Hamilton's home until I healed, while keeping quiet and only calling in to check on everything and everyone every now and then. And I can say that I managed to get through it all without risking anyone getting hurt or just something worse. Because I simply pretended to be sick and didn't need anyone to come and help me because Hamilton was taking such good care of me.

Although he really was coming home on his breaks from work to check on me, or either he would call to see if I needed anything when he was unable to leave work. – While through it all I understood that time was racing, and eyebrows would raise if I didn't eventually show my face again at home or at work, sick or not.

While I also knew that once I healed, I wouldn't be returning to spend another night with Hamilton ever again. But with him hitting me in the same spot a few times, there were bruises that I wanted to be completely gone that took longer to heal than I expected.

But then when I felt comfortable enough to leave, and saw that he was comfortable enough to believe that I had forgiven him and everything was all good again.

I waited for him to go to work one day, then I wrote him a very long letter right before I left him forever, and with no good intentions of returning. Because I knew that things would only get worse if I'd stayed with him and potentially ruined everything that I'd worked so hard to build with my family, and it would've been all because I'd fallen in love with the wrong person. And I wasn't about to let my bad decisions produce reckless behaviors from my *BAMT's*, or from my brothers over harming Hamilton in a permanent way after finding out what he had done to me.

I was determined to keep my mouth closed about the entire incident, and just tell everyone that we had broken up because he cheated on me, so we split forever. While they would also know that I didn't want to communicate with him under any circumstances if he ever decided to call or stop by to see me.

I had planned to stay quiet because all I wanted to do was be removed from Hamilton, that fight, and our relationship all together.

But that wouldn't turn out to be the case after I had left him that day, although my guys on the other hand was so happy to see me walk into the Parlor that you would've thought that I'd been gone for a year.

They all joked around saying that they thought that Hamilton had kidnapped me and told me to forget about them, and while as unfunny as that was to hear them talk like that, after going through what I'd just gone through. I still laughed as much as I could at their jokes, but I was feeling so hurt and disappointed inside.

I soon changed the subject and began to walk around the Parlor while being brought up to speed on how everything was during my absence. Even though I was calling to check in when I was away, but I still needed to officially catch up.

Then I later gathered Tru and Keenan to join me while I went to show my face at PMF, and to get caught up on how everything was going there as well. And while shaken from being abused, or maybe I was just being cautious, I knew that I was no longer willing to go anywhere without Tru or Keenan being with me.

At least not until after I knew that Hamilton and I were in the clear of him trying to come for me. With the weirdest thing being that I'd purposely left my gun at home even when I had a chance to get it, because I just had no desire to carry it like I used to.

And I didn't need a gun for protection as much as I did in the past because now my guys, or either Hamilton was always with me. So I just stored it so that I could get to it quickly at home if I ever needed it.

But that is where it stayed even after my fight with Hamilton, while Tru and Keenan knew exactly where the other two guns where located in the house for if they ever needed it to protect us.

But ultimately, I didn't feel like neither of us needed a gun for Hamilton, but I still wasn't about to be alone until after I knew for sure that he wasn't looking for me.

CHAPTER
15

After going back home to get cleaned up and situated after being away for so long. I was happy that everyone was handling their parts in making sure that our customers and our employees were happy at the Parlor and at PMF.

And I tried to stay home and relax my brain after checking on everyone and everything, but since I'd been away resting long enough at Hamilton's house. I went over to the Parlor to do some work.

But then a minute or so after walking inside of the Parlor. I turned around at the reception desk and looked up and saw Keenan walking out of the front door, passing right by Hamilton, who was walking into the Parlor.

And my heart started beating so fast, and I had no idea where Keenan was about to go, while Tru and Turtle was in the back with clients, so I was about to be alone with him again.

Nevertheless, I stood there and watched him walk towards me, but thankfully as soon as the entrance door closed. Keenan opened it and came right back inside, he must have remembered me telling them that Hamilton was no longer welcomed to call or stop by to see me, or to receive any services at the Parlor.

But Hamilton immediately started apologizing and telling me that he couldn't believe that I'd left him, and through a letter at that.

And although he was looking extremely emotional and hurt, I didn't care because I was taught better than to fall for a wolf in sheep's clothing twice. – Until he began to apologize for hitting me, because he didn't care who was around or how embarrassing he looked begging for my forgiveness.

He kept saying that he promised to never treat me like that again, but I immediately tried to stop him from talking.

Then I asked Keenan to give me and Hamilton about two or three minutes alone, because I knew that Keenan was hearing what Hamilton was saying.

So again, I asked Keenan to leave and give us a minute, even while he asked me what was Hamilton talking about.

But I told him that it was nothing, and that he should just leave and come back in a few minutes because I wanted to talk to Hamilton alone.

But with the distraction of Hamilton asking me why did I block his phone calls, and why did I leave him a letter instead of waiting for him to get off work.

Keenan stayed and kept saying things to Hamilton, although Hamilton was talking to me and not Keenan. But I knew that my nightmares of my relationship with Hamilton possibly messing up things that I'd worked so hard to build would manifest, if Hamilton didn't shut up in front of Keenan. Especially with us having customers in the back, customers who only knew Keenan for his grand smile that everyone loved.

But Hamilton was about to bring out a dose of frowns inside of Keenan that not even Turtle or Tru would be ready for.

And that's when I walked outside in hopes that they both would follow me.

185

And they both did while the questions from Hamilton or Keenan didn't stop, Keenan asked me if Hamilton had put his hands on me. While Hamilton responded to him with if he did, then it wasn't any of Keenan's business.

And while I stood in front of Keenan, knowing how he felt about Hamilton anyway.

I told him that Hamilton didn't hit me, and that he should now go back inside because everything truly was OK.

But with his focus being more on Hamilton, and what he was saying. I started yelling at them both and told them that they needed to tone it down at my place of business, when they knew that I had customers inside.

Then Keenan told Hamilton that if he finds out that he'd touched me inappropriately, then he was going to touch him, and that's when Hamilton told Keenan to touch him right then if he thought that he could handle him.

But no matter how small I was compared to them both, or how angry they were. I got in Keenan's face and damn near begged him to go back inside and just watch us from the window if that's what he wanted to do. While I kept telling him that Hamilton honestly hadn't hit me.

I told him that Hamilton was just mad and was saying anything just to piss him off, while I tugged, pushed, and pulled him all the way back inside of the Parlor. And I was beyond mad and couldn't believe that Hamilton would just show up so soon and so amped, but he needed to leave while Keenan was still controllable as he somewhat listened and went back inside.

And thankfully he stayed inside while I went to tell Hamilton to leave, although Hamilton was still in somewhat of an uproar over Keenan, but he decided to finally listen to me when it was just the two of us.

I told him that the only way that we would be able to regain anything was if he calmed down and listened to me.

And when he did calm down, I said what I had to say about how sweet of a person that I thought he was to me and everyone else, until he showed me his hands like he did.

But all he wanted to do was apologize and tell me that it would never happen again, as he displayed several red flags after his apologies because at any time that I didn't agree with him after he'd apologized for everything.

He got angrier, instead of trying to take a break to stop and see how and what could be done differently to fix the problems. – All he wanted was for me to agree with him, and since he had never been so mean nor showed me any signs of becoming violent toward me before our fight. I didn't need any more red flags to know how much I didn't need to be in that kind of blindsided relationship with him.

No matter what he said or did, nor how successful, sexy, or how much in love he was with me. There was no way that I would allow him to take ownership over my life like he could potentially do, so I needed for him to move on immediately. Because I honestly believe that when a person shows you who they really are, then you should believe them. Especially their actions, believe their actions more than their words.

And he showed me twice what he was capable of when he'd slammed me to the floor, apologized, then came at me again even more violently after that. So I was already over his I'm sorry act. – But keeping in view of how he wasn't going to budge in keeping the peace until I agreed to unblock his number from my phone, regardless of what I was saying to him. He said all he wanted was to be able to call and talk to me and possibly get together to hash everything out better than they were.

And I eventually agreed to unblock his number, but only if he would agree to leave because I needed him off of my property, and I also needed for him to leave quietly and not return. So that means that if I had to falsely agree to never block his calls ever again, then that's what I did.

Although I knew that I was going to permanently block him again, but not until after I figured out how I would show him how serious I was about our relationship being over.

I just needed to do it without having fear of the consequences that I may have to face after showing him who's the boss, so at that point I just walked over to his car with him, while he stood there watching me unblock his number before he would get into his car.

Then when I was done unblocking his number, he got into the car, rolled down his window and changed everything with his lethal tongue by looking me in my eyes and saying that if he couldn't have me then no one could.

And I was flabbergasted, so I placed my hands on his door and stared at him for a few seconds before asking him did he really just say that to me.

I told him that he sounded just like an abuser talking about if he couldn't have me then no one could, but he said that he didn't mean it like that. But how else could a person take such a comment?

So I told him that he must have read me all wrong by thinking that just because I loved him, and stayed with him after our fight, then he must have thought that I was some sort of weak fool. But he kept interrupting me and saying that he didn't mean it in a threatening way.

He said that he only meant that he would keep bugging me until I realized that no one could love me like he could.

However, it really didn't matter to me what he meant by it because comments like that, along with how he had blocked me from leaving and trapped me in his house.

His words just destroyed us even more in our disaster, and right then my emotional switch was flipped to kill or be killed to prove to him that I do the owning in my life.

And that's when I became up for his challenge, I'd put on a fake smile and told him to just call me when he got home.

Because in my head, I knew that I was about to personally fuck him up.

I knew that my choices regarding Hamilton brought forth a lot of my weaknesses, but what he didn't know was that I was the wolf in sheep's clothing.

And I only bowed down and let him get away with so much because I wanted to protect him, and I wanted to protect my guys and my brother's from harming him.

I cared more about how hard we've all worked, and I wasn't about to let them hurt him and potentially go to prison on my behalf is what he didn't understand.

And since Hamilton was my problem, I wanted to be the one to officially shut his behavior and his heart for me down.

And by then I knew that I wouldn't be able to do it alone after seeing how bold he can be, so involving my *BAMT's* could no longer be out of the question. For they would be the ones to help me to officially stamp Hamilton's brain with NO means NO, especially when it's coming from Honey.

Because the sweet little Tristan Bass that he knew and loved was not as much of a push over as I appeared to be, after getting to see him for who he really was.

Therefore, I couldn't wait to show him how bad he'd messed up. Because I could already see that he would be the one to put me in my grave mentally, physically, and financially after a while of me not following what he wanted and when he wanted it. So I really had no choice but to become fearless and completely done with his crazy love shenanigans.

And since he knew that I had my cell phone in my hand, he called me as soon as he pulled off of the parking lot. But I told him that I needed to go into the Parlor to get Keenan together, and that I would call him as soon as I was done.

He then tried to keep me on the phone longer by explaining how he wanted us to get back to loving each other again.

But again, I told him that we would just have to discuss it later. While I eventually went back into the Parlor and knew right then that I had to first fix Keenan, then I would fill him in later about what happened after he'd settled down.

Because the current condition of his mindset was a bit too rowdy to tell him what really happened with Hamilton, as well as when, why, and how I plan to fix it. – So I asked him to go home and wait for me to get there, while I stayed and waited for Tru or Turtle to finish their session so that someone would be up front in case another client arrived.

And when Tru came out first, I told him that I would talk to him later, but at that moment I needed to talk to Keenan. So I would need him for about an hour or so, and I told him that I had already called Paxton to come in to help them.

Then after that I went home, locked the front door, and told Keenan to come into my bedroom and lock the door behind him as well.

He then came into my room and sat on my bed and started looking at me with a confused look on his face when I told him that I really needed to talk to him about everything that's happened, but I couldn't do it until I had his unbothered attention. I told him that I needed his mind free and clear from anger, but his leg kept bouncing like he was still on the edge and mad. But he was also intrigued to be in my bedroom again, so I walked over to unlock the door. Then I left the room to go into the kitchen to fix him a strong drink with alcohol, because I needed him more relaxed.

And although he wasn't a heavy drinker, I knew that he would relax more even after having only a few sips of alcohol. Because I really didn't need for him to lose his cool when I explain what happened and how I wanted to fix it, so when I was done fixing his drink, I went back into my room.

I locked the door back and gave him the drink while proceeding to tell him that after I get him back to where I needed him to be mentally.

Then we were going to talk, and talk serious business that I really needed for him to keep a leveled head about, no matter how bad it gets.

And after a few minutes he had only taken one or two sips from his glass, but he immediately kept asking me what kind of business was I talking about, because he already knew that it was about Hamilton.

And it was obvious that he couldn't just let their argument go, so he took my words of handling business no matter how bad it got in terms of being that Hamilton did cross the line of disrespect regarding me.

But before I knew it, I'd told him to shut up and stop speculating, and just drink and relax. While I got up and walked over to my stereo and turned it on. I'd put on some music that was always sure to get me hyped to dance my way into whatever I wanted, since it was time that he got the full experience of what helped to place us financially in the space that we were in from the beginning.

I was sure that it would relax him and place him back to our past, during the days when we were having sex before Hamilton was even an option. – So after walking back over to him and placing my hands on his legs, as I watched him now take sip after sip from his glass as if he was getting nervous knowing that it had been so long since we had been sexually intimate.

Because I knew that he could immediately feel what was brewing, and I could tell that he was already starting to forget about Hamilton.

And with my sensual seductive vibes, I knew that I would soon be able to form a plan against Hamilton. And Keenan would be my strong-arm of choice, but I needed him to be smart and all about doing only exactly what I would request.

But it still wasn't time for me to talk to him yet, so I just continued to seductively rub and caress him.

While I stood in front of him and of course began to dance to the beat of the music as I began to take off my clothes little by little.

Then I grabbed the back of his neck and hopped on top of him as we sat at the edge of my bed. Then I pushed him further onto the bed because I wanted to stand up in the bed and directly over him while I sublimely rolled, popped, and grind my way into having a decent conversation with him now with sex on his brain instead of anger.

And it was eventually translated into him wanting nothing more than for us to stay connected like we used to during our fun sex days. So right then, as soon as I saw that warm-blooded look in his eyes.

Along with the rock-hard penis impression that was in his uniform pants, I then completely stopped everything and jumped off of him and out of the bed and walked over to the stereo and turned it off.

But the room wasn't quiet because all I could hear was him vehemently yelling. "No, no, no, don't stop! We're just getting started!"

We both burst into laughter because it did seem bad that I'd taken him there, only to stop just as we were really getting excited and ready for more of each other.

But then I promised to make it up to him after our talk, but I had to stop and talk to him while I had his vulnerable attention.

So I told him that I trusted him and wanted him to assure me that he wouldn't take what I was about to tell him and run with it.

Because if he did, then he would be on my shit list for taking things into his own hands and making them worse.

While I also told him that he was free to suggest whatever he wanted to suggest, but nothing would happen either way until I said so, just as usual like with everything else.

He then agreed to listen and to help in any way that he could without making things worse.

So I told him that Hamilton had trapped me in his home and beat me up a few weeks prior to that day. And that's why I didn't come home because my face, leg, back, and my arm was too bruised. And I didn't want him or Tru to see me then go and act just as stupidly back toward him in retaliation.

Then I told him that I also wanted that information to stay strictly between us, for him and soon Tru would be the only other person to know the real reason why Hamilton and I broke up. I also stated how I really tried my best to hide it from them, but Hamilton just wasn't planning on letting me go as easily as I'd thought. And I'm sure that he could see that for himself by how ready Hamilton was to do whatever he had to do for us to get back together.

And then insomuch as a few seconds, I thought for a moment that I had made a big mistake by talking to Keenan, because his overdone face prompted him to ask me why in the hell would I still communicate with Hamilton at all after that.

He said for me to allow Hamilton to put his hands on me, while making me stay at his house afterwards was odd because he knew that wasn't like me.

And he said that it was only making him angry all over again, because he thought about how hard it must have been for me to stay with him that whole time due to trying to protect them.

So when he told me that he was ready to do whatever I needed done. I told him at that point all I needed was for him to mentally deal with what I was telling him, so that when he sees Hamilton again he wouldn't be trying to get at him more than he already wanted to.

And as he was provided with that information, I kept repeating to him that I just needed for him to hold his tongue and his hands together whenever he saw Hamilton again, because I wanted to be the one to return his type of pain back onto him.

But I wasn't going to be able to do that if I had to worry about him letting Hamilton's egotistic ways get to him every time he saw him.

Keenan then assured me that he would continue to follow my lead and try his best to ignore Hamilton, but I told him that he needed to do more than just try to ignore him.

I needed for him to completely ignore him and just let Hamilton back himself into a corner all by himself.

I explained how I also wanted to be the one to explain everything to Tru, just as I'd explained it to him, while he nor Tru would never ever tell my brothers the real reasons for why Hamilton and I wasn't together anymore.

I wanted us to strictly handle everything by ourselves, and hopefully just keep moving forward like nothing ever happened.

Finally, as Keenan had agreed to everything without being so angry.

I decided to make myself feel better and him as well by completely taking our minds back off of Hamilton and our problems. And placing our minds and bodies back onto each other.

So the next thing that I did was reach into my nightstand for a condom, then he and I relived the fun rodeo sex that we used to have. And it was excellent as we both could tell that our bodies missed each other a lot.

And we both orgasmed long and hard enough to know that we would continue our sexy connections more often now that Hamilton and I were completely over.

Then after we finished, I sent him back to the Parlor to finish helping the guys, and with instructions to keep his mouth closed about everything that had just taken place.

While I on the other hand formed a plan to show Hamilton that his sweet little punching bag of love, had become bitter and ready to show him something that he wasn't quite familiar with.

CHAPTER
16

Only an hour had passed before Hamilton decided to start back calling me, but I let his first few calls go straight to my voicemail. Until I was ready to put on an act of fooling him into thinking that he still had me under his foolish love spell.

And when I finally decided to speak with him, he continued with his same ole song and dance about how sorry he was for his behaviors. But it was still followed by him ignoring me when I told him that I forgave him, but I still only wanted us to be just friends at that point until further notice.

But he said that he didn't want to hear any talking about us being just friends due to how much time we'd spent together, and how quick and hard we'd fallen in love with each other. Yet, I told him that some time apart would still help us to decide what it was that we both really wanted out of life.

Although I understood why he wanted to fight so hard for our relationship to work, because everything that he was saying and feeling was exactly how I used to feel.

I never thought that anybody could make me feel like Rico made me feel, but Hamilton damn near even surpassed him, so I just knew that he was the one for me no matter what.

Even with his jealousy of my guys, which was normal considering that they were living in my house, and working for me. But everything else was good between us until he'd slammed me to the floor like I was nothing.

While even after that I still couldn't think of any signs or red flags that I probably ignored of him potentially becoming violent towards me before that day.

All I saw was his mild temper when he couldn't get his way, but he always gained control of himself immediately. But then again there wasn't a lot of mad moments in our lives, so I never saw him as a threat.

But I ended up talking to him over the phone for as long as he wanted to, until he began to ask to see me again.

He said that he wanted to know why I kept saying that I forgave him, but I still broke up with him and was now acting like I didn't want to be around him anymore.

But it didn't matter what I said to him because he wasn't trying to hear it if it wasn't in line with what he wanted to hear.

So I told him whatever I had to tell him, as well as answered his phone calls and text messages for about a full week after that.

Then that following week, I accepted his invitation to go on a lunch date with him, but only if it was in a public place of my choice.

And as you can imagine, he came to the restaurant smelling good and looking very handsome and successful by the way he carried himself.

He showed no signs of being violent at all once again, while he did seem very remorseful as he talked about how much he missed us being together like we used to be.

He had even bought me some beautiful diamond earrings and a necklace that would out shine any other piece of jewelry that I owned.

But before he had let me open the gifts, as he was pulling them out of his pocket. He had warned me that when I saw what he'd gotten me, I was probably going to try and reject it.

He said that he just wanted me to know that he wasn't going to take the gifts back if I refused them, and that he really did get it to show me that he was sorry for what he'd done.

But instead of falling for his materialized apology like he expected I would, I was only putting on an act when I accepted the gifts and acted like I forgave him.

And as usual, throughout our entire lunch date he only heard himself, while at one point he even called and made reservations for us to meet and have breakfast that next morning without even asking me if I was available or not.

As if we were back dating again due to his apologies and gifts.

But I told him that as friends we could hangout sometimes, but I still wasn't ready to start back dating him.

However, instead of acknowledging what I was saying, he said that he would just go and pick up our food and bring it to me if I didn't show up for breakfast that next day.

But then I warned him of what could potentially happen again between him and Keenan if he kept being so persistent and cocky, instead of just giving me some space to make a decision on what I wanted.

But all he wanted to know was besides that what else could be done to fix our relationship, so I just stopped trying to change his mind and just accepted his gifts and ended up playing along.

I told him that I still couldn't make breakfast that next day, but I could do dinner if that was okay with him. And we agreed that dinner would work for the both of us, while I didn't say another word about us not being together anymore. I also didn't put on my new earrings and necklace right then, I told him that I was going to wait and just wear my gifts to our dinner date.

And while I really was happy to have the gifts, my smile wasn't genuine at all as I pretended that he was winning me over with his continuation words of never giving up on us no matter what. And while that necklace continues to be the most expensive piece of jewelry that I own even now, I must say that Hamilton's issue wasn't that he should've warned me that he wouldn't be accepting his gifts back. Because contrary to his beliefs, I was never going to reject the gifts in the first place.

The issue was that my guys had made me enough money through Abigail and her friends alone, that I could've bought the earrings and that necklace, along with anything else that I wanted with my own money.

So what he should've been saying was that he was going to go and get some counseling to try and get some anger management help, instead of taking his normal power outlet that usually worked for him.

But I was never as blown away as I appeared to be at the gushing beauty of it all, because whether I could afford it on my own or not, he failed to see that material things are not what makes me happy.

But I was done arguing with him, so I kept pretending to take it all in stride as we both eventually left each other feeling excited, and ready to be boyfriend and girlfriend again.

We even hugged and kissed before we parted, after I'd sat on his lap and told him that I was glad that we'd made up, because he had really pissed me off.

He said that none of that stuff would never happen again, as we both vowed to forget about it. And then we went our separate ways to go and prepare for our date that felt like an official getting back together date. So I immediately went home and prepared my guys for a night that none of us would never forget, especially Hamilton.

And I probably should've started calling him Snow like everyone else at that point, because it was about to get real cold for him.

I called Cosewh and told her that I would need her for the next three days, although Tru and Keenan would be working also. But without going into too many details, I told her that she should still call Turtle in to help David and Paxton if they get busy.

Because although Tru, Keenan, and I would be around; we would be unavailable to work with any customers.

And my only reason for wanting Tru and Keenan free for the next three days was to watch my back, and theirs in case Hamilton would try to show his face at the Parlor again after my plan.

The plan that they would first help me to stain him with as I prove my not so healthy point of it being time for some actions regarding Snow, and his disrespect.

Therefore, after I'd waited until my guys had gotten home and was all showered, comfortable, and ready for bed as usual.

I then called them both into my room to come and talk to me like I always do when we need to talk, so that I could let them know what was about to happen and why.

And neither of them had any complaints or suggestions as I stressed how I wanted everything that we were about to do to sting Hamilton hard, but I also wanted to be clear that our actions could come with some hard consequences, even if we were successful in our attempt.

But as sure as any sure could get, they both were more than ready to help me, and even more ready to face their consequences if things turned bad for us. Keenan didn't care either way, just as long as he had a part in at least getting to punch Hamilton in his face a few times like he did to me.

And instead of me once again trying to explain to them that I wanted to be the one to return Hamilton's type of pain back onto him, I just told them both that what we were about to do would hurt him way more than physically punching him would.

And while they both were excited and eager to execute my plan, or maybe now I should say our plan after we'd stayed up for about two hours strategizing together.

I intentionally placed ideas into their heads that I usually wouldn't be on board to do.

But we had planned as much as we could step by step on what would happen immediately after Hamilton and I was done eating, along with what should happen if our plans didn't go accordingly.

So the next evening, I had put on the sexiest dress that I could find in my closet. Accessorized by the gifts that Hamilton had bought me, as if I wanted to feel and look clean, sexy, beautiful, and just ready to have a good time when I got with Hamilton for the night.

We ate, danced, and drank only a little because I particularly wanted us both sober.

So I advised him to not drink a lot during dinner so that we would be able to drink as much as we wanted to after dinner, and at his house safely without the worries of having to drive home drunk.

He agreed that we could just grab a bottle to take with us back to his place, and just as I'd planned, we enjoyed ourselves then went back to his house.

And just when he thought that he still had me and everything else back under his control, after we'd walked into his place, and was preparing to get more comfortable.

I opened my purse and pulled out a very stringy piece of lingerie, with a stringy thong to match.

He began to smile really big, and seemed intrigued when I told him that I was about to disappear to go and change clothes for him, and that I was going to keep on my new jewelry with my lingerie.

Joyfully, he said that he could just leave the room and let me change and do whatever I needed to do in his room.

But that wasn't how my plan was supposed to go, so I told him that he should stay and use his own room and bathroom to get comfortable, while I would just go into his workout room down the hall to change. Because I wanted to make a cute but grand entrance when he sees me in my strings and heels.

And he said that he was cool either way, he was just happy to see me happy and ready for him again.

And without any more thought he went along with whatever, and just let me go to prepare and do my own thing, while he started taking off his clothes and getting more comfortable.

I then immediately went into his workout room, where I frequently used his equipment when I was stuck there.

And that's how I knew that there were two windows in there, because I used to open them to let in some fresh air every now and then when I would get too hot.

I immediately walked into the room and unlocked both windows, while also making sure that no one would have any problems opening them if they tried to sneak in from the outside.

Then I ran back over to the door to open it, and began to get undressed with the door wide open in case Hamilton decided to walk by. Because I really didn't care if he saw me or my lingerie at that point, I actually wanted him to see me in there changing clothes as if nothing strange was happening anyway.

And as I had already prepped Tru and Keenan on exactly what to do, when, and how carefully and quickly to do it.

So that I wouldn't have to entertain Hamilton in his bedroom for too long by myself. – I felt like it was perfect timing when Tru and Keenan entered into his home.

They came as soon as we started getting each other in the mood to enjoy ourselves.

Tru and Keenan had been instructed to make sure that they had closed and locked the windows back that they came through before they would enter into his bedroom with us.

While I would have Hamilton totally open and vulnerable so that it would be difficult for him to fight us back, even if he tried to while being almost naked.

And while he did have a house alarm, I made sure to distract him when we came in so it was never set, even when I was changing clothes he never passed the room to go and set it. While there was also no need for them to worry about him having any weapons around because we would be too busy enjoying la-la land, and I knew that he'd kept his gun in his closet anyway.

So it was easy for my guys to walk straight into his bedroom while I was on top of him as they interrupted us.

And when they came in I immediately rolled off of Hamilton and got out of the bed and stood to my feet as we were still only kissing and rubbing at that point, I then walked over to my purse and pulled out a pair of handcuffs.

While Keenan kept the gun that he was holding pointed directly at Hamilton the whole time, as he laid in bed completely astonished at what was happening to him. He also couldn't do very much besides watch Tru pull out some rope, and trot straight over to his bed.

Tru then wrestled Hamilton onto the floor so that he could tie him up, while I helped placed his hands behind his back and his wrists into the cuffs way too tight, but I had to cuff him good.

But Keenan kept getting closer and closer to Hamilton's head with the gun when Hamilton kept trying to fight us, although he was only supposed to point it at his legs to make him cooperate. Because I still didn't want Keenan physically touching Hamilton at all yet, but when I saw how he had come so close that he'd actually placed the gun against Hamilton's temple, like he was literally about to shoot him in his head.

I immediately no longer cared how tight I'd put the cuffs on Hamilton because my eyes were on Keenan, while Tru had Hamilton's ankles and legs tied up, so at that point his body was just as secured as his hands were.

But I still didn't feel relieved until Keenan put down the gun, and had helped Tru to move Hamilton to the other side of his bedroom like they were instructed to do.

I told them that I wanted him placed in a perfect position to get a good view of what was about to happen in his bed, but before my guys would take a seat on the bed and wait for me.

I asked them to keep the cuffs on him tightly, but loosen them only a little while they sat him up as straight as they could get him.

Then when they were done, I stood in front of Hamilton and told him that he should've just let me go when he had the chance. As I presumptuously walked back and forth in front of him while saying some really hurtful things to him.

But when I told him how he made me feel when he'd slammed me to the floor, and when he was hitting me in my face.

Tru and Keenan both charged at him like they were some angry bulls, and I tried to protect Hamilton. But I couldn't help him at that point, although them beating on him wasn't in our plans unless it became necessary.

So I started yelling and fussing at them because they were supposed to stay calm no matter what I said or did.

But I had cussed and fussed until I'd gotten them both back sitting on the bed and waiting for what was next.

And Hamilton just kept looking at me with his bloody face in disbelief, but he didn't try to yell or scream for help, nor did he try to escape.

All he kept saying was, "Tristan, don't do this".

And I don't know if he didn't try to scream for help because if he survived, he knew that he would seek revenge, or if he was just afraid of us and knew that screaming would be pointless anyway. But as everything calmed down, and had gotten back on track with our plans.

I then walked back over to Hamilton and told him that it no longer mattered to me who he was, or who he knew, or who his family was, or how much money they had.

Because he needed to know that I wasn't to be fucked with, although he could relax because I wasn't going to kill him or let my guys kill him.

I advised him to simply just accept that our relationship was over, and he needed to let bygones be bygones after we were done, if he knew what was best for him.

I then told him how much he should understand that the girl that he knew, no longer existed, then I ask him if he had anything to say about our relationship.

But he just sat there bleeding, then he eventually answered and said that he didn't have shit to say.

But he kept talking, he said that I didn't have to take things that far if I really didn't want to be with him anymore. He said that he got my point, and that he didn't want to be with me anymore anyway.

I told him to keep it that way, even though I shouldn't have had to slam his heart to the floor for him to understand, then I walked away from him and went to sit on the bed with my guys.

I then turned to Tru and kissed him so that we could pick up from where Hamilton and I stopped, while Keenan got up and grabbed my feet and turned me around so that my whole body could be on the bed.

I then laid back further onto the bed and continued to enjoy Tru rubbing and kissing me all over the top part of my body, while Keenan started from my feet and began to kiss and lick me all over from the bottom.

And as we all knew to keep an eye stayed on Hamilton during the entire time just to be safe, we continued with Keenan sliding his tongue between my stringy thong and my vagina.

While I began to open up more with my chest poked out for Tru as he had his hands and mouth occupied with my breast.

And when I had opened my legs more for Keenan, he immediately took in a mouth full of my vagina.

While I stared directly at Hamilton with my ecstasy face because Keenan knew exactly what to do with his mouth, so I really couldn't ignore what I was feeling even if I wanted to.

And Hamilton did look very disappointed and angry.

But I didn't care because he had disrespected me and thought that he owned me, so at that point I was about to disrespect him and his bed and show him who really owned who.

But then, as we indulged more and more into our gratified actions, Hamilton yelled and said. "OK Tristan, I get your fucking point!"

Tru then let go of my breast and abruptly walked over to Hamilton and started hitting him in his face again, and told him to shut the fuck up. And when Keenan rushed over to stop Tru from trying to beat him up, Tru kept saying stuff in French like he always does when he's mad and no one can understand him.

Although I've never complained about his angry language because he always looks and sound sexy to me anyway.

So I usually just sit and listen to him and observe him while Keenan is usually the one who gets frustrated and says that Tru could be saying that he's about to kill everybody, and we wouldn't even know it.

But Keenan pulled Tru back towards the bed and told me that I was always worried about him acting up, when it was Tru's crazy ass that I needed to be worried about.

And at that very moment my plan of crushing Hamilton's heart was a success in my eyes. As he witnessed how even during those moments, me and my guys were strong as he had watched us all burst into laughter when they began to argue more, and I'd began to fuss at them with a smile on my face while shaking my head.

He heard and saw how much their arguing was pissing me off, but we just couldn't do anything but laugh after I'd told them how we couldn't even commit a damn crime without them arguing. Especially with me aggressively grabbing them both by their arms like they were my children.

And that's what I wanted Hamilton to see, he saw exactly what I was giving up to be with him. Because he knew that I really was working hard toward being only his one day, but he wrecked it.

However, my guys and I laughed at ourselves and at Keenan's comments about how much we always under estimate Tru, and how he moves about.

Although personally, I understood Tru and how he moves, so I just continued to laugh at it all.

But keeping in view of what was happening, I told them both to get back in the bed with me and proceed with what I wanted because I was ready to do them both and leave.

Tru then took his shirt off while Keenan was already undressed and wearing only his boxer briefs.

Then Tru pulled some condoms from his pocket and laid them near us so that they could just grab one when we needed it.

But then I had pushed them all onto the floor and reached into Hamilton's nightstand, where we keep our condoms that he'd paid for.

I then grabbed a few and laid them next to us as we kept pleasuring and enjoying each other in his face.

And when I saw that both Keenan and Tru's penis was hard and ready to go, I yelled for Hamilton to look at what I had to go home to, while I held Tru's penis in my right hand and Keenan's in my left.

But he looked away and refused to watch us, even though regardless of if he looked or not, what we were doing couldn't be denied.

Although I did see him taking a few glances over at us after that, especially when Keenan put on one of his condoms and submerged himself inside of me like he was the one who owned me. But then in the mist of us enjoying ourselves, they did get a little too carried away because as soon as Keenan eventually pulled out of me wearing his condom. He got up and told Hamilton to salute him for what he'd just done.

While Tru and his thing of always having to prove that he was from Africa, and very different from them both. He had literally picked me up from the bed and attempted to get an orgasm from me while holding me up directly in Hamilton's face.

And our only issue was that he didn't put on a condom, nor did he ever pull his penis out of me even when I did reach my peek of an intense orgasm in front of them that only Tru could produce.

And as that was all combined with him ejaculating along with me and inside of me, right then it was all over for me and I was ready to leave and never return.

I had immediately un-wrapped my legs from around Tru while he lowered me to the floor so that I could stand up and get prepared to leave.

We then gathered everything that we'd brought into Hamilton's home. — Gloves, rope, and everything else including anything that I'd left behind when I left him the first time.

I got what I wanted then told Hamilton that I never wanted to see him ever again, then Tru followed me to my car as he'd gotten into the back seat and laid down so that no one could see him even if they saw my car leaving Hamilton's house.

I had put on my seat belt and pulled off from his house like I would do on any other normal night.

I then proceeded with our plan for me to just go and park where we had designated for me to park and wait for Keenan to come and get into the car with us, so that we could go home as if nothing had never happened.

Then afterwards, when Keenan met with us, he had gotten into the car and said that everything was fine.

He told us how he had kept the gun on Hamilton after he'd cut him loose, but then he had put the gun into his pocket because he wanted Hamilton to come at him. — Since he was no longer tied up, and there wasn't a gun being held on him, but he didn't.

He said that once we left, Hamilton just sat there looking at him like he was a wounded puppy, so he just left him there.

CHAPTER
17

It had been a long time since I'd heard anything from Hamilton, or have seen anyone that he knows, including his family members.

Then suddenly one day at the Parlor, Paxton was preparing a massage session for a Mrs. Snow. And I immediately stopped what I was doing and went up front to see who Mrs. Snow was, and my heart began to beat a lot faster as soon as I saw that it was Hamilton's mom.

She'd reached out to me for a hug as soon as she saw me, and then she said that she never forgot that she had told me that she would stop by to get a massage one day.

So I told her that I was happy to see her, and glad that she'd finally decided to come and check us out. Then I had called for Paxton to come up front, and I told him to take extra special care of her, and he said that he would give her a VIP special care treatment.

We both then continued to catch up with how things were currently, while Paxton left us to go and finish preparing for her massage.

She told me that she was a little upset with how things ended between me and Hamilton, and that he'd asked them to not contact me because our relationship had taken a very bad turn, and he knew for a fact that we would never be together again.

And with all things considered, she said that they just wanted to do as he requested and stay out of his personal life, instead of getting too involved like they had made the mistake of doing once before.

While she also added how he would get so mad, and never wanted to talk about me or our relationship every time they brought it up, so they all just figured that I cheated on him or something like that.

She said that since it had been so long since he'd said anything about me, or since they saw me. She knew that it was really over, so she figured it was okay for her to come in for a massage now that everything seemed to have settled down.

And as a lot of moms tend to do even without realizing it sometimes, she began to talk to me a little too much about what Hamilton had been up to lately.

She explained how he had brought home two different women to meet them within two weeks of each other, but she hasn't seen neither of the women ever again.

Ultimately, in her opinion she wanted me to know that she felt like he and I should've just worked through whatever broke us up. Because she and his dad felt like he just wasn't the same after our break up, and not just because it was too soon for him to be dating those women right after me, but because she knew that there were more women than just those two.

As if he was trying to disregard his pain by being with a lot of different women, along with drinking very heavily.

But then she crushed everything when she asked me if I'd been watching the news for the past two weeks, and I told her that I have and I haven't.

I stated how I would turn it on, but a lot of times I would walk out of the room or just eventually turn the channel if I was ever really sitting down to watch television.

Especially lately within that past week or so, because I had been feeling ill, and had been lying around watching a lot of movies, but I didn't watch a lot of news.

She then told me that she figured that I must not have heard about what happened, although she was supposed to be out and about to help take her mind away from what Hamilton was going through.

But she said that she couldn't just come there and talk to me and not mention what her son was going through, especially after seeing how I clearly hadn't heard about it. Then I asked her what exactly was he going through, and why was he on the news.

She said that the news channels showed his car accident on their programming twice, but they mainly showed the bad accident and where it happened. They didn't really say anyone's name as far as who was in the accident because they all survived.

She said that they did eventually say Hamilton's name on the air, and showed his picture one time and talked about his recovery and getting back to his position at the bank. And how they all wished him a speedy recovery.

But she could see how I probably hadn't heard about it because it was very brief, but in contrast to what my guys and I did to Hamilton. I still felt bad for him, and even a little sad to hear her talk about him being temporarily in a wheelchair.

She explained how the doctors told them that he would never be able to walk the same again, even with rehab he may have to permanently use a cane. — She then clarified how Hamilton was still in good spirits, and was determined to one day walk without a cane, although he understands that he has a long road ahead of him to get back to how he used to be.

She talked about how they were all helping him and sticking by him to get him back on track, and she also extended an invitation for me to stop by their home to see him anytime I wanted to. But I told her that I wasn't sure if that was a good idea because Hamilton was right, he and I really didn't end on a very good level of friendship.

Although I understood why she felt like time and circumstances may have healed things, so I lied and told her that I would call him to check on him.

Then I added that during our conversation I would see if he wanted to see me or not, so I told her that if she was okay with it, do not mention to him that she had saw me. – While she requested the exact same thing from me, because she was supposed to stay out of his personal life.

After that, she said that her intentions really were to only come in for a massage, because she really wasn't trying to be a matchmaker.

Even with her feelings of how she used to think that he and I would one day be married and have her some grandbabies.

She looked at me and asked me if I remember her saying that to me when she had first met me, back when she was only hearing Hamilton constantly talk about me and our relationship.

And I told her that I did remember hearing her say that to me, because I was so happy that everyone liked me, and when I heard her say that, it made me feel like a part of their family.

She then immediately threw in how a part of her still believed that could happen, but she was just going to try and let go of those thoughts.

And as things went on, I told her that I wasn't going to lead her on because he and I were far from marriage and children, but I did see and understand her perspective. So I stated again that I would call to check on him for real because I really didn't know that he had been hurt. And just as I understood her, I knew that she understood my position as well.

The only difference was that it seemed like she meant every word of our conversation, while I was only honest about half of what I was saying.

I wasn't planning on calling him or stopping by to see him, but I really did honestly feel bad for him. Until she had talked me right out of that feeling before our conversation was over.

By telling me how she hasn't had a conversation about babies or marriage, or even tried to interfere with anything in Hamilton's personal life since his divorce.

She said that his ex-wife hurt her heart by claiming that she'd miscarried because Hamilton had pushed her down some stairs, when he knew how pregnant she was. – She explained how she thinks that his ex-wife lost the baby on purpose, because the baby probably wasn't even Hamilton's, because he would never do such a thing.

And I knew right then that she was delusional, and I didn't need to be talking to her anymore because at that point I was completely turned off to feeling anything for Hamilton, or his crazy and violently deranged family.

Especially after she said that his ex-wife initially told everyone that she'd accidentally fell down the stairs, until she was in recovery at the hospital. She said that his wife had pulled her to the side and told her that Hamilton needed some help mentally because he had pushed her down the stairs on purpose.

But she said that she didn't believe her because she thinks that she was cheating on him, and she was just looking for a way out of being in a committed relationship with any man, or even a woman as far as she was concerned.

"Because she was a bisexual whore", and those were her exact words. So again, I was starting to feel extremely offended, and I wanted her to get away from me immediately as she'd began to explain how his ex-wife said that the only reason she decided to open-up to her was because she was afraid to tell anyone else. While ultimately, Mrs. Snow still hasn't said anything to anyone about Hamilton pushing his ex -wife down the stairs. Because even until this day, everyone still thinks that her miscarriage was just a bad accident due to her losing her balance.

She said that she really was sorry that they had lost the baby, but she was happy that their relationship was finally over after suffering such a loss.

Adding how his ex was always so arrogant and wanted to stay away from them, like she was too good for them or something.

While all along in my head, I was thinking that just because his ex-wife came from a family with money, that didn't mean that she didn't come around them very often because she was arrogant.

Nor because she was a bisexual whore who wanted to be with a woman or anything like that. She probably just couldn't come around them due to being hurt from her son's temper, just like I probably would've been if I had stayed around any longer.

So with just the thought of me thinking of how she would feel about me if I had opened-up and told her what he'd done to me made me sad, and we weren't together nearly as long as him and his ex was.

Therefore, I knew that she would think that I was lying and the truth wasn't in me for trying to ruin her son, just like his ex, whom he'd been with for years and years before me.

But that ultimately meant that I was over her and their entire situation, so I was glad to see Paxton come around the corner and get her so that they could get started.

Because all I could think about was that Hamilton had me feeling so sorry for him due to losing a child. After I'd damn near cried in his arms about how everyone was mad at me, including me being mad at myself for having an abortion. While he had gotten emotional and was also about to cry when he talked about how much he wanted a son, but he guessed it just wasn't time for him to have one.

So with those thoughts in my head, I just never wanted to be around or talk to Hamilton or anyone else in his family ever again. And I was really glad when his mom finally left my Parlor, because I was already sick on and off from day to day for about a month as it was, and she didn't make me feel any better because my emotions were spiraling out of control by the time she'd left.

But after having so much baby talk with her, I knew that I was missing my menstrual cycle, and needed to take a pregnancy test to make sure that I wasn't in fact pregnant with a baby whom she may think is her grandchild.

But the baby would be Tru's and not Hamilton's because Hamilton and I always used protection just as I did with my *BAMT's*.

Except the night when Tru ejaculated inside of me in front of Hamilton when we officially broke up. But when it comes to all of that, Tru and I both could've gotten pregnant that night after the way he had African prided his way into a grand orgasm from the both of us.

But instead of assuming such a notion regarding me being pregnant, simply taking a pregnancy test was going to cease my suspicions as I also began to calculate the exact date of that one and only time when Hamilton and I had only one condom in the night stand.

And we had been having fun playing around and had actually ripped the only condom we had, but we continued. So for a moment I thought that one and only day could make it possible for me to be carrying Hamilton's baby, if the test comes back positive.

But the more I thought about it, the more I thought about how I'd had a cycle since then. And I could also remember that he had pulled out of me and we both saw his semen cum out and onto my body as we finished, while I can also remember washing it off of me.

Unlike Tru, who planted every drop of his semen inside of me, while not only me, but we all saw that take place.

However, I wasn't extremely worried about who the dad could be because I didn't know if I was pregnant or not.

So ultimately that same day that Mrs. Snow left me thinking about everything. That night when I got home, I brought out three different pregnancy tests that I'd purchased from the store after I'd left work.

And for some reason, I always lock my doors when I'm trying to figure something out—so I had locked my bedroom door. As well as the door to my master bathroom while I pissed in a cup and individually tested all three tests, and waited for the results.

And I was beyond nervous at that point because deep in my heart I knew that I was pregnant, due to missing my menstrual cycle and always feeling sick and lethargic.

My heart, mind, and my entire body just felt pregnant. So I knew that I was going to need some professional help even before reading the results.

While I also knew exactly where to go to find help, although that didn't stop me from being nervous and afraid of how my life was about to change if I had a child.

But with me wanting to seek help on my own without my brothers or anyone else telling me that I need help concerning my childhood issues.

I knew that I was maturing and being smart, so I didn't panic when I looked and saw that every stick had a positive result saying that I was pregnant.

I stayed cool and calm while I didn't jump up and down or get excited about how I would present such good news to my child's father like they do on TV.

I just sat on the floor for a few minutes until I could gather my thoughts, then I eventually got up to go and get both of my guys so that they could experience that moment with me.

I yelled for them then waited at the entrance of my bedroom door for them both to get up to come and see what I wanted, because I wanted to walk into my bathroom with them both at the same time to share the news.

And when we walked into the bathroom, they both became excited and very happy to see pregnancy tests and empty pregnancy boxes spread out like they were. So they immediately realized that I was revealing to them that I was pregnant.

And as they both stood in just as much shock as I was in, I looked at Tru and asked him if he was ready to become a dad, while I also told them that I haven't been to a doctor to confirm anything.

But I kind of knew that I was pregnant anyway, while I also told Keenan that he would be assisting us in raising the baby as if it's his baby too, because he or she will have two dads. Although Tru was probably the biological father.

But Keenan looked at us both with his usual smile that was just as genuine as the smiles that Tru and I had, but he immediately said that Tru probably put a baby in me on purpose, because they know how to do that kind of stuff in Africa.

He then laughed and asked Tru had he been planning to not wear a condom that night since the plan began, because he felt like he had been planning to do me like that in front of him and Hamilton's face ever since I told them about the plan that they'd helped me put together.

While he also began to tell me how Tru was always doing slick little things behind my back to prove that he's my number one, so he was convinced that Tru getting me pregnant was definitely done intentionally.

But even with those thoughts we all laughed and just enjoyed the moment, as Keenan's humorous comments did softened everything.

Until he kept saying that after I have the baby then he wanted me to get pregnant by him next.

He said that he knew that he couldn't just ask for a baby as if it was that easy. But he told me and Tru that if Tru gets to have a baby with me then he felt like it would only be right that I have a baby with him too.

And it was all fun and funny at first, until the laughter was over and it was time for us to realize that there was about to be a baby added to our family for real, and we needed to get prepared for such changes.

But before we could do that, Keenan wanted me to know that he was making a real request of wanting me to really consider getting pregnant by him in our future.

But I told him that getting pregnant right after I have my first child would be the furthest thing from happening in this world, regardless of how he or anyone else felt about it.

Because all I wanted to focus on was our current situation only, so I told him that we would have to discuss that some other time. And he understood my point and the situation at hand because he didn't ruin the moment by continuing to press the issue, and that made me very happy.

He let it go and remained just as excited about our first child as if he was the biological father too.

CHAPTER
18

E normously sitting over six months pregnant at this point, and I never would've thought that receiving counseling would seriously help me as much as it has just to talk about everything that's happened from my childhood until now.

But letting go of my regrets of aborting my baby years-ago is what really helped me to get prepared for this baby, because I've forgiven myself and I have realized that I shouldn't live in the past any longer.

Especially at this point since I've been bonding and talking to the person inside of me that I have fallen in love with for the past almost seven months. And I want nothing more than to meet him and to raise him right.

Just like my nieces and nephews that we all spoil, but they're not spoiled rotten because they are good kids that are very smart and respectful.

And that's what I want for my son also, and now everyone is very excited and just as ready to meet him as I am.

And while I remain happy and open minded; coming to therapy about everything seems to be one of the best decisions that I've made during my pregnancy.

Seeing as though I'm receiving great advice from not only a known professional, but a great friend. Although it has been mentally exhausting at times when I've had to relive a lot of bad times during our sessions.

But still I'm just as normal as everyone else, even during those times when I believed everything that my uncle Snap placed into my head as a child.

And after meeting my brothers, and falling right into the circle of how they lived. It wasn't right, but it felt good because I received a lot of love that felt extremely better than the love that I was receiving from my uncle, although sexiness and money became my new normal as a better Honey.

But blaming myself and feeling negatively about my choices was never going to help anything, so I'm happy to now have such a permanent change of heart.

Because now I even prefer to only be called Tristan, although I don't get mad when people forget and accidentally call me Honey. Because I understand how for some people Honey is the only name they know, yet at the same time with a smile on my face. I have no problems with correcting everyone by telling them that I no longer prefer to be called Honey.

And I'll politely correct everyone for as long as I have to, until they all have my real name embedded into their brains.

So I guess what I'm ultimately saying after telling you all of this as if you haven't heard it all before. But what I'm saying is,

"Thank you for listening and guiding me through my journey to get comfortable enough to even want a baby, while also understanding that although my lifestyle isn't typical. I'm just as normal as everyone else who has problems."

"You're welcome!"

Is how my therapist responds to me as we come to an ending of yet another great session, as it is time for me to leave and go back home to my guys.

"Your progress has been spectacular, Tristan, and you should continue to leave my office feeling accomplished. And be proud of how much you've earned the way that Tru and Keenan respects you. And be just as proud that you and your guys are great parents because the baby hasn't even arrived yet, and I can already see what kind of life your child will have from how you all are even now as parents."

And with my last words to her being. "Well, thanks again Suuri, I appreciate that."

I now leave my therapy session feeling refreshed and thankful that I can come to her office and release a ton of information, and not have to worry about anything said coming back to me negatively.

Nor do I have to worry about my secrets being shared with others because I've been knowing my therapist Suuri for years, although I never got to officially meet her until a few years after I'd graduated from the same high school as she did.

Although she was two grades ahead of me, but just to give you a little background on how she became my therapist.

I've known Suuri since we were teenagers, back when she was the President of a lot of stuff in high school.

She and her sisters were involved in everything, although just like them, I was involved in a lot and had a lot of so called friends back then as well.

And I was just as popular as they were because I was smart, cute, and dressed real nice because I had my own money to do whatever with it. So that gave me even more power to be classed as greatness just like them.

But when Suuri graduated, her sisters were still there and I was never best friends with any of them or anything like that, but we were all cool and got along great.

In addition to that, a few years after I'd graduated, I officially met Suuri when she came into our club and into my domain for a private dance.

And I just couldn't believe that she would even be in such a place, and even more so paying me better than some of the guys were paying to get a fully private dance.

And when you're in my domain, I never hold back or shy away from anything. But she accepted me for who I was and for what I did, and I respected her for liking it.

Although she never made her visit a regular thing because I never saw her at the club again after that. But I will never forget that she came in for that dance, nor will I forget that she was a little too comfortable for it to have been her first time doing such a thing.

But after that, I never really thought of her or had any other dealings with her until she became popular for being a good lawyer.

She was known for keeping people out of jail even when she knew they were guilty, and she's big on client confidentiality, so people loved her.

And we reunited after I saw her on TV talking about how she was leaving the court room and becoming a Therapist, because that's what she's always wanted to do, even during her college years.

She said that she comes from a family full of lawyers, so she knew that she would be good at it, but her passion was in helping people who have a hard time understanding themselves. And that's why she went back to school after moving into that area to become a Therapist, a Therapist whom I contacted and now she has helped me to love myself even more than I already did.

Although I'm still cautious of what I say to anyone no matter who they are, but thanks to her strong reputation of knowing about her client's kidnappings and murders that even the broadcasters on TV says that she won't even comment on.

I knew that my little complicated life wouldn't be a problem for her to keep to herself.

Nonetheless, I leave Suuri's office happy and ready to get back home to my guys, whom I'd promised that I would share the news of our baby's name with them after my appointment was over.

Since they have been waiting for me to decide between three different names that we have chosen, and I finally decided on one so they don't have to wait any longer.

Especially with me being so close to officially turning seven months soon.

And everyone still calls our son, baby, so I really wanted to get home so that I can go and hang out at the Parlor. And then when my guys are done and ready to shut everything down for the day. I want to be there to share with them that I've chosen to call him TJ, because his real name will be the exact same as mine.

Tristan Jerrie Bass is my name, so Tristan Jerrie Bass Jr. will be his name; and TJ fits perfectly for Tru junior as well.

Even though I love the name Isaiah, and I acknowledge that's Tru's birth name. But he said that he would honestly be cool with whatever I want to name him, so Tristan is what I want, and TJ is what his nickname should be.

So while leaving Suuri's office, I look down at my big belly and rub it and officially start calling my baby TJ at this point.

While I stand outside of the medical building and wait for my car service that has already been called to come and get me.

Then just as I look up from rubbing on my belly and talking to TJ, lo and behold I see Hamilton coming to stand in the same area to be picked up by a car service as well. — Along with some older lady who was already sitting a few feet away from us on a bench waiting to be picked up.

Hamilton comes and stand right next to me holding a cane and looking like he has lost a lot of weight, but he's still handsome. And not looking nearly as bad as I thought he would look after listening to his mom explain his injuries after that accident.

But he has had time to heal so I guess he really was determined to get better, even as he does walk with a limp and needs a cane. The only thing that hasn't healed is his brain because he immediately asks me if I'm carrying his baby.

And I just stand for a moment and don't say anything at first, then I answer.

"No, this isn't your baby. How could this be your baby when we always used protection? And now that I'm almost seven months along, the timing adds up to this being Tru's son."

"First of all, we didn't always use protection, we had a moment when we didn't use a condom. And secondly, you can lose the agitated attitude because I already know how you feel about me."

He says. "I'm just surprised to see you here, especially pregnant because I had no idea that you were pregnant until right now. But now that we're here, I want to know if that's my child that you're carrying? Because in my mind at this moment the dates between us could vary if you're seven months along."

He continues to talk while following me as I walk away from him to go and sit on the bench opposite of the older lady.

He says. "Tristan, I have a right to want to know if that's my child or not because all it takes is one time, so he could be mine."

"You don't have a right to shit!"

I yell. "So just leave me alone because if this was your baby, I would've told you by now! Tru is the father, while you of all people should know that after witnessing him put this baby in me with your own eyes! And Hamilton, regardless of what you say, the dates don't vary! Tru is the father so get over it!"

I continue while shaking my head. "And I'm sorry about what we done to you, as well as the car accident that you were in! I really am sorry about your bad luck, but this is not your child!"

"I don't accept your apology Tristan, because you're not sorry! And I know that you don't love me since you've whored yourself out to 'your guys', so you can just keep your apologies because I don't need it!"

"I didn't say anything about loving you, but you're right, I don't give a damn about you so get away from me! And if you call me a whore again, I'm going to snatch that cane from you and beat the hell out of you with it!"

I now grab my bag and attempt to get up from the bench.

"This is not your child so we have nothing more to discuss here, so goodbye Hamilton."

But he reaches and grab my arm and pulls downward so that I can stay sitting, and says. "So you really hate me this much all because I hit you?"

"See Hamilton, that's just it, you did more than just hit me. But you never seem to realize the entire scene of it all, and just because I'm angry with you, that doesn't mean that I hate you. I just don't fuck with you anymore, and I'm now mature enough to forgive and move on. So move."

I jerk my arm away from him and attempt to get up again.

But he holds onto me once more. "OK listen, I won't keep trying to stop you from leaving, but I think I deserve better proof of if you're carrying my child than just your word for it."

"I'll provide you with proof after he's born Hamilton, and after you see that he's not yours. I'm going to need for you to let go of our past once and for all so that we can all live happily ever after."

I now get up and walk away to go back and stand by myself as I continue to wait for my ride.

But crippled or not, Hamilton is the same persistent guy that he's always been even before his injuries, because he limps after me saying.

"I get it, and I won't bother you ever again if he's not mine, but if he is then I can't just let you shut me out like I don't exist."

"Okay, well maybe we'll just come to you for another visit and kill your ass this time, how about that?"

I utter with much frustration, because I know that he won't stop until he finds out if TJ is his or not.

"Your threats don't scare me even if you are serious, because underneath all of that anger. I know that you have a heart because I felt it, so even if you do have them to kill me over wanting to know about my own child, it's only going to hurt you every time you look at him and see me." He proclaims as if he already knows that TJ belongs to him.

"Like I said, I'll provide you with legal proof of who the father is after he's born. And don't be so sure of how much you think you know me Snow, as you've made that mistake before. And while we're at it, let's be clear. I'm not trying to scare you because I don't make threats, I do what's needed to get my point across. So just know that you're not the only person that has a little power to work with these days, so I'll be in touch."

I now turn around to walk back into the building, but my driver pulls up just as I was about to walk back inside.

"Well, I'll be looking forward to hearing from you Tristan." Hamilton says as I walk to get into the vehicle to leave.

"Indeed you will Hamilton, indeed you will."

I now leave while glad to be headed home because I'm not as in shape to stand up to Hamilton as I appeared to be. Seeing how as soon as we pull off, I begin to cry while feeling afraid, and needing to talk to Suuri because I thought that she had fixed me. And although I know that she's with a client, whom I saw sitting and waiting to see her as I was walking out.

But I still call her because I don't want to alarm my guys with me coming home crying and unable to gather myself due to my pregnant emotions now after seeing Hamilton.

But I receive Suuri's voicemail, so I become even more unbalanced because the option of holding back information to protect either of my guys from confronting Hamilton shouldn't even be a factor again, but it is.

And with Suuri not answering, I just sit in the back seat crying and rubbing my bellying as TJ begin to move around like he knows that there's something different occurring outside of my usual calm and happy life before I saw Hamilton.

But by the time the driver arrive at my house, I go inside to proceed with my plan to change clothes, then walk to the Parlor and wait for us to close so that I can give them the name that I'd picked.

So I wash my face and get as comfortable and as normal as I can get before I go to the Parlor to help them close everything.

And as everything goes just as they would on any other normal day of the week at closing time, when it's just the three of us, we share a few laughs.

Then I eventually tell them that I'd picked the name TJ for our baby, while I also blurt out that I had just saw Hamilton earlier when I was leaving the doctor's office.

And surprisingly, I don't think or hesitate to tell them what happened, nor am I afraid of what could happen if they know everything that was said.

I simply tell them that I saw Hamilton, and how he really took an interest in wanting to know if TJ is his son or not. While I'm also clear with them about how intense it was when I saw him, although he didn't hurt me or do anything stupid while he was just really surprised to see me pregnant.

Then Tru ask me if I think that Hamilton will now start popping up all the time at the doctor's office, now that he has seen me there pregnant and without them.

"It was totally a coincidence that we'd bumped into each other, so I doubt that I'll run into him again when I go back." I answer while shrugging my shoulders.

"Well, I don't think that you should go back to the doctor by yourself because I don't trust Hamilton."

Keenan says.

"Even if I have to drive you there and sit in the lobby until you're done, then I feel like that's what we should do now that he's suddenly back from the grave."

Keenan says with a smirk on his face. "Didn't you tell us that he died in a car accident anyway?"

While he already knows that I said that he had almost died in a car accident, not died.

"You know that he didn't die in that accident Keenan, and I really don't want to talk about Hamilton right now. Besides just letting you guys know that I saw him, because I feel like we should be focusing more on TJ right now."

"You're right."

Tru says as he places both of his hands on my belly and starts talking to the baby.

"Keenan was right little man, I put you in there on purpose."

He now begins to speak to TJ in French, and starts laughing and looking at us because he knows that I don't mind. But he knows that Keenan gets agitated and very flustered with him when he does that.

"I know that you want us to think that you're joking."

Keenan says. "But I know that you did that shit for real."

"No one can just pick a day and say, today is the day that I will get her pregnant." Tru says while moving over as Keenan kneels before me and starts talking to TJ as well, with now his hands on me instead of Tru's hands.

Keenan says. "Look here TJ, you may call Tru daddy, but I'm your daddy number two. So you don't have to figure out all of that crazy talking that he's doing because when it's time for you to learn how to talk for real, just know that your D2 is the one who you need to listen to, okay."

"He's going to learn how to talk from you both, and just in case you're wondering. The TJ stands for Tristan Jerrie, just like we talked about."

I now get up and playfully push them both out of my way and tell them to come on so that we can go home.

"Tristan junior, Tru junior, it's all the same to me because if he's anything like you."

Tru says. "Then his name is a well honored name."

"Thanks, Tru."

I respond as I gather my things and wait for them by the door. "But like I've said before, Isaiah is a beautiful name, and I really do love it seriously. But I can't help but to go with Tristan, as TJ does fit him as a nickname that honors the both of us."

"Right!" Tru agrees with me.

Then after they check everything for closing, we all gather by the door to set the alarm as usual before leaving.

Because after what we did to Hamilton, we decided from that day forward that we would stick together, especially at night in case he did want to retaliate. – While Tru and Keenan both usually wear shorts under their uniform pants, so that they can keep their guns on them after what we did.

And I've been cool with that as long as they're safe in doing so. Because I don't carry my gun or any other weapons like they do, since we haven't had a problem out of Hamilton since we left his house.

Because after several months passed without any signs of Hamilton, I didn't care if they carried or not because I really did think that he had moved on until now.

But still, it has become such a habit that we wait and walk home together whenever we're leaving the Parlor. That we still just do it even now, when we really don't have to do it anymore.

And as we set the alarm, and walk out of the door and locked it, Keenan says to Tru. "You strapped?"

Then a voice from the side of the building emerge as we watch two people come from around the corner, and they both have a gun in their hand.

"He better not be strapped."

One of the unmasked guys says while running toward us.

While right at this moment, I immediately see a car pull up fast and stop quickly in the rocks, although I don't recognize the car.

But I can see Hamilton's face as the driver thanks to the street lights.

Keenan now immediately stretch his arm back and grabs for his gun, and the unmasked guys are clearly shaken and wasn't expecting for him to seriously pull out a gun so fast.

Suddenly gunfire begins, and I don't know who pulled the trigger first, but I do know that Keenan really scared them both judging from their facial reactions.

I also heard Tru say "no", when Keenan asked him if he was strapped, but regardless of who had what, or who shot first.

Keenan pulled his trigger and didn't stop pulling it until he'd hit one of them, because one of the guys went down and never got back up.

Just before TJ and I also go down, with me screaming while Tru lay on top of us bleeding from the back of his head.

And I now shake him as hard as I can so that he can get up, while I'm also trying to see Keenan, but Keenan is damn near at their car still shooting at them.

Before he swiftly comes back to help me and Tru after the car is gone, as the surviving guy had ran to get into the car with Hamilton and they left the guy that Keenan shot lying there.

"Fuck!"

Keenan screams frantically as he pulls Tru off of us and grabs me to see if I'm shot. Then as we both see that I'm okay, Tru still isn't moving.

"Tru!" Keenan scream.

"They shot him in his head Keenan! They shot him in his head!"

I scream in just as much horror as Keenan, while we both try to revive Tru however we can. Until I finally think to call the police, for they are probably already on their way due to the alarm sounding at the Parlor.

"Please wake up Tru! Please!"

I continue as his blood is spread all over the top part of my body.

"I'll try CPR!" Keenan says while placing him fully on his back, while I speak to the 911 operator on my cell phone.

But no matter what Keenan does, Tru just isn't moving.

He looks dead and we both already know that he's dead by his appearance, but accepting it just isn't a reality.

Even when the police shows up and puts a sheet over his body before the ambulance arrive for me, it's still unbelievable to us.

He and the guy that Keenan shot died right in front of us, and all I can think about is if it wasn't for Tru jumping in front of me and continuing to hover over me and TJ like he did, then we probably would be dead also.

And now everything is in complete chaos while they take me to the hospital, but I told Keenan to call everyone so that they can come and help us.

But as I arrive at the hospital they place me on black-out, and Keenan has my phone so I can't personally call anyone for myself.

Nor can anyone get in touch with me due to the hospital's black-out policy of not giving out any information at all to anyone, including family.

Just in case the shooter tries to come to the hospital.

But I know the shooter isn't trying to find us because those guys really didn't expect Keenan to have that gun.

And I could tell by the look on their faces that they didn't expect this to happen, but it did, and now my precious Tru is gone.

"Please let me make a phone call!"

I shout at the nurses and doctors.

"I want to call my family because I know they're worried about me!"

"I'm sorry Ms. Bass, but you have to wait until we're done making sure that you and your baby are okay."

The Indiana looking nurse that's helping me to sit up says.

"I spoke with your boyfriend and he will be in here after he's done talking to the police, but he said that he's called your family."

"But I need them here with me right now, please let me use the phone for myself!" I continue while I can't stop crying and worrying about everything.

"I'm sorry Ms. Bass, but you have to calm down to keep you and your baby safe. I promise you will be able to use your phone very soon."

I now cry even harder while rubbing my belly and thinking about Tru and how he was lying on top of me dead like that. And I miss him already, although a part of me still feels like he's not actually dead for real.

And I know that I saw the hole in the back of his head when I looked at him, and I heard the police confirm it.

But as infrangible as he and I are, having a permanent separation from him just doesn't seem right, and I can't really accept it.

Then a little later, I finally see the police, Keenan, Cosewh, Gerald, and Ali come into the room looking worried and sad.

And I try my best to follow the doctor's orders and continue to stay calm, or they will make everyone leave and have me wait to see them again.

But it's very hard to stay calm when Tru is dead, and we can all feel it, especially me.

So things just don't get any better anytime soon.

Aside from receiving the information of them finding Hamilton's cousin's car that he was driving, along with them finding Hamilton and his cousin. Whom Keenan had also shot twice before they fled, because the police found him bleeding while they were also mourning the loss of their loved one as well.

CHAPTER

19

Thanks to the accurate video footage that they have of the attack on us, the police have everything they need to convict Hamilton and his cousin for Tru's murder.

While Keenan also got into a little trouble for firing his gun as well, although the gun that he was carrying was registered.

The video footage does show him chasing after them when he shouldn't have chased them, so he did get in trouble.

But he still didn't receive any harsh punishment for his actions.

Nor did they charge him for shooting the guy who died, because the video also showed that he was acting in self-defense when he only pulled his weapon to protect us.

And although he had chased them, he stopped shooting when he got to the rocks.

So they believed him when he told them that he was only trying to make sure that they were gone as he feared for our lives.

And it was their voluntary inclinations that prompted Keenan's actions in the first place.

And while Momma Bass, Sabrina, and Autry makes most of Tru's funeral arrangements for me. Especially as I stress over now knowing that Hamilton and his cousin has confessed to coming to my Parlor only to scare us, but they had no intentions of anyone dying as far as what they told the police.

And although I feel like they're actually telling the truth, because they were very surprised by Keenan, but I still want them to suffer because all we saw were guns and guys that came to harm us.

Hamilton told the police that they came over only to threaten us just like I'd verbally threatened him earlier that day, when we were discussing if TJ was his baby or not.

They said that he said that he would never try to murder me or his unborn child; because they were being charged with murder and attempted murder.

As well as a few other charges after the police viewed the video footage that we provided, along with the footage from other locations that they retrieved video from during their investigation.

And it was hard for me to return home from the hospital and not have Tru at home with us, because absolutely nothing felt right anymore.

I also closed the Parlor for two weeks for several different reasons, while I understand that my employees need to work because they have bills to pay. As well as some of their clients have real medical treatments that they receive that's actually referred to be done as their doctor's orders.

So the Parlor will re-open as soon as possible, as well as I'll have Cosewh to hire some extra help because personally accepting it all. — And seeing how much everyone loved Tru places me in no position to guide anything or anyone right now.

Not even at PMF, so the presence of Cosewh and my family and friends are the most necessary things for me to have right now.

And they have all stepped up and helped me and Keenan even more than I expected. While my brothers, Momma Bass, and Autry told me that they were going to alternate in staying with me until TJ gets here. They didn't ask me if it was okay, or if they should wait until Keenan and I could gather ourselves first.

They all headed to the hospital the exact night of the shooting, when Keenan called everybody to inform them of what happened.

And they have all been with me and very helpful and supportive, and hasn't left me at all, but I still don't feel happy or pleased about any of it.

Not even about Hamilton and his cousin being locked up, because none of it should've happened anyway.

Although Tru saved our lives, he had a lot to live for so I really don't understand why he had to die like that.

And that's why I need to see Suuri and try to work through understanding how I will ever be able to move forward every day as I walk pass where he died. – I own my home, and business is too good to relocate, so my days spent inside of the house to avoid having to see where he laid will probably be long and many.

And as Suuri eventually makes a house call to come and help me, she suggested that we redo the entire front entrance of the Parlor after Tru is laid to rest. As well as change the colors and a few other things inside of not only the Parlor, but the house as well, to give it a fresh feel.

And she says that it's not to forget about Tru or his existence, but doing so may help me to cope, so that I want see such a hurtful visual every time I walk by.

Including inside of his room at home if I felt comfortable with doing such a thing.

So I had Cosewh to form a budget and prepare to give the Parlor a new appearance soon, while nothing at all will change in Tru's room until I'm good and ready to make that change, because I'm surely not ready for that yet at all.

And I know that everything will take a little time to complete anyway, especially with everyone's focus being mainly on me, Tru's burial, and the delivery of TJ.

So I do try to give as much direction as I can on Tru's funeral, and on the future changes of the Parlor. But I mainly let them handle it all, while I step away from it and listen to music while trying to put all of my focus onto TJ, and how we will both be okay.

Although I'm nervous because it's getting close to the time for me to deliver him, and I'm happy to still feel him always moving around and kicking, and the doctors say that he's still very strong and healthy.

But now only having two days until Tru's funeral, I want to be more stable and able to handle everything without breaking down and agitating him anymore than I already do.

"How are you feeling Tristan?" Keenan comes into my room to check on me.

"I'm okay, much better than I've been these past few days. How are you?"

I now reach out my arms for him to come and lay with me.

"I'm OK, too, it's just going to be hard putting Tru in the ground knowing that he won't be able to meet TJ."

He says while lying close to me with his arm around me and TJ.

"I just can't believe they rolled up on us like that Tristan. And you know that if I hadn't pulled out my gun, then Tru may still be here. And none of this would be happening if I hadn't acted off of impulse and almost caused us all to die."

"Keenan, this isn't your fault, its Hamilton's fault. He wanted to make a point by scaring us but it backfired, and that's on him because his family is in mourning just like we are. And now he and his cousin are suffering the consequences of their actions, so please stop blaming yourself."

I now grab his hand. "Tru would be very proud of you for what you done because all we saw were guns being pointed at us, and you're the only one who could protect us in the way that you did, because none of us knew what they were going to do with those guns."

"That's how I feel about it sometimes."

He says. "But I can't stop thinking that this wouldn't have happened if I would've just let the punks scare us and move on."

Now suddenly Autry, Sabrina, Elaine, Mia, Cosewh, Gabriel and about two or three more ladies come bursting into my room, and they all have baby gifts in their hands.

"Oh, I'm sorry y'all!"

Autry says as they all come in so jolly and ready to surprise me. "Keenan, we didn't know that you were in here!"

"We'll wait and come back later!"

She says. "We should've knocked first anyway!"

"Nah, y'all are okay, come on in because I can talk to her when you're done."

Keenan says while I now interrupt him and agree with Autry, because he hasn't taken the time to seriously open-up and talk about his feelings like he was doing, and I don't want him to stop.

"No, really, you guys come on in and do your thing!"

He insists, while getting up from lying next to me. "I promise, we can catch up after you're done."

"But Keenan, we haven't had time to really talk about everything, so they really are willing to wait."

I hold onto his arm, and want to be here for him because no one has seen his beautiful smile in a long time. I mean he smiles, but not like he used to, and I can tell that the ladies really didn't know that he would be in my room hugging me and talking.

"Come on y'all let's go."

Autry says as they all turn around, then she looks at me and says. "Tristan we'll be back later, we wanted to surprise you with a small baby shower to uplift your spirits, but we'll be here all day so take your time."

"Okay, thanks a lot. I appreciate that."

"No, come on in here, y'all!"

Keenan says as he stands up and walk around to the side of me and tells me to relax and just enjoy my family, friends, and his son.

"Your son?" I ask while smiling.

"What happened to D2?"

"Off course my son!"

He says. "When Tru was alive I was going to be daddy number two, but now after what's happened, I can't be D2 anymore. I have to step up to the number one spot because I know that Tru would want it that way for real."

"You're right Keenan, he really would want that, but probably after y'all argue about it first."

I state as we both laugh.

"Sometimes it used to get on my nerves when y'all would argue about him doing things to show off how much he was my number one, but now that he's gone. I'm really going to miss those arguments."

"So am I." He says while laughing.

"He was always doing some unnecessary shit just to prove a point."

We both burst into even more laughter while he adds. "And that shit worked all the time T, because I would fall back and just let him do his thing just to avoid the argument sometimes, but even now that he's passed away. That shit is still working on me because as much as I hate that French gibber jabber talking, I'm going to have to learn how to speak some of it to teach TJ, because I know for a fact that he wanted him to learn it. And if for no other reason, he would have him talking like that just to get on my nerves. But now I have to do that for him."

"Well that's really sweet of you Keenan, and I'm sure that he's looking down on us smiling right now because he knows that you have to be feeling some kind of way if you want to learn how to speak French."

I continue to laugh. "And you want to teach it to TJ, too! Oh yeah, you just made his heavenly day by feeling the way that you're feeling right now!"

Keenan says. "Yep, because he just made me do the one thing that he knows that I hate, but I'm going to do the shit anyway just to avoid the argument!"

Smiling and loving the good atmosphere that is no longer drenched in sorrow, our reminiscing of Tru helps us both so much.

Keenan says. "Anyway, will you all come all the way back into the room?"

He looks at Autry and everyone else who's crowded around my doorway.

"I keep telling you all to come on in here, so why are you still standing around the door with your hands full, instead of just coming all the way into the room?"

"Because we all know how you and Tru feel about Tristan, and for y'all to lose him is devastating. And seeing how everything happened the way that it did, we came in here to do what you guys have already done on your own."

Autry continues. "We came to put a smile on her face, so there's no way that we want to interrupt you guys. But we'll stand here and be nosey since you keep insisting that we stay."

"Right!"

Elaine chimes in. "Because I already told myself that before we go back home, Don and I are going to buy you a Rosetta Stone Kit that will teach you how to speak another language! I mean, I wasn't trying to listen to your conversation, but I can't help but to hear everything since we're just standing here!"

"Well just come on in here because you probably won't hear too much more because we have plenty of time to talk later, that's why I keep saying come on in here! But even now you all are still crowded around the damn door, instead of just coming inside!"

Keenan yells with a smile. "We're good, come on in and do whatever you're about to do! And Elaine, after we get Tru settled, I do want to know more about this kit that will teach me the gibber jabber."

We all now giggle because even they can tell that he just doesn't like speaking in French at all, but on the other hand he wants nothing more than to learn how to speak it in honor of Tru and TJ.

"There are several different kits and programs that will teach you the gibber jabber."

Elaine says while laughing along with us. "But we'll get you a good one that's the most popular, and that'll teach you successfully."

"OK, well thanks."

He continues to smile and yell even louder.

"Now can you all please get ya asses out of the door way and come all the way inside, please!"

"Yes!"

They answer while coming inside of my room with a lot of goodies for TJ, and I can't do anything but cry tears of joy as they all put down everything to get situated.

Still uplifted and filled with laughter, everyone continues to place their attention onto TJ, and how he will be learning things and being spoiled by Keenan and everyone else as well.

And although everyone can see how much I look like I can go into labor at any moment.

Some are still in shock that I am seriously about to have a baby for real, so that within itself makes it all more exciting that I have finally decided to have a child.

And that's why the baby shower turned out to be such a great success, because of the love and excitement of it being such a long time coming.

It was like everything had been planned months in advance, because we played games and everything.

Then as the night goes on, everything stays upbeat while Momma Bass even slept in my room with me and TJ.

It wasn't until the night before the funeral that I wanted to sleep alone, because I needed time by myself to get prepared on my own to be able to bury Tru.

And to just stand strong like I've always been since he'd met me, as well as I want to be strong and support everyone else who knew him and loved him.

Because everyone had gotten to know Tru for themselves, and they saw how much he loved being a part of our family.

And they couldn't do anything but love him just like they do with Keenan, so to prepare myself to see Tru one last time.

I do a few pregnancy exercises, I listen to some music, and I look at a lot of pictures of Tru.

I pray, I reminisce of so many of our good times and bad times. And I just ultimately release my feelings of not being able to let him or any of his belongings go.

Because by the end of the night I was prepared to let Keenan and my brothers go ahead and pack up some of Tru's things like they'd previously asked me if they should do, and of course I said "hell no" to everyone who asked.

But now, I feel like after we peacefully put him to rest.

I'm willing to slowly but surely allow them to pack his things without me freaking out on everyone.

I now feel somewhat ready, willing, and able to step up to the challenge of burying my number one. — While understanding that he's now free of all the cares and worries of this world, and he can now possibly get to be with his blood relative who died of a drug overdose.

And I know that he loved and he missed him a lot, so now for that reason alone, I want nothing more than to send Isaiah off properly. And looking good so that his cousin will see how well he eventually turned out to be, after he stopped using drugs and met me.

And with that notion, I eventually look into my own closet to find the prettiest black dress that I can fit, because I also wanted to be pretty for Isaiah one last time.

So the next morning as we all prepare to say our final goodbyes, I fix myself up as beautiful as I can.

Then I put several snacks into my purse, along with a box of Kleenex, and off we went. And as prepared as I'd gotten to finally let my Tru go, it was very overwhelming to see him lying in that casket dead as my last sight of him continued to hurt so badly.

So I truly ultimately reached the zenith of my grief at his funeral.

I even thought that I was really going to go into labor at one point, because I couldn't control my thoughts or my body.

I lost control of everything.

I really had to force myself to sit down and try to stop thinking about how he would never be able to meet TJ, nor would TJ ever be able to meet him. — Combined with my emotions of how if it wasn't for Tru, TJ and I maybe would've died, so I had to take my mind back to being in the hospital.

And hearing the doctors say that if I'm stressed then so is my baby, and that's the only thoughts that were helping me to stay calm and not keep getting overwhelmed with grief.

But we eventually got through everything without me actually going into labor at his funeral, as my family and friends ultimately helped me to send him off properly.

While Keenan and I move forward with him wondering who will help him with his duties at the Parlor, including how things will proceed as far as their extracurricular activities with my rich friends.

But I had placed a few things on hold because Momma Bass, Autry, Sabrina, and my brothers have been serious about rotating their visits with me until TJ arrives.

So until my family leaves, the only money that will be made is through our regular forms of legit business.

While my rich friends are just going to have to wait, or just move on to some other sex outlet because our days of taking their easy money may have permanently come to an end.

Because my mind and heart is now more on how we will raise our son, whom we will continue to call him by his nickname TJ. But I have now decided to change his full name to Tristan Isaiah Bass.

And he's truly the center focus of my wants and needs, so those sexual extracurricular activities are truly no longer a desire.

CHAPTER
20

"Oh my goodness, he's so handsome!" Autry says. "He's only two days old, but he's looking around at us like he already know everybody!"

"He probably does!"

I reply back to her while sitting up in the hospital bed, and watching TJ be passed around while everyone admires him and how wonderful he is.

"Everybody in this room has talked to him, sang to him, or either was always rubbing my belly. So he's probably connecting your faces to all of the voices that he's heard already."

"Okay, well it's my turn to hold him again!"

Cosewh says. "Seeing how Gerald and I are the God-parents and all."

"Um, when did you make that decision Tristan?"

Elaine stands up and walks over towards Autry and Cosewh with her hands reaching out for TJ also, like it's her turn to hold him.

She says. "Just give me my nephew/son because Don, the kids and I can't wait until he can come and stay with us sometimes on the weekends."

"Nah Elaine, and Cosewh, just because she's the God-mother to your son doesn't mean that automatically makes you and Gerald the God-parents either!"

Autry continues while looking at both Cosewh and Elaine's arms stretched out for her to pass TJ off to either of them.

"He just whispered in my ear that he doesn't want me to give him to y'all anyway, so you both can just fold your arms closed and sit down while we figure this whole God-parents thing out."

"I haven't really made a decision yet, Cosewh is just messing with you all because I haven't said anything else about picking his God-parents, so she just claimed it. The baby shower was like two months-ago anyway, and a lot has happened since then so I haven't thought too much more about picking God-parents after we discussed it at the shower."

"Well, he's here now, so right now is a good time to pick." Autry now analyze the situation while looking into her arms at TJ like the ball is already in her court.

"I agree with Autry!" Elaine shouts.

"Me too!" Cosewh agrees with them.

"Me too, and me too!"

I hear about three more times as everyone agrees with Autry. Including Momma Bass, who also yells out, "me too!"

"Oh no, see now y'all done got my Momma involved in this mess, too!"

I laugh out loud while taking a pillow and putting it over my face and pretending to suffocate myself.

"I'm just kidding baby, just like my other grandbabies he's already mine, I just wanted to get in on the calms." Momma Bass says as she adds a few more giggles to the conversation.

"Well wait a minute Tristan before you pick, because Mia and Gabrielle went to the cafeteria, but they're on their way back now so hold on for a minute."

Autry says while Cosewh and Elaine sit next to her waiting. "They're about to walk through the door then you can pick."

"But who said that I was about to pick his God-parents right now?"

Still shaking my head and laughing. "I'm still admiring him and his presence of even being here at all, but all y'all can think about is who's going to be the God-parents?"

"Nope."

Elaine interrupts, while also laughing and shaking her head like we're not going to just end this until I choose his God-parents.

"That's not all we can think about."

She says. "Because we're all admiring him too, because he's like our little miracle baby, so choose."

"I'll do no such thing, and I'm serious because this is a great thing happening here."

I now sit up even more in the bed, and begin to get emotional and start to cry while Mia and Gabrielle walks in with their food.

"I know that we're all laughing and having fun, but I also know that some of you are kind of serious. And wants me to choose for real, but I can't. It just means so much to me to have so many friends and family members who support me because not everyone have that. And if it wasn't for Momma Bass, I wouldn't be here nor would TJ because I wasn't born into this kind of love. So if it's left up to me to choose right now then I'm choosing all of you, because he's going to need you all, and whomever he's with at the time. Then that's his God-parent as far as the people who are in this room."

"Okay, so what you're saying is that I'm his God-momma right now since I'm holding him. But when I give him to Cosewh, then she's the God-momma at that time?"

Autry asks while still holding on to TJ, instead of sharing him.

"Exactly."

I respond. "And when he's with me and Keenan, then you all are the God-parents all at once, it's a group effort!"

"Well, the only reason I won't complain about having to share him is because I understand how you feel about your family, so it's cool."

Cosewh says. "Although Autry does have a problem with sharing because she still hasn't let me or Elaine hold him since we've been sitting here."

Autry laughs along with us while Momma Bass hands me a tissue to whip my face. While Autry finally does let Cosewh hold TJ, as the conversation continues on why I've chosen them all to be his God-parents.

But the conversation is short lived because my brothers and Keenan now walks into the room holding a car seat for TJ to go home in.

While the nurse also walks into the room with them, and she informs me that a few people would be coming in to speak with me as they do routinely with all of their patients before they're discharged from the hospital.

Then as always, my angel, Momma Bass says something that was music to my ears.

Although I truly do love everyone that's present, but Momma Bass says to the nurse that they will all be gone shortly, so that TJ and I will have some time to ourselves.

She then tells everyone in the room that they should all prepare to leave soon, so that I can get some rest.

And now the nurse goes over the information that she has for me, while my brothers and everyone else continues to gush over how cute TJ is.

And I am glad to hear that so many people will be coming in to speak with me before we're officially released, because one of the main reasons that I want to be left alone with the nurse is because I have a few questions that I would never ask her in front of everyone.

So I will just hold onto my questions until everyone leaves, while the nurse continues to routinely go over everything that she's supposed to.

And when she's done, she takes TJ away from everyone and with her to do their normal baby stuff that's provided for all newborns.

Then Momma Bass says. "Okay baby, we're all about to leave and go back to your house and clean up before you guys get home tomorrow. Because you would faint and have to come right back to the hospital if you saw how messy your place is right now."

"Oh my God, how bad is it?"

"Let me put it to you this way, I know how much you love your nieces and nephews."

She says while shaking her head. "But even you would put them all out if you saw them running all over the place like they've been doing, and they've only been here for one day so far. That's why Don and Deon just reserved a few rooms at a hotel near your house for the next two days."

She then continues by saying that they will all be gone in two days to give us a break because she knows that I've barely had any time to myself at all since the shooting.

But she said that she personally wants them all in a hotel until we can get comfortable with how everything will be now with a new baby in the house.

And personally from my perspective, I know that if she made them all check into a hotel, then they must have really been messy.

And I'm in no condition to be cleaning up when I get home, so I guess a hotel really is the best option for now.

With the good news being that they will all still be able to see me and TJ more than they've saw us in a while, because all my nieces and nephews really are just as excited as everyone else. Because they would always have a thousand questions about their baby cousin every time I would let them rub my belly when I was around them, so I know that they really want to see him outside of my belly.

They just won't be spending the night with us, and that's fine due to the circumstances right now.

But for now, Momma Bass gathers everything and everyone to leave at this point.

And we all say our goodbyes until we see them tomorrow, while only Keenan and I stay at the hospital.

Now finally feeling a bit normal, and ready to keep living life as best as I can, while I can slowly feel my energy restoring already. Although I know that my body may take a minute to snatch back, I'm not sure yet.

But I do feel good about myself and I look good to myself so I will dwell in that.

"So, Keenan, how does it feel to have your space invaded by the family?" Giggling while I also ask him to sit down and relax.

"Are you kidding me, I love it!"

He says. "Even when they're messing up my stuff, I still love it!"

"Who messed up your stuff?"

"Well, he didn't exactly mess up my stuff, but Elaine is going to be in for a big surprise from Little D when they start cleaning up the house."

"Oh Lord, what happened now Keenan?"

"Well, this morning when I walked into the kitchen everybody started asking me what kind of cologne was I wearing, but I wasn't sure which one that I'd grabbed and tossed on.

Especially since I'd only put on a little bit, so I really wasn't paying attention to the bottle because whatever it was, I didn't use much. But they all liked the smell and kept asking me what kind was it, so I went to my room to get it for them."

He says. "But then after they were done with it they sat it down on the dining room table next to a bottle of dishing washing liquid. And although I saw it sitting there, I left it there because I didn't want to rush it back to my room as if I was being stingy with it after they were done sniffing it."

"Wait."

I stop him and ask.

"Why was the dish washing liquid on the dining room table?"

"You don't even want to know Tristan."

"What do you mean I don't want to know?"

I yell. "Oh my God, so my house really is dirty for real?"

"No, calm down, because it's definitely not dirty. But it's messier than it would be if you were there. Because we all know how you are, but the kids are so excited and just glad to be out of town and kicking it with us, that they were running, playing, and just really enjoying themselves."

He says while smiling.

"But you know Momma Bass is about to get it together so don't even worry about it, the house is fine. The only big mess is still kind of small, although like I said, Elaine will be in for a surprise that she won't be too happy about. But other than that, I promise you it's not as bad as it sounds. Anyway, no one was paying attention to the cologne or the dish washing liquid, not even me. Until later when I'd walked up on Little D and saw him sitting under the table with the dish washing liquid bottle, but it was almost empty. But I didn't see any liquid anywhere, but I knew that the bottle was almost full the last time I saw it, and I could smell my cologne as if it had been opened and emptied also. But I knew that wasn't possible because of how hard it would be even for an adult to actually open the bottle and pour it out. So I bent down to pull Little D from under the table, and I saw him spraying my cologne into Elaine's shoe. And that's when I noticed that he'd also poured the dishing washing liquid into her shoe as well. And I knew that she was going to be mad at him so I hurried up and pushed her shoes, the bottle, and my cologne further under the table so that no one could see it. Then I rushed him out of there and into the bathroom to wash his hands and stuff."

"But Keenan, why did you push it further under the table, instead of going to find Elaine?"

"Because he's only three years old, and I didn't want him to get in trouble."

"It's so cute and funny that you're trying to protect him, but you should've said something instead of hiding it, so that he will know not to do that again! Although Little D already knows better than to do that, because as active as he is, I don't think that he's ever done anything like that before!"

"I know, and that's why I didn't say anything because he's a busy kid. But he's not a bad kid, so I didn't want him to get in trouble because he knows not to do that again, so I just pulled him away from the scene and cleaned him up."

I now laugh at him and Little D.

"I be letting him get away with a lot too Keenan, because he's so funny and little. But I still discipline him so that he'll know right from wrong. Although it is funny how you quickly pulled him away from the scene as if it was a crime scene or something."

"I was just trying to help him out, but he's still going to get caught anyway because there was nothing that I could do about the smell of my cologne all over him no matter how much soap

I used on him. So whenever they do go back into the dining room they will put the puzzle together and know that it was him, although I did go back and grab my cologne from under the table and took it back into my room. And I put the dish washing liquid back under the sink. But Tristan, I started thinking about why would Little D put soap and cologne into Elaine's shoes? Maybe her feet stink and he just don't know what else to do about it?"

"That's terrible Keenan."

I continue to chuckle. "Although that is something to think about, but maybe only that pair stink, I don't know. But what I do know is that if TJ ever does anything like that then you better not hide it or both of your asses are mine!"

"Nah, with TJ, I would've handled it totally different."

He says while smiling.

"But seriously, I just want to say something right quick."

"Say what?"

"I just want to let you know that I really am happy to be a part of your family more than you know, that's why I would never be bothered by having my space invaded because I love them like I love you. And I know that I've said this before, but I can't say it enough because I truly do thank you for changing my life T."

"Okay Keenan, now stop it."

I begin to get emotional.

"I just said that I was starting to feel normal and ready to get myself together, instead of sitting here crying every five minutes and not staying focused."

"I'm not trying to make you cry, but that's truly how I'm feeling. And after all this time of going back and forth with Tru about how he's proved himself to be your number one, it's now weird to actually step up to the challenge of being that for you."

He says. "But I do know what it takes to be that for you, because we have our own thing going that's similar, so I got your back no matter what happens as we move forward."

"Thanks Keenan, and I know that you have my back."

I grab a Kleenex and wipe my tears, then throw the Kleenex at him while shaking my head and smiling.

"Now I'm all emotional again, and I can't wait to ask the nurse will my hormones be back under control soon because I'm always crying or laughing. Then I'll be sad, then so happy and filled with so many up and down emotions all over again, and I don't like being all over the place with my feelings like this."

"Trust me, I know."

He says.

"You were already changing a lot of things after you found out that you were pregnant, even before Tru was killed you was already different in a lot of ways. Nothing bad or frustrating, but we could all see the differences in you, and now you're even more different. I mean you're still hard as a rock and very outspoken, it's just in a different way than usual."

"I know, Suuri said that it's because I'm maturing. And that I've had all of the men, women, and money that I want. But now with a baby, I desire different things in life and that's a good thing."

I now look into his eyes while I explain my actions.

"I believe Suuri when she says that I'm maturing, because I've been on the fence about how we're going to be as we move forward now that TJ is here. And now that we have three new staff members at the Parlor that Cosewh feels good about, we can now permanently change how we operate."

"Well, I like all of the changes because you and your whole family have been treating me more like I'm your one and only boyfriend. And instead of you normally correcting them and telling them that we're just 'close friends', although everyone knows better than to believe that lie after all this time anyway."

He says. "But I like what's happening right now. Well, I love it."

"That's because you have been more so like my one and only lately, especially after all that we've been through. And I don't know if it's my hormones or what, but I've been feeling this way for a while now. Because I really would prefer that it remain being only you and I for now, because I don't desire to have more *BAMT's* like I used to. Although you still may have to pull a few *BAMT* duties every now and then, depending on how much we're offered. But for the most part I'm thinking about ending that side hustle all together, and just keeping you strictly for myself."

"I'm down for whatever you want Tristan, even though I think I love where this whole thing is going. It's about to be just me, you, TJ, and the other baby that we're going to have."

"Okay Keenan, now you've added another baby, slow down because that's definitely not what I said."

"I know."

He says while smiling.

"It just feels like that's where this is all headed, just like before you came to the hospital, you asked me to lay in the bed with you so that we can talk and catch up. And we ended up watching television all day and night before we finally talked and then made love like I was your one and only, and no one else in this world mattered."

"That's true, it was just like that, and it was fun too. I think that's probably why I went into labor a few hours after that because we'd finally had some good love making during this pregnancy without my belly making everything so uncomfortable. It was perfect, nothing was uncomfortable or out of place. And I wanted no one in this world as much as I wanted you, and I still feel that way. But um, Keenan, I'm not about to have another baby anytime soon. And you can take that however you want to take it because that won't change and I'm so serious about that. Although I'm not saying that it won't happen one day, but the possibility of it being right after TJ is just not even up for a discussion. Even as we do seal our relationship into being more serious than ever like a normal couple, that part of us is not going to be a problem. But I need for you to really know and understand that I'm truly not getting pregnant anytime soon."

"I'm not talking about you getting pregnant again right away, because we're still trying to figure out what's what with TJ. I'm just saying that I like where this entire relationship is headed, and I know that everything takes time, so I'm just speaking my mind that's all."

The nurse now walks in holding a clip board and a fruity juice box.

"So did everyone just disappear on us?"

"Yep, you heard my mom. She wanted to finally give me, Keenan, and TJ some time to ourselves. Because tomorrow when we get home our house is going to be filled with a lot of excitement for the next two days. And to be honest, I was ready for them to leave because I want to get some rest so that I'm able to stay up and fully enjoy them when we get home. As well as I wanted to get the final results from the DNA test between TJ and Isaiah."

"I don't know why I'm so nervous, but I'm ready for the results too."

Keenan says while rubbing his hands together. "Although either way it goes he's still my son anyway, but as much as I believe that Tru did this on purpose, a part of me is afraid that it may say that he's Snow's."

"I was a little afraid of that at first too, but now it really doesn't matter because he's ours regardless Keenan. And in my mind, Hamilton has a very small chance because he and I were very careful that one and only time that we chanced doing it without a condom. But even more than that, I can tell by the way that TJ's lips are shaped. It's like God knew that Tru was going to pass away so he left an almost identical part of him behind to live on."

"Everybody says that his lips are just like Tru's, and I can see that too because he does look like him. But still, I'm nervous."

He says.

"Nurse Scott, can you please give her the results right now?"

"I sure can."

Nurse Scott says. "And instead of me telling you the results. I'll just give you these papers for you to read the results for yourself because every nurse here knows how much you hated having to wait for these results, so we just made a copy of everything for you to keep for your records. And since we knew that you wanted him to be Isaiah's, we wrote something on the bottom of the paper for you guys."

I now snatch the envelope from her hand and rush to open it, while Keenan gets up and comes closer to the bed to read the results with me.

"CONGRATULATIONS!"

That's the first thing that I see and read as the nurses have drawn smiley faces and put congratulations stickers underneath the results.

Even before reading the actual results, I see that and become happier as Keenan and I both scream out. "Yes!"

Especially after seeing that Isaiah is 99.9999% TJ's father, and I start crying, Keenan starts crying, and even Nurse Scott is crying.

"Thank you Nurse Scott! This is a weight lifted from my chest, although I already knew who his father was, but due to some of my past mistakes it calls for a need to be proven that I was right about this! And although I've heard people say that newborns are too young to look like anyone for the first few weeks. But it's obvious that TJ not only have Isaiah's lips, but in my opinion he has his whole face!"

I explain to her while removing my cover so that I can sit up and get out of the bed for a little while.

I now hand her a Kleenex and show her my phone with a picture of Tru on it.

"Oh wow!"

She says. "They really are identical!"

She continues while whipping her eyes.

"After hearing you talk about what happened to you all, I really wanted Isaiah to be his dad too, so when I saw the results for the first time. I screamed out just as loud as you guys just did, I was so happy to see that 99.9999%!"

"Good!"

Keenan says. "Now when can we see TJ again?"

"He's down the hall with the doctor right now, but you can see him whenever you want to see him. I only needed to take him away for a moment, but when I'm done in here, I can go and get him and bring him back if the doctor is done. And if the doctor hasn't gotten to him yet, then I'll bring him back here and the doctor will just come to your room to see him whenever he's ready for him, if that's what you'd like."

"Yes, that's what we want."

Keenan says while we watch Nurse Scott write something on her clip board before leaving the room.

"He's my son and I'm going to always be known as daddy to him, and I was still going to teach him French regardless of the results anyway. But Tristan, I'm telling you right now these results just made me the happiest man in the world to hear that Snow is not the father."

"I feel the same way, I'm just so happy!"

We now continue to go back and forth about how happy and relieved we are, as we eventually watch Nurse Scott re-enter the room with TJ.

And she gives him to me while I sit in the rocking chair next to the bed, while Keenan is kneeling in front of us. And when Nurse Scott leaves the room again, he places his head in my lap.

And while I hold onto TJ, Keenan holds on to us both and tells us that he loves us and will always be here for us.

"Thanks Keenan."

I now place a kiss to the top of his head.

"We love you, too."

Thank you for reading!

And I would love to hear from you, please reach out and let me know what you think!

Leave a review!

ABOUT THE AUTHOR

Meko is delighted to connect with her readers, and her connection is exclusively set apart to provide a variety of books designed to entertain, inspire, and help readers to grow at their own pace.

For more general information about Meko, and for more of her fiction and non-fiction books. Please visit her online at www.eaglelifepublications.net.

Thanks again!

HONEY